A Gown of Spanish Lace

JANETTE OKE

A GOWN of SPANISH LACE

JO

A GOWN OF SPANISH LACE
A Literary Express, Inc. Book
(a subsidiary of Doubleday Direct, Inc.)
Reprinted by special arrangement with:
Bethany House Publishers
A Ministry of Bethany Fellowship International

PRINTING HISTORY
A Bethany House Publication / July 1995
The Janette Oke Collection / April 1998, November 1999

Cover art by Dan Thronberg, Bethany House Publishers
staff artist.

If you would be interested in purchasing additional copies of this book, or have any questions concerning the Janette Oke Collection and your membership, or if you would like to correspond with the author, please contact us at:

The Janette Oke Collection
Literary Express, Inc.
1540 Broadway
New York, NY 10036
Telephone #973-473-4800

ISBN: 1-58165-030-2

Printed in the United States of America

In memory of my father.

A true gentleman, a special daddy,
a lover of nature, and an avid reader,
who good-naturedly humored
my “romance” with the West.

JANETTE OKE was born in Champion, Alberta, during the depression years, to a Canadian prairie farmer and his wife. She is a graduate of Mountain View Bible College in Didsbury, Alberta, where she met her husband, Edward. They were married in May of 1957, and went on to pastor churches in Indiana as well as Calgary and Edmonton, Canada.

The Okes have three sons and one daughter and are enjoying the addition to the family of grandchildren. Edward and Janette have both been active in their local church, serving in various capacities as Sunday-school teachers and board members. They make their home in Didsbury, Alberta.

A Word From the Author

In the WOMEN OF THE WEST fiction series, I have attempted to present several different facets of pioneer life. A rough, rugged element of the "new frontier" was also a significant part of the history of the West. With that in mind I have included this story, which takes a look at the coarser life of the new land—the lawless side. What happened when good and bad collided?

This story is not born of sudden inspiration. My fascination with the West began when I was a teenager, and because of my growing love for the land and the people, I read everything I could find that dealt with the subject. The fictional accounts I discovered were written in one genre—westerns. So it was natural that my very first idea for a story was also in that vein. In my mid-teens, I romanticized about a West far different than the one in which I had grown up.

When it came time for me to begin my own writing, I chose to deal with the settlers—those courageous people who carried with them far more than their walking plows and cooking pots. In many instances they also had a deep personal faith in a sovereign God. They built towns in sheltered valleys and shaped the rugged open plains into productive farmlands.

So I put aside this story plot—supposing I would never

have use for it. That was forty-plus years ago.

But over the years the idea continued to push itself forward. Each time I gently nudged it back into some hidden recess of my mind. Finally, I came to the conclusion that God might have some use for it. I began to pray for His direction.

I knew I would have to honestly present the ruthless mind-set of the outlaws to make the reader understand the real danger of my characters—the ones who were victims and the ones who struggled to free themselves from such a life. Could this be presented in such a way as to show the hopelessness and helplessness of those who choose to live without law—without compassion—without God? Was there a reader of westerns who could benefit from this approach? This story?

The answer seemed to be yes. If even one reader finds some encouragement or direction—or hope—then the story will have served a purpose.

If you happen to be that reader, may you know at the outset—I have prayed for you.

Janette Oke

Contents

Chapter One

A Girl and a Town

The schoolhouse was set in the ideal spot. The simple wood-slab walls blended in with the slate gray of the rocky hillside behind it. A wooden step led to a heavy, hewed oak door with its leather-strap pull and squeaky iron hinges. The building faced east and looked out over the downward slope. The blend of nearby trees was broken by the silver of the now-quiet stream that could at times become a tempestuous surge of flood waters. A simple wooden bridge that after every spring runoff had to be rebuilt, or at the least repaired, spanned the water. Farther down and beyond stood a cluster of more wood-frame buildings. The town's businesses melted together along one long, winding street, seeming to point the way to the town's single church marking the outskirts on the east. Rows of simple homes spilled out blue-gray smoke lifting lazily into the brightness of the morning sky. All seemed quite still except for an occasional stirring here or there announcing that one or another of the town's occupants was busy on some self-appointed mission.

The scent of autumn's fallen leaves hung delicately in the air to mix with the tang of the woodsmoke. Bright gold of aspen interchanged with the greenery of spruce and pine, filling the valley with color that continued on up the slopes of the hills enfolding the little town. Birds, wishing to remain long enough to feast on the last red berries from mountain ash or wild chokecherry before making their flight south, sprinkled the morning air with song, reminding the saucy squirrels that the summer's bounty had to be shared.

On the wooden steps of the school, a young woman stood, cast-iron bell in hand. Though she looked to be little more than a schoolgirl herself, her face held a look of serenity and her eyes reflected her sense of responsibility.

But for the moment she appeared to have forgotten the noisy little group of children who chased about the small yard that had been coaxed from the forested hillside. She seemed to have forgotten even the bell in her hand and what she had come out to do. Her eyes gazed out over the scene before her to drink in every aspect of the picture. It was a beautiful morning. A beautiful autumn. Yes, and a beautiful, sleepy little town. Smithton. She loved it. Everything about it.

She stirred and sighed deeply.

Finally her eyes turned to the frolicking youngsters. Her students. She loved them, too.

With a flick of her wrist the bell brought them to attention. The clear ringing lifted eyes in the streets below to the little schoolhouse on the hill. She could see the few pedestrians raise their heads, or stop midstride to glance upward before hurrying on their way. She knew that the contentment she felt, the love for the town she claimed as home, was shared by those who walked the morning streets below her.

The bell caused a change in the noise that came from the schoolyard. It didn't lessen—simply altered in tone as boys and girls of various ages and dispositions hastened to fall into line, eventually to be led with some measure of decorum into the classroom.

The young woman marched directly to the front of the room and turned to face the scurrying troop. After depositing lunch pails and outer wraps at their assigned spots, all students hurried to the simple wooden desks that were their centers for learning. The little crew stood at attention, hands fidgeting slightly or hanging limply at their sides.

The teacher's eyes scanned the group quickly. They were all there. No one missing because of colds or grippe. That would come with the winter months. She reminded herself to take full advantage of the days of good weather and good health.

"Good morning, class," she said evenly, trying to keep the joy she was feeling inside from spilling out too enthusiastically into the words.

"Good morning, Miss Benson," they replied in ragged unison.

"We will salute our flag," announced the teacher and turned her back to her class to face the faded cloth that had been proudly mounted on the wall above the blackboard.

The flag would have hung rather forlornly had it not been firmly supported and carefully secured by caring hands. Ariana Benson knew the local school officials were proud of that flag. Not all schools in the territories could boast a flag of their own. It might look worn and a bit scruffy to outside eyes, but this flag had done honorable duty. It had once led the way for a contingent of blue-coated soldiers who had fought to bring law and order to the West.

The voices of the fifteen students joined in with their teacher as the pledge to flag and country was solemnly repeated. Though Miss Benson could not see her students, she was confident that all fifteen stood rigidly at attention, hand held over heart as the words were spoken.

As soon as the salute ended, the teacher turned and lifted a Bible from the corner of her desk. She had already marked the passage for the day, Proverbs, chapter three, and she read it now in a clear voice, accentuating the words she particularly wanted the children to hear and understand.

When she reached the fifth verse, her eyes lifted slightly from the page to quickly scan her small audience. "Trust in the Lord with all thine heart," her tone encouraged, "and lean not unto thine own understanding. In all thy ways acknowledge him," she went on, "and he shall direct thy paths."

As she closed the Book and looked out over her class of students, willing them to hear and heed the words, she wondered just how fully she understood the verses herself. Silently she vowed to remind herself of them frequently in the days to come, to gain deeper insight into their meaning for her.

She could recite the verses by memory. Her father and mother had seen to that. Now she needed to get them from her head to her heart. To learn to do as the verses admonished.

"Let us pray together," she invited in a soft voice, and fifteen heads bowed as one, and fifteen young voices lifted together in the Lord's Prayer.

A general shuffling followed as students took their seats. The teacher's full attention was turned to the lessons of the day.

After the students had been dismissed at school day's end, Ariana remained behind, poring over lesson books as she corrected grammar and sums. When the last assignment had been properly marked, she turned her attention to preparations for the next day's lessons. It required hours of careful planning to make sure she had meaningful, productive studies for each of the students in the eight grades. And as it was Ariana's first year as a schoolteacher, and her sixteenth birthday had just passed, at times the task seemed almost overwhelming.

But she loved to teach. She was thankful her parents had sacrificed in order for her to get her teacher's certificate. Ariana could imagine doing nothing else with her life. The light in a child's eyes when a new discovery was made was worth all the long hours and every effort on her part to make learning fun and exciting.

The last glow of twilight was fading from the skies before Ariana finally closed the last book, picked up her wrap, and carefully fastened her hat in place with its two pins.

She was weary. Yet she had exciting news to tell when she reached home. Little Jeff Newcome had recited the entire alphabet on his own for the first time. She had worked and prompted and struggled and prayed. She had begun to fear that he would never master the letters. But today—today he had stood proudly and carefully worked his way through the alphabet. She had asked him to repeat, fearing that the one time might have been some fortunate accident. But he had made his way through the list again. Ariana felt nearly as triumphant as he did as she handed him the wrapped sweet from Barker's Store as his reward.

She carefully pulled the heavy door shut tightly behind her. The cumbersome door with its worn hinges did not cooperate well, and the leather pull tended to slip through one's hands in resistance. Ariana tugged again—just to be sure it was properly in place. She turned her eyes to the rocky path that wound its way down the hillside, over the footbridge, and into town.

It was darker than she had expected. The sun slipped quickly behind the hills, bringing night to the town before it was so evident on the surrounding prairies. Ariana quickened her step. She did not wish to be the cause of her mother's worrying.

"It's Saturday," Mrs. Benson said, her tone gentle but firm.

Ariana lifted her head from the book opened on the table before her. Her eyes held a question, though she did not voice it.

"It's Saturday," repeated the woman. "Don't you think you can lay your books aside for one day?"

Ariana stirred restlessly. She did wish she could forsake

her reading. Her eyes were weary from perusing the printed pages. She lifted a hand to rub the ache from the back of her neck.

"I haven't enough knowledge of the Industrial Revolution to challenge my two eighth graders," she responded.

"I would think any knowledge of the Industrial Revolution would be more than what they know now," put in Mrs. Benson.

Ariana pushed the book aside. She straightened tired shoulders and reached up to tuck in a stray lock of hair. Inwardly she once again bemoaned the fact that the tresses were too soft and wayward to stay pinned. Outwardly she turned her attention to her mother.

"You've been at that book all morning," her mother continued.

"Was there something you wished me to do?" asked Ariana, who was careful to tend to her share of household chores.

"No. No—except give yourself a bit of rest. You can't keep studying all the time."

With a sigh Ariana closed the book and stood to her feet.

"You are right," she admitted reluctantly. "But it is so—so hard to keep up."

"You'll be getting sick if you don't get some fresh air and exercise," her mother went on.

Ariana let her gaze steal to the open window. Her mother was letting fresh air sweep into the home, spilling its fall fragrance into the room along with the breeze that rustled the curtains.

"It's not the same as walking in it—breathing it in," her mother said as though reading Ariana's thoughts.

Ariana's eyes stayed on the window. Another beautiful day called—it beckoned. She longed to forget her responsibility as the town's schoolteacher and follow her heart up the winding trail and into the woods. She knew the little creek would sing. The fallen leaves of aspen and birch would rustle beneath her feet. The sky would present just enough fleecy clouds to make one's imagination have full run. Ariana longed to be out in the sunshine—the freshness of the day. It would be so easy to feel like a kid again. She longed for that. Longed to lay aside her adult responsibilities for just a few hours.

She stretched and gave her shoulders a little shake. She had another hour's reading to do to be properly prepared for Monday morning.

"I really—" she began.

"You really need to get out," her mother encouraged. "Surely a break will make you fresher for finishing the studying later."

Ariana considered the comment, then nodded slowly. "You're right," she said, her voice trembling slightly with eagerness. "I'll just—take a little walk. I can finish up later."

She gave her book another little push as though to inform it that she was done with it for the present.

"Where's Papa?" she asked.

"At the church. Putting final preparations on his Sunday sermon."

"Can I take him a cup of tea?"

"He'd like that."

The older woman smiled and moved toward the kitchen to prepare the tea while Ariana went to her room to gather a shawl and change into something more suitable for walking. By the time she reappeared, her mother had a small tray with a teapot wrapped snugly in a cozy, a single cup, and a slice of toast smothered with wild blueberry jam.

"Remember it gets dark earlier than it did," her mother warned as she kissed Ariana's cheek.

Ariana nodded.

Once the door closed behind her, Ariana breathed deeply. Her eyes took on a new sparkle. Her step quickened and her chin lifted. Her mother was right. The fresh air and fall sunshine would do her a world of good.

Chapter Two

A Boy and a Camp

Tall trees shadowed the winding trail hidden from view of all eyes save the lone eagle drifting on soundless currents of morning air far above the crags and rocky slopes.

To those below, the hillside was unbroken from its wildness—uninhabited by humankind. Uninformed eyes would not have detected the slight indentation that resulted in a passageway, small and tucked securely away against the face of steep outcroppings of rough and ragged rock, leading into a secret valley.

It was the perfect setting for any who wished to keep their whereabouts concealed from an outside world. Outlaws. Bandits. Desperadoes. Blackguards. Brigands. Freebooters. Highwaymen. They had been called many things throughout the years—but always the names carried with them the same sense of hostility and hatred. They were seen as parasites—by terror and force living off the sweated brows and calloused hands of honest workers.

But the young man who removed his stained hat, who squinted his eyes against the harshness of the midday sun, cared little about any of those names. He paid no heed to the expressions of hatred. The words of contempt. He had been raised in the hidden camp, had known no other life, no other family—if one could call the band of rough, cursing, hard-riding, desperate men a *family*.

He had been sent to the rise by his father to survey the valley below. It was not unusual for a close eye to be kept on the valley floor. A sentry was always posted to be sure there was no chance of discovery. He took his shift like every other man in the outfit. But still—there was something different about the order this time. He had yet to sort it through, but he had this strange gut-feeling. . . .

He could see McDuff, already posted on the shelf of rock that overlooked the entire area—hills, streams, valley, and connecting valleys. There was only one way into the camp. If anyone was on the trail that paralleled the small creek below, McDuff would spot them. So why did his father feel this added vigilance was needed? Had his pa reason to think they had been followed? Or was his pa simply using this as an excuse to get him away from the camp for a while? But why? What could his pa be planning that he didn't want discovered?

The young man fanned his bronzed face slightly to get some coolness on his sweating brow. The day was unusually warm for fall. Indian Summer, they called it. Indian Summer that could get as hot as any mid-July day. He stepped back into the shade of a large pine before increasing the action of the Stetson. Even a small movement could be detected in an otherwise motionless setting.

As his eyes traveled over the slope before him, they took in everything—the flit of a bird, the stirring of tall grasses as some cautious, small creature moved about seeking food, the rollicking bounding of an energetic squirrel. He even saw the shift of hand from McDuff on his ledge perch as he brushed away a pestering fly. McDuff could be careless. His rifle was lying in plain sight on the ledge. Not that anyone from below could see the Winchester, but what if the shifting of the afternoon sun should reflect off the barrel? McDuff needed to be more cautious. The young man frowned as he thought about the danger carelessness could bring to the entire group. He wouldn't refer the matter to his pa—that might cause an unnecessary fuss. He'd speak to McDuff himself when they were both back in camp.

After another thorough study of the valley, he was content that they had no cause to be concerned about unwanted visitors.

Guests were not welcomed at the camp of the band. Not even those of similar stripe. Years of living on the edge had proved that no man was to be trusted. They had learned to guard their own backs even from those of their own company. And one never left a trail that was too easy to follow, or rode without checking frequently over a shoulder.

He moved slowly from the shadows and replaced the stained Stetson. His steps were lithe, deliberate, and smooth. His body fit and muscular. He intended to keep it that way. He abhorred the wasting away of manhood, of body and mind that he observed in those with whom he shared the simple log buildings of the small camp. He attributed their slovenliness, their softness, and their paunchy bellies to their lives of boozing and idleness. Except for the frequent night excursions that supplied the needs of the group, they did little but lounge around and take their occasional watch. He had no intention of becoming like them. Secretly he admired the strong bodies and straight backs of the braves in the local Indian tribe—but he knew better than to express that thought to his pa.

His pa had no love for the Indians. That was evident each time one was seen or talked about. His father, dark and swarthy and given to black moods, would spit in the dust, curse profusely, then spit again. "Only good Indian is a dead Indian," the boy had heard all through his growing years. He knew better. Yet he was smart enough not to argue with his pa.

"Well—nothin' goin' on down there," he murmured to his mount as he reached one hand to gather the reins. The horse tossed its head and snorted.

With one easy movement he was in the saddle. The horse danced in his impatience to get going, but the rider held him in check. For some reason he could not understand, he was reluctant to head back into camp, even though he had planned to spend a good share of the afternoon practicing his draw. With the raid of the night before, he was now supplied with ammunition. His pa allowed him no shells for target practice when their store was low.

He loved the feel of the cool, ivory-covered pistol butt in his hand. He loved the tension he felt in his own coiled body as he hit leather. The click of the hammer as the gun whipped upward—the feel of his finger being at one with the cold metal as he squeezed off a shot. He felt close to his gun. As though it really was an extension of himself. He felt closer to his gun than to any of the men down in the valley shacks below him. It had been his only "toy" as a child, his source of entertainment as a boy, his challenge of skill as a young man.

Now part of him itched to take full advantage of the new supply of ammunition. Yet part of him held back. Something strange was going on. He could almost taste it. He had to try to think it through. To see if he could work out the puzzle. Nothing had been said to him directly—but he could sense it. Could feel it. And it had something to do with him. His pa seemed unusually morose—black in his mood of the morning, even though the raid of the night before had been even more successful than any of them had dared hope. Not a single man—nor horse—had been lost or even hit. They had returned with supplies that would last them clear through the winter if necessary, and cash to add to the ample collection that each man guarded with his life.

It had been a good night's work. And no man even appeared to try to tail them. So why the tension? Why the scowls among the group? He just couldn't figure.

With a word to his horse he moved forward. He wasn't going back into the camp. Not yet. He'd give things a chance to cool off down there. Give his father time to be mellowed by whiskey.

He turned the buckskin back down the trail, but he knew he would take the left branch once he hit the bottom. He would head for the spot where the spring formed a deep crystal pool and take a leisurely dip in the frigid waters. Maybe it would clear his head and help him to think.

⁂

"I don't know why yer growlin'."

The man named Sam was the only person in the small company of men who would have dared to speak to "The Boss" in such a fashion. Perhaps he dared because they had traveled together for so many years. Perhaps he knew that under the sweating, stomping, cursing exterior was a man who might—on occasion—be willing to listen to some reason. Perhaps Sam was just too hardened to care what the other man thought of his comments. His gun was faster, and both men knew it.

"He's a coward," spoke the prowling boss with a curse and a spit into the thick dust on the floor of the room. "Jest a yella-bellied coward."

"Ya know thet ain't so, so I'll not even favor thet comment with a re-ply," spoke the first man as he sliced a section from a wad of dark tobacco. He poked the tobacco back into a torn pocket and stuffed the chew into his mouth, tucking it firmly between his stained teeth and droopy lip.

"He covers it. He covers it well—but he's a coward all the same." The big, brooding man cursed again and kicked at the only chair in the room. It toppled, breaking once again the leg that had been patched over and over.

"Dawgone it, Boss," said the smaller man, irritated. "Don't know how many times ya think thet I can mend thet thing." It was his turn to curse. But his voice was softer, less menacing.

"Fergit the chair. It's the boy we're talkin' on." The big man stopped his pacing and turned to the man who sat on one of the log blocks that made up the other seats in the dark room. He leaned close to the tobacco chewer and his eyes shot sparks of fire.

"He covers it." He almost shouted the words into the face of the smaller man. "He—"

"Back off," said Sam, the smaller of the two, giving a push to the heavy chest leaning over him. "I ain't nohow wantin' to share yer whiskey. Not when you've already downed it."

The big man glowered but straightened and moved back slightly. His hand was trembling. He cursed again, this time more from habit than venom, and moved off to moodily peer out the one window with its broken, smoke-blackened glass.

"What'd he do wrong now?" inquired the smaller man, still seemingly undisturbed. He spit into the corner.

At first the big man just glared as though the other should understand. Then he spoke angrily. "He had a chance to finish thet no-good gunslinger yesterday. To finish 'im. What'd he do? Wing 'im. Jest winged 'im. He's a coward."

The smaller man didn't share the opinion. "Look, Boss—iffen the Kid is wrong—he's wrong. But he ain't a coward. I've known him 'long as you have. I've watched him grow. He ain't no coward—an' you know it well as I do."

The big man continued to stare out the window.

"He can shoot straighter and draw faster'n any man I know," Sam continued from his perch on the log stool. "He's strong as a bear an' springy as a wildcat an' he has eyes like an eagle—never misses the flutter of a wood moth. He hears the slightest rustle. Leaf can't fall in a tornado without he hears it, and besides all thet—he's got this uncanny sense—this feelin' in his bones when somethin's amiss. Why, you'd a walked right into an ambush over there in Widder's Pass hadn't been fer him. And you'd never got away from thet posse in—"

"Shet up," barked the man known as "The Boss."

"Jest remindin' ya," said the tobacco chewer mildly, spitting again into the corner.

"Well—ya needn't. I know all thet, Sam. Think I've been somewhere else whilst he's been growin' up? I know all thet."

"Then what's stickin' in yer craw? I don't figger."

Silence hung in the air while Sam worked his tobacco, and Will Russell, the boss, stared off into the distance. The latter ran a hand through thinning, dark greasy hair. "I dunno," he said at last. "Jest this—this sick feelin' in my innards. This—this funny fear—thet iffen it came to it—he'd back down."

"Back down?" Sam aimed a stream of tobacco into the corner. The big man whirled and moved toward him, his voice lowered, though one could not call it soft.

"Ya ever seed him shoot a man?" he hissed, the sound raspy and harsh.

"Well—shore. He's got the quickest hand—"

"Have ya seed him shoot a man?" the big man insisted.

"Shore. I told ya."

"Dead?"

There was silence. Sam stared at the scowling face before him. "Don't think dead. He jest—takes out their shootin' arm."

"Exactly. Exactly."

Sam shrugged his shoulders. The stiff leather vest lifted and fell with resistance. "So what's yer beef? They sure don't do no more shootin' fer a while."

"But he's never taken 'em *out*. Never."

"So—"

"So—don't ya think folks notice thet? Don't ya think word gets around? Here's a feller quick with a gun—but he never shoots to kill. Every gunslinger in the West is soon gonna be in on thet little secret."

The big man kicked at the sprawled chair, sending it careening across the room to smash into the log walls of the cabin.

He cursed and Sam joined him.

"Good thing this here shack is built sturdy or ya woulda kicked it down by now," Sam complained.

"Make some coffee," snarled the big man, and Sam stirred himself from his seat and moved toward the blackened stove near the cabin door.

The big man crossed to lift the chair and study the damage. "Fix this thing when ya get around to it," he told the smaller man. "I hate sittin' on a wood block. Most as bad as sittin' on a rock."

Sam shrugged, nodded, and shoved some wood into the firebox. He filled the blackened pot with water and slashed open a small bag holding coffee grounds and liberally dumped some into the pot.

Silence followed until Sam had finished his duties and returned to his log seat.

"We oughta get us a few more chairs," he said more to himself than to the big man.

"Hard to carry behind a saddle," the boss growled. He reached out a hand to drum his fingers in agitated fashion on the boards of the wooden table.

Silence again. At last Sam spoke.

"So yer worried about 'im?" he asked. His voice was lower now—his manner less defensive.

"I worry," admitted the big man in response.

"I still think he can handle hisself."

"Maybe," replied the big man. "But odds are agin' it."

"How so?"

The fingers beat more rapidly on the tabletop.

"Doublin' up. One man forces a draw—another comes in—gits his attention. First man has a chance for a slow, careful shot with his good hand. Takes 'im."

"Come on, Boss," scoffed Sam. "How often ya seed thet happen?"

"It could."

"Sun could come up in the west, too, I reckon—but I ain't seen it do it yet."

"Could happen," insisted Will.

Sam got up to check the coffee. It wasn't boiling yet.

"Sure gonna be good to have a decent cup of coffee," he muttered. "Thet stuff we been drinkin' tasted 'bout like slop."

He brought two chipped, stained cups to the table.

"Know what I think?" he asked softly.

There was no response, so after a few moments of silence he continued. "I think yer jest worryin' too much. The boy is doin' jest fine. Can't think me of a better tracker—smarter woodsman—more careful feller at watchin' his back—why—bet there ain't an Injun—"

He stopped. The big man had begun cursing and spitting. Sam quickly changed the course of the conversation.

"It's jest 'cause yer his pa thet yer frettin'," he hurried on. "Boys are gonna think yer a stewin' ole woman iffen—"

The big man stirred restlessly and his curses grew louder. Sam went for the coffee, hoping it was boiling. He may have pushed a bit too far. It was time to back off.

"I know he can take care of hisself," the big man growled. "Iffen he chooses to—thet's the rub. He's gotta learn thet ya have to take yer man. Dead men don't carry grudges. No smart man leaves him a trail of one-armed men carryin' a full pail of bitter with 'em. Sooner or later one of 'em varmints is gonna turn up and he ain't gonna be lookin' to play fair."

It was a new thought for Sam and the first one he agreed with. He poured the coffee and moved to put the pot back on the stove.

"Too hot to be drinkin' coffee," he muttered to himself, even though he sniffed the deep aroma with appreciation.

He returned to his seat and took a drink of the scalding liquid. The coffee burned all the way down, causing his eyes to water. When he recovered he spoke again.

"So what ya plannin'?"

There was silence while the big man fingered his cup.

"Gotta force his hand," he said at last.

"Force his hand? You mean—make him take his man?"

The big man nodded, his eyes dark and smoldering.

"And how ya fixin' to do thet? You gonna call him out?"

Will Russell answered that ridiculous question with a dark stare.

"Okay, okay," hurried Sam. "So thet was dumb. I take it ya got a better idea."

The big man sipped his coffee slowly, smarter than to gulp it as Sam had done.

"Well—" prompted Sam.

"What's the one thing thet a man—almost any man—would kill fer?" asked the boss.

"Money?"

The big man cursed. "We got thet," he reminded Sam. "Stashed away. An' we can get more—anytime we take a notion."

"Then—?" Sam let the question hang between them.

"A woman," said Will simply.

"A what?"

Sam could not believe what he had just heard. The boss only nodded.

"Ain't no woman within miles of here," Sam reminded him.

"Thet means we gotta find one."

"Find one. How?"

"I ain't got it all figured out yet, but it'll come."

"An' if an' when ya do find one—how ya aim to get them together? An' what makes ya sure he'll—go fer her? He ain't got no idee what a woman's even about."

The big man gave the smaller one a withering look and then turned back to the table as though the absurd comment deserved no reply. He hiked his large frame a little closer to the table and returned to drumming his fingers in an irritating fashion, his brow furrowing with deep, dark thoughts.

At length he turned. “We’ve got a lot of figurin’ to do, Sam,” he said, then nodded his head toward the coffeepot to indicate he’d be needing his cup refilled.

Chapter Three

Ariana

Saturday walks became an anticipated part of Ariana's week. She no longer resisted her mother's counsel. She had learned that she was more productive after a stroll in the neighboring woods or along the local stream. Often she invited one or another of her students to accompany her. It became a time to build relationships and teach lessons that could not be learned in the schoolroom. Ariana prayed that she might be able to teach not only about life but also about the Giver of Life. Not just scientific facts of the world but about the One who established the Laws of Nature. Not just mathematics but about the One who made the consistency of mathematics a possibility.

"God has given us an ordered world," she said often, and she hoped her students would see and understand what she was trying to convey as they looked at the world around them.

If there were any whose children attended the little schoolhouse on the hill who thought that the preacher's daughter was bringing "too much religion" into the classroom, they never voiced it. Even the owner of the local saloon suggested that "a little law and order wouldn't hurt" his two offspring any. He thought the world was bound to quickly chip away any "excess goodness" they might obtain.

"We need us some high principles," said the school board chairman in a community meeting. "And I for one don't know where to find 'em 'ceptin' in the Good Book. Far as I'm concerned, thet little gal can pour in 'em all the Bible learnin' they can hold. Make upright citizens of 'em, the way I see it."

Others seemed to agree. Ariana thought of her teaching in the local school as an addition to her Sunday school class in her father's church. Not all the townsfolk felt Sunday services a necessity. So her Saturday walks were one more means of bringing valuable lessons to her students who might not be attending church.

There were those few who had little patience with the biblical teaching. But it could also be said that, by and large, those individuals had little use for any teaching at all.

"Can't 'magine a boy his age goin' off to school. When I was his age I drove a team of mules and put in sixty acres of crop each summer," huffed one elderly man.

"What do young gals need all thet book learnin' fer?" scoffed another. "Don't help none with makin' a pot of stew or hoein' a garden."

Ariana chose to ignore such remarks. But she often had to bite her tongue to keep from responding with a lecture.

"If the West is ever to be civilized and prosperous," she wanted to say, "we need people who are educated. Educated not just in book learning—but in moral living. That's the only hope for taming the West and making it a place of fulfilled promise for future generations."

Ariana determined to do all she could to prepare her students for the future, whether or not every townsperson approved.

"You have such pretty dresses."

The words were spoken with such wistfulness that Ariana almost felt like apologizing. She had chosen Chloe Travis, a seventh-grader, for her Saturday walk companion.

The girl was sallow skinned and frail and came from a poor home on the edge of the town. Ariana supposed that the girl's slight frame was due to the fact she never really had enough nutritious food. Her father seldom worked, and her mother sat in the shade of the front porch from sunup to sundown.

"The poor woman must be ill," Ariana's mother had said with honest concern. "No one who is well would be content to sit and let the family do without."

Ariana secretly wondered if her mother was being generous. Now and then a pot of stew or a roasted chicken was sent to the home from the parsonage. There was little verbal response from the adults in the family, but the looks on the faces of the hungry children were enough thanks for the preacher's wife.

Ariana turned to the girl in the patched, faded frock. "My mama sews," she said simply.

"Wish my ma could sew," the girl replied.

"Perhaps if—" But Ariana was not allowed to finish.

"Naw—she wouldn't. Not even iffen she had a machine, she wouldn't. She don't like to do nothin'."

Ariana was tempted to gently correct the grammar, but in order to do so she would have needed to restate the girl's comment. She couldn't do that.

"Yer really lucky," went on the girl.

"Yes," said Ariana with deep feeling. "I am . . . really lucky . . . only . . . only I don't see it as luck. I see it as—"

She stopped. She had been about to say that it was because God was good to her. How could she say that? How could she claim that God loved and cared for her—and left Chloe struggling along in a family that did not even function? Ariana bit her lip.

"Shall we sit down and rest for a little while?" she asked instead. "Mama sent along a little lunch."

The girl's eyes lit up, and Ariana could see her tongue pass quickly over her upper lip.

They found a place to sit, and Ariana brought out the cold beef sandwiches. She held one out to the young girl and watched as she hungrily devoured it. Ariana broke off a small piece of another sandwich and took a bite. She felt hungry too. The crisp fall air had a way of increasing one's appetite. But she held herself in check. There would be plenty of food waiting for her when she returned to her home. Who knew when Chloe might get another meal?

Ariana's thoughts were on the previous conversation. She wished to say more to the young girl. Something that would make sense. Something that might give her reason for hope. Ariana hardly knew where to start.

"You know, " she said at last as she passed the rest of the sandwiches to Chloe, "you said I'm lucky—and I am. I have been . . . blessed. My parents are wonderful. I love them dearly. I have been blessed. . . ."

She let the words fade away as she thought on them. Then she turned again to the young girl and spoke. "It wasn't—well, always so. Did you know that?"

Ariana took a deep breath before she went on. "My parents—my birth parents—were . . . were killed in an Indian raid . . . when I was a baby. The whole wagon train of people were . . . killed."

Ariana saw the eyes of the young girl open wide with surprise—then horror.

"What happened?" Chloe asked around the rest of the roast beef sandwich.

"We were traveling west. For a new life. A new beginning. I . . . I don't remember, of course. I was just . . . just a baby. But one night—for some reason—the Indians attacked. There had been trouble in the area. I don't know what had happened. Some Indians had been killed. They blamed it on the scouts from the train. So they . . . they decided to get revenge." She paused a moment.

"Anyway, the people were killed," she told the young girl. "All but me and Aunt Lucy."

"Who's Aunt Lucy?" asked the young girl, her voice little more than a whisper.

"Aunt Lucy was a . . . a dear old woman. Not really my

aunt. And not really old, I guess, though she seemed old. She was a friend of my mama's. I think of her as my second mama." Ariana's voice threatened to break. "She took care of me until I was five years old. I . . . I don't know how she managed. She was crippled—from a fall and—"

Ariana stopped again.

"When the Indians attacked," she was finally able to explain, "Aunt Lucy snatched me up and ran. There was a cliff—all rocks. Aunt Lucy bundled me close and jumped. Jumped right off the cliff. Both of her legs were broken. The Indians were so sure the fall would have killed us that they never even came down to check. Just looked over the edge, Aunt Lucy said, and pointed and shouted. Blood-curdling yells, Aunt Lucy said.

"Then they . . . they finished their . . . their raid and set fire to the wagons. A storm was approaching and soon it was pouring rain. Some of the wagons didn't even burn.

"Later, Aunt Lucy heard someone come to the train. Local ranchers or maybe soldiers from the nearby garrison. She didn't know. At first she was afraid it might be the Indians returning, but they spoke English. She heard them cursing as they looked at the . . . the carnage. She called and called until she was hoarse, but she was already weak and she couldn't make them hear her.

"For three days we lay there. It was hot. Aunt Lucy dipped water from a small puddle and gave me drinks from her cupped hand. She was sure I would die before help came.

"On the third day a band of soldiers did come by. Aunt Lucy was able to make herself heard, and they came to us. They checked the wagon train. There were no other survivors, but they . . . they saved a few things that had been my mother's. Aunt Lucy insisted that they bring them when they took us into town.

"Gradually Aunt Lucy's legs healed enough that she could struggle along with two canes. She never did regain her health—she had been hurt inside, too—but she cared for me for those five years. I don't know how she managed to make enough pennies to keep us fed—though I do know that she often went without.

"Aunt Lucy was getting weaker and weaker, and I often heard her praying—for me—that God would take care of me when she was gone. Then a miracle happened. At least, Aunt Lucy said it was a miracle. A preacher moved into the town. Aunt Lucy went to see him and he . . . he and his wife agreed to take me. They had no children of their own."

"The Bensons?" asked Chloe, her eyes large.

"The Bensons," nodded Ariana.

"I thought they were your folks."

"They are—now," smiled Ariana.

"Where's Aunt Lucy?"

Ariana's eyes filled with tears. "She died about two months after I went to the Bensons," she said softly.

The young girl shook her head. "That's pretty awful," she said.

"Yes," said Ariana. "Yes—it was. For my folks—for all of the people on the wagon train. For Aunt Lucy. I've been the one who has been blessed—and I . . . I really don't know why. Not yet. I hope to one day discover just why—why God chose to spare a baby. What does He have for me to do? I keep telling myself there must be a reason—and I think I've found it. I think it was so I could be a teacher. So I could help you—and others—to know—to really understand that God is real. That He cares about us—no matter what our circumstances."

Ariana laid her hand on the young girl's faded sleeve. "He really does care, you know."

Chloe stared into her face.

"He loves you, Chloe," Ariana said gently. "He knows all about you—and He loves you. Can you believe that?"

The girl hesitated. She looked down at the limp dress, the shoes with holes in the toes. Then she looked back into the solemn blue eyes and nodded slowly.

"May I walk ya home?"

Ariana had just stepped out the church door. She looked up into the tense face of the tall young man who stood before her. It was not an attractive face. Willis Boyd was probably the last person she would have hoped to make such a request. His skin was blotchy with youthful acne, and his ears were much too big for the size of his head. Crooked teeth were stained from tobacco juice, and his hair looked like the only washing it ever received was when he was caught in the rain.

Yet something about his pathetically hopeful look made her smile softly and swallow hard. How could she refuse him—just because of his appearance? It would be cruel. Especially since he had just recently been showing up at her father's church.

She was about to reply when someone brushed his way between them. Bernard Dikerson stood before her. He smiled and pushed back smooth dark hair with a well-groomed hand. Ariana couldn't help noting the sharply creased trousers, the tailored suit jacket, and the natty cravat. Bernard Dikerson was the son of the local banker, newly arrived in the town. Every girl had her hat set for the banker's son.

Bernard said nothing—just gave the derby in his hand a slight tip with the flick of his wrist and jovially offered her his arm.

Ariana prayed a quick and beseeching prayer—*What should I do, Lord?*—then lifted her eyes to survey both young men. Inwardly she struggled. *I . . . I should befriend Willis. He'll be so shamed if . . . everyone is looking our way . . . he'll . . . he might not come to church again . . . yet . . . yet Bernard . . .*

Willis had stepped back, his face red with embarrassment. Bernard stood, arm still offered, a look of total confidence giving him a boyishly charming expression.

Trust in the Lord with all thine heart, came the soft inner voice to Ariana.

But I . . . I . . . this is an opportunity I've dreamed of, argued Ariana silently. *If I . . . yet . . .*

Ariana cast another quick glance at the flushed Willis, then gave Bernard the benefit of a full smile.

"I appreciate your kind offer, Mr. Dikerson," she said as sweetly as she could, "and under other circumstances I would be honored to accept. But Mr. Boyd had already asked to escort me home. Perhaps another Sunday."

Ariana smiled again and moved to take the limp arm of Willis Boyd. He flushed again, this time with pleasure.

O Lord, breathed Ariana as she walked away with her head held up in spite of her desire to lower it and cry, *Bernard likely will never speak to me again after this. . . .*

Trust . . . trust, came the silent words. *Trust in the Lord with all thine heart and lean not unto thine own understanding. . . .*

Ariana's head lifted higher. She swallowed back tears of disappointment and turned to the eager young man beside her.

"Have you had a good fall, Willis?" she inquired sociably, but she honestly found it hard to concentrate on his reply.

Ariana and her students worked hard to prepare for the school Christmas program. It was a great success, and even some townspeople without any children in the school came and enjoyed the singing and recitations. The following week Ariana was heavily involved in another program held in the little church. She was relieved when both events were over. Now she would be able to relax and focus wholly on her family's celebration of Christmas.

That evening she was turning from the church door, supposing that all had gone on home except her father, who still lingered to care for last-minute cleanup, when a voice spoke softly from the shadows. "Would now be a convenient time for me to ask to accompany you home, Miss Benson?"

Bernard Dikerson stepped into the light of the winter's moon and looked up to where she stood on the step. Ariana's breath caught in her throat. Bernard Dikerson had made no further approach since the incident a full two months earlier.

Ariana swallowed and nodded her head slowly. Then fearing that he could not see her nonverbal agreement, she forced the words through trembling lips. "Yes . . . yes, I guess so."

"Splendid," he said with enthusiasm, and moved forward to offer his arm.

Still tongue-tied, Ariana stepped down to accept his invitation.

"I do hope you haven't judged my silence as disinterest," he began as they walked together.

"I . . . I really . . ." Ariana stammered, but she didn't know what to say. She had thought about it—she could not deny it. She had wondered. She had felt disappointment. How could she respond without admitting more than she wished to?

"I know how busy you've been with the two Christmas programs—which both were delightful, if I might express my humble opinion," Bernard said. He chuckled softly.

Ariana smiled to herself. Somehow she couldn't imagine him having a humble opinion—about any subject. But he did sound genuinely interested in spite of the formal words.

"So I thought I should try to be patient. But I have been watching you—with admiration."

Ariana tilted her head slightly so she might catch a glimpse of his face. He did sound sincere. It made the breath catch in her throat.

"Now that your busyness is over—I do hope you will have some time for . . . for . . . some pleasantness. Work with no play can—"

"Oh, but I love teaching," Ariana interrupted.

She felt his hand move to press her fingers that rested on

his arm. "Of that I am convinced," he said, smiling down at her easily. "But perhaps it is time for you to discover a . . . a few other loves."

Ariana was puzzled and had no idea what he might mean by such a remark.

They reached the walk leading to the door of the parsonage. He stopped and Ariana was forced to pause beside him since he still held her hand firmly.

"Will you—would you like to come in?" she asked, though she felt uncertain about her offer.

"Not tonight. It's late—and you must be very tired. But I will be in touch. Soon."

He emphasized the last word. Ariana's breath caught in her throat again. He released her hand and tipped his hat.

"Good-night, Miss Benson," he said, very properly.

"Good-night . . . Mr. Dikerson," replied Ariana.

As she mounted the steps of the front porch, she felt the whole world spinning at a delightful pace.

"When?" asked Sam as he sat with his boss at the wooden table.

"Next big snowstorm," came the gruff reply.

"Storm? You outta yer mind? Ain't a body in his right mind thet'd ride out in a snowstorm. Ya know what storms can be like in these parts."

"I do. An' thet's why we're choosin' one. No way we're gonna be tracked nowhere in a snowstorm."

"Well, thet all depends. A light snow an' they can track ya right on in here like ya laid it out fer 'em."

"We won't pick a light snow."

"An' how ya gonna know 'head o' time whether it's gonna be heavy or light?" snorted Sam. But he knew it was almost uncanny how the boss could read storms.

"I kin tell."

Sam snorted again. “Sounds risky to me. Body can freeze to death in them storms.”

“We’ve been in storms before and we ain’t freezed yet.”

“What ya mean, we? I ain’t goin’ out in no winter storm, I tell ya. Not me. Not fer—nobody.”

The flickering light from the open fire cast eerie shadows across the dark face of the bigger man, making the scowl more pronounced, the dark eyes more menacing. “If I say ya ride—ya ride,” he growled. “Nobody made you boss—yet.”

Curses followed as each man expressed his anger in dark words.

“Who’s goin’?” Sam finally asked, conceding the fact that he would ride if the boss said ride.

“Jest you and me.”

“Jest. . . . Thet’s plumb foolhardy. Two ain’t enough to even—we’ll die in the storm fer sure. Not to mention the girl. She’ll never make it—an’ she’ll keep us from makin’ it, too.”

“Quit yer squawkin’,” the big man barked. “You ain’t gonna die before yer time. Iffen yer number’s up—then it’s up.”

“But I sure don’t plan on helpin’ it out in a snowstorm,” Sam argued once more.

“Better than a shot in the back.”

“Maybe not. Least a shot in the back would be faster.”

Sam moved to throw another log on the fire, sending sparks flying up the smokey chimney.

“Next storm,” Will repeated. “You be ready to ride tomorrow. We’re gonna move in closer and take thet ole trapper’s cabin down by the river. We’ll work out from there.”

“Thet’s Injun country,” interjected Sam.

Will placed his whiskey bottle on the table while he spit and swore at the mention of the tribe that made their home in the valley. Then he took another long draught of the fiery liquid.

“Be ready to ride tomorrow,” he barked. “I got it all worked out. Yer sure about the girl?”

Sam nodded. “She’ll be there,” he answered slowly.

Will lifted the whiskey bottle to his lips again. But when he discovered it was already empty, he flung the bottle angrily into the corner, scattering shards of broken glass about the cabin.

Chapter Four

The Snowstorm

Will turned to his son. "Not certain jest when we'll be back," the big man said to the tall young man before him.

Laramie made sure his face betrayed no emotion, but he was not pleased with the fact that his father and Sam were riding off with a winter storm imminent.

"Any orders?" he asked quietly. He would not openly question his father's decision, even though he felt it was downright foolhardy. He had a strong feeling Sam agreed with that assessment, though the man had not expressed such to him. Still, Sam stomped and cursed and looked particularly menacing as he saddled his own mount. The packs had been tied securely on the backs of the two other animals.

"No orders," said Will curtly. "You know the ropes."

The young man nodded. This was his father's way of saying that he was in charge.

His eyes turned back to the waiting horses. His father's horse pawed at the ground and blew, his nostrils flaring. He too seemed reluctant to leave the shelter of the buildings but was impatient to be off if a trip had to be made. Sam's horse stood head down, eyes nearly closed against the cold wind. He was getting old, but Sam refused to give him up in place of a younger mount.

The two pack animals crowded in against each other as

though seeking warmth. The young man's eyes narrowed slightly as he studied the two animals. Why two? The packs weren't that cumbersome. One horse could have easily carried the load. And there was something very odd about the one. A blanket covered the entire pack—as if something was being concealed. But hidden from whom? He was puzzled, but he knew better than to ask.

"Ya sure this rope is—" he began nonchalantly and stepped forward to check the rope that reached across the pack. He let his hand run over the contents beneath the blanket. Again his face gave nothing away, but he had discovered the mystery of the blanket. There was a saddle underneath it, camouflaged by small packs that rested on it. And it sure wasn't a pack saddle. It was a riding saddle. Why did his father need a third horse for a rider?

He stepped back and nodded to Sam, his way of casually acknowledging that the rope was secure. Sam cursed softly.

"Ya think I'm fergittin' how to pack a horse?" he grumbled.

The young man did not answer. He knew that none was expected. The rule of the gang was to keep quiet unless talk was required. He had already broken one of the rules. He had questioned a superior. Anyone but Sam would have been more than upset by the interference.

There were no goodbyes. No calls of "Safe trip," or "Be seein' you." The two men mounted their horses in silence; each picked up a lead for a pack horse and moved out onto the trail that wound away from the crude buildings. The few men left behind did not stand and watch them go or even wave a hand to send them on their way. They turned back to whatever their own activities had been, which in most cases was simply to be in where the fire would warm the frigid air.

"Skidder—best git up there and spell off Rawley," said the young man as they entered the cabin.

"He ain't been up there any four hours," protested the man called Skidder.

Laramie stopped. He looked straight into the eyes of the

man a few feet across the cabin. Something changed about the young man's stance. Not that his face—or even his body—gave much away, except that he was ready. Ready for whatever he might face.

They both knew there was some bad blood between them. The entire gang knew it. Had always felt it, though no one was quite sure what had started it. Now the whole cabin tensed.

"I don't think I asked how long he's been out there," Laramie said, and his words were coolly controlled. "I jest said thet it's time he was relieved."

He stopped and his eyes sent their own message. The others in the cabin shifted slightly. The young man appeared loose and easy—yet coiled like a snake about to strike. Everyone knew that the few words of question from Skidder had challenged the younger man's right of leadership.

Laramie spoke again, suggesting that he was not anxious to start a row—but he was in charge. "It's cold out there. We'll take shorter shifts," he said in explanation. He hesitated, and then drawled slowly, but with meaning, "Unless, of course, yer anxious to have yerself one extry long shift."

Skidder shuffled nervously but seemed to feel some relief. Had it been Will he had questioned, his dead body likely would have been cooling off out behind some barn by now. Will, as boss, had never been known to give a gang member a second chance. And Will never stopped to explain an order. "Only one boss in this here outfit," he said coldly to any new member that might be taken in. "An' you ain't it." The meaning was always clearly understood.

Skidder, who had been around gunmen for most of his life, had already figured out that the Kid, as all the camp called Laramie, would not shoot to kill. Still, he had no desire to have his shooting arm all messed up.

Without another look toward Laramie, Skidder reached for his heavy mackinaw and his rifle. The room stirred again. It seemed that bloodshed had been avoided. Shadow pulled out a deck of cards, and James pulled a log stool up to the table to let the man know that he wanted to be dealt in.

Laramie moved toward the fire and reached for another piece of wood. This one was over—but he'd have to watch his back even more closely in the future.

❧ ❧ ❧

In another cabin some distance away, Sam threw another log on the fire and shivered visibly in spite of sparks that shot upward.

"This here cabin's got enough cracks to run a bear through," he grumbled.

Will paid no attention to his complaining. He sat with a bottle of whiskey at his elbow and every now and then stopped to take a long, bored draught of the liquor.

"Fella gotta wear his hat to keep his ears from freezin'," Sam went on. He rubbed his hands together to keep the circulation going.

"Why don't ya sit down and quit yer grousin'?" Will said sourly.

"Gotta go git us some more firewood, thet's why," Sam threw back at him. "How many days we gotta keep this fire goin' anyway?"

" 'Til it storms."

"An' when ya bringin' in this here storm of yers?" Sam's sarcasm was more felt than heard.

Will scowled and shifted. Sam wondered if he had pushed too far and was relieved when Will's right hand reached for the whiskey bottle. The man couldn't hold a bottle and a gun in the same hand.

"Soon now," he answered, almost civil. "I can feel it. It'll be soon."

Sam said no more but picked up the hatchet and went out to look for more firewood.

❧ ❧ ❧

Ariana sighed and stacked the day's marked assignments into a neat little pile on the corner of her desk. She was glad to have the grading completed so she could get home. The sky had darkened and the temperature had dropped. Even though she had recently added more wood to the potbellied cast-iron stove, it was unable to keep the room warm. Her feet cold, she stomped them on the floor once more as she sat at her desk.

She had some assignments to get ready for the next day and a Scripture passage to choose for the morning reading, and then she could bank the fire and be off home. She pulled her sweater a bit closer about her body.

The heavy door creaked open and Ariana raised her head. Along with a few flakes of snow, two men in long, heavy buffalo coats and black hats pulled down over bearded faces stepped through the opening. Ariana knew she had not seen them before.

"Hello," she said pleasantly, thinking them to have lost their way. "Can I help you?"

There was no answer. The two men moved farther into the room. Ariana could sense that their dark eyes were sweeping quickly over the interior, taking in everything they saw. Something about them made her feel very uncomfortable. She stood.

"Can I help you?" she repeated. "If you are looking for the town—"

The smaller man looked longingly at the iron stove. Ariana saw one hand reach out toward it, as though to take full benefit of its heat if only for a moment.

"Please, feel free to warm yourselves before you go on," offered Ariana. In spite of herself, she felt a tremble of fear pass through her.

"Reckon we won't take time fer warmin'," said the bigger man gruffly. "Got some ridin' to do. Now iffen you'd jest git yer coat, miss—we'd welcome ya to join us."

Ariana stared in unbelief.

"What—?"

"Git yer coat, miss." The order was growled more loudly from the gravelly voice. Ariana froze to the spot.

"I think ya better do as told, miss," advised the smaller man. "It'll be easier on ya iffen ya co-operate."

"But I . . . I can't go with you. My family is expecting me—"

"Then yer family will jest have to wait a spell," said the big man. Ariana saw the end of a pistol peeking out from the furry sleeve of his heavy coat.

"But I—"

Ariana stiffened and pulled herself to her full height. She took a deep breath and told herself to hold steady. Not to panic. But at the same moment her whole body trembled. She was afraid she was going to faint.

She closed her eyes and grasped her desk with both hands. *Trust in the Lord*, she managed inwardly. That was as far as she got with her prayer.

"Git yer coat," barked the big man again. "An' I'd advise thet ya git any other wraps thet might keep out the weather. We got us some tough trails ahead."

"If you think I have any intention of riding off—" began Ariana, finding courage she did not know she possessed.

Her words were interrupted by a hoarse laugh. The big man turned to the smaller one. "Ya got us one with spunk, Sam." He laughed again. "I like thet. Should work in our favor—later." Then his eyes turned cruel again. "But not now. Now—ya git yer coat."

Ariana lifted her chin and tried to still its trembling. "I will go nowhere with you," she managed.

The big man reached out a hand that closed firmly on Ariana's wrist, making her wince with the pain. Roughly he jerked her toward the hook where her coat hung. She struggled against his iron grip, writhing this way and that in an effort to free herself. The grip on her wrist tightened, sending spasms of pain shooting up her arm.

With one last mighty effort, Ariana spun around and raked her fingernails down the face of her opponent. She saw the prickles of blood appear on the broken skin before he wrested her to the floor.

Dark curses filled the air. "Sam, gimme the rope," he shouted.

The other man stepped forward, an ugly frayed rope dangling from his hand. For a moment he stood looking down at her, chewing on his stained mustache. Ariana was fighting against tears. Her wrist felt as if it had been broken.

"We be needin' this, miss—or are ya gonna be reasonable?" asked the man named Sam.

Ariana nodded mutely. The big man pulled her roughly to her feet. "Then git yer coat—and I ain't sayin' it agin," he growled.

Ariana had no choice but to obey.

"Take everything thet ya be needin', miss," said the smaller man. "Ya won't be back fer a while."

Ariana felt there might be just a trace of sympathy in his voice. Instinct told her to respond quietly to his orders. Perhaps, if she did not resist, in time she would have an ally.

She quickly moved to get her coat, her eyes darting over the room to see just what she might take with her that could be of use in the uncertain future. With her wrist throbbing painfully, she managed to pull on her heavy coat and do up the buttons. Then she pushed a few items into her cloth carrying bag. She really had very little at the schoolhouse. Just as she was about to move off, she noticed her Bible and quickly slipped it into the bag as well. She had the impression that it might become more important than ever to her.

She felt as though she were in some horrid nightmare. Nothing seemed real. She prayed that it wasn't. That she would soon wake up to her usual life. But the pain in her wrist was a reminder of how real her present circumstance was. She had to do something. Had to protect herself someway. But what could she do?

Her hands trembled and she felt weak and faint. There was no point in screaming—no one was within hearing distance. There was no use trying to fight—she'd never be the winner. And there was no way she could break and run—at least not now.

She was being kidnapped. Cruelly, frighteningly *kidnapped*—by two desperadoes. She knew not why and she knew not where they were taking her, but her whole being trembled at the questions tumbling through her mind. What would they do with her—to her? Would she ever see home again? What would her parents think? Her poor mother! Her pupils? Bernard Dikerson? Her—

No. No, she must stop thinking. It would drive her insane. She had to pray. She had to trust God. She had to.

But it was hard to concentrate on Bible passages as she was roughly pushed out the door and toward waiting horses. It was hard to pray sensibly. It was even hard to think.

"Oh, God," was all she was able to whisper.

She was boosted up on one of the horses and given a blanket to cover her legs and feet.

"Wrap yerself in this. It's bitin' cold," said the smaller man.

Reluctantly Ariana obeyed.

"Ya ride?" snarled the bigger man.

"Some," replied Ariana in a trembling voice.

He nodded as though that was good enough. "Yer gonna ride now," he said in his rough voice, and he grabbed the lead rope attached to her horse and gave a jerk. They were moving out. One man in front of her, one behind.

It was snowing quite heavily now.

Mrs. Benson let the curtain fall back into place. Her eyes were dark with worry as she turned back to the kitchen stove, where the evening meal waited. She was troubled. Ariana was never this late. And it was snowing. Fairly hard now. She didn't like it. She moved toward the living room to speak again to her husband. Maybe he should go—

When she reached the door he was already pulling on a

heavy coat. "I think I'll just walk on out and meet her," he said, making the words sound reasonable.

Relieved, she smiled at him. "You'll take the lantern?" she asked simply.

He looked out the window at the falling snow. It was getting darker. He nodded slowly.

"Might be a good idea," he said. "I suppose she's been busy and just lost track of time. Doesn't realize that a storm has moved in so quickly."

Mrs. Benson knew he was trying to reassure her. She also knew he was aware that their Ariana was not one to lose track of time or the weather.

"She might have slipped and twisted her ankle—or something," she responded. "It's awfully—"

"Now, Mother," said her husband gently. "Let's not borrow trouble."

His words could not erase the worry from her face or the pang in her heart.

She quickly lit the lantern and brought it to him. "She might have stopped at the hardware store," she said, trying her own explanation. "She did say she needed another bottle of ink."

"Likely got talking with one of her students—or friends—and has—" He floundered to a stop.

Mrs. Benson could tell he was going to add "lost track of time."

"I'll check there first," he said instead.

She watched him go, anxiety making her body tense. Ariana had never worried them with tardiness before. It just wasn't like her.

Ariana's mother turned back to the kitchen. She would busy herself with finding a way to keep the evening meal palatable.

Chapter Five

Searching

All through the long night and into the next day they traveled. Ariana had lost all sense of direction or any clear knowledge of time. Once they stopped, and the man Sam dismounted and came up to Ariana.

"Best slip off those shoes and put on these," he informed her. Ariana was so cold she couldn't comply. It was the man who pulled the shoes from her feet and slipped on soft-furred moccasins. He tucked her shoes into one of the packs on the extra animal. Then he handed Ariana some heavy fur mittens. "Put these on," he ordered, and Ariana managed to obey.

At least they were protecting her—in some ways. But why? Why was she taken? What was their reason for picking up a simple schoolteacher? They must have confused her with someone else. Surely there would be no demand for ransom. Her father was simply a village parson—not a wealthy man. He had no money to pay for her release. But if a ransom was not the motive, then why was she taken?

The very question made Ariana's blood run cold. Was she to experience a fate worse than death?

"Oh, God—please not that," she breathed into the cold night air.

It was again dark when Ariana saw the dim outlines of a

cabin. She was helped to dismount by the man named Sam and led—almost carried—into the cold interior—no better than the outside as far as temperature went.

Sam busied himself with starting a fire and nodded his head toward the flame as he spoke to Ariana.

"Jest don't git too close, too quick. Might faint."

And he left her with the big, surly man while he went out to the horses.

The big man said nothing. He did not even remove his coat or hat. He crossed to a wooden frame in the corner that made some sort of crude sleeping platform.

"Gonna git me some shut-eye," he said, and even those words sounded threatening. "Don't go try nothin' foolish. I've shot more'n one man in my sleep."

Ariana shivered from more than just the cold. She bit her lip to keep from crying and huddled more closely to the fire in spite of Sam's warning.

When Sam returned he made a pot of coffee. Ariana was surprised at how good it smelled. She wondered how her stomach could even respond to it under the circumstances.

When the coffee had boiled he poured her a cup, then rummaged in a pack he had brought in and handed her something. It didn't look good—and it didn't smell good either. Ariana's stomach revolted, even though it ached for something to eat.

"Pemmican," the man informed her. "Boss ain't got much use for Injun ways—'ceptin' pemmican. Lets me make it the way I learned from—" He stopped, then shoved something else into her hand. "Hardtack. Eat it. It's all yer gonna git fer a while, an' yer gonna need yer strength."

Ariana cast a glance toward the corner. She could hear snoring coming from the big man. She took a tentative bite of the hardtack. It was tasteless and hard chewing, but it wasn't too bad. She took another and washed it down with the coffee.

She glanced toward the big man. Dared she—dared she ask Sam questions?

"I . . . I don't understand . . . what this is all about," she ventured in a quiet voice. "There must be some mistake. I . . . I'm not who you think I am."

Sam chewed off a big bite of the pemmican and spent some time trying to get his teeth to work up the piece before he even attempted a response.

"An' who do we think ya are?"

"I . . . I've no idea. I . . . I'm just a schoolteacher," she stumbled on.

"Got nothin' agin' schoolteachers," said the man, taking a swallow of the hot coffee to wash down the pemmican.

"But why—?"

"Now, miss—don't ya go frettin' yerself over it none."

He took another bite of the pemmican.

"Don't fret myself!" exclaimed Ariana, raising both her position and her voice.

Sam cast a quick glance toward the corner, reminding Ariana that she'd best watch her step.

She shrank back into her crouched position before the fire. In spite of her strong resolve, tears began to fill her eyes and trickle down her still-cold cheeks. She brushed them away with a trembling hand. Sam continued to eat his pemmican.

Ariana said nothing more. It was Sam who first broke the silence. He had finished munching on his trail provisions. He had even finished his third cup of coffee. Now he pulled the back of his hand across his unkempt mustache and sniffed.

"How's yer wrist?" he asked, as though it was an ordinary question.

Ariana's eyes showed her surprise, but she said nothing.

"Let's see it," he suggested.

She hesitated for one moment, and then held it out obediently.

He took the wrist in his two hands and ran his thumbs and fingers over the area, bending it forward, then back, nearly making Ariana cry out. He pushed it to one side, then the other, his fingers feeling each bone and muscle as he moved it. Ariana fought the tears.

"Don't think nothin's broke," he said at last, "but it's gonna pain fer a while."

There was no apology. No offer to give any assistance with the pain. He released her hand and went back for another cup of coffee.

As he poured out the thick, steamy liquid he spoke again. "Iffen I were you, I'd jest curl up there beside the fire and try to git some sleep. Once daylight comes I 'spect we'll be movin' on out—an' we got a mighty tough ride 'head of us."

Ariana nodded. The fire was making her feel drowsy.

"Here," said Sam, "use this," and he tossed his big buffalo-hide coat on the floor at her feet. Ariana reached for it and awkwardly spread it out before the fire.

Mrs. Benson opened the door as soon as she heard her husband's steps. Her eyes quickly scanned the darkness, but to her dismay he stood there in the snow alone.

"What—?" she began, but he brushed past her and into the room.

She saw his face then and knew that he was just as concerned as she herself was.

"I . . . I didn't find her," he admitted.

"Did you try the store?"

He nodded. "I went to the store first."

"Did you go to the school?"

"Of course I went to the school." His anxiety made him a bit curt, which was most unusual. His words, spoken in sharpness, brought terror to her heart.

Tears formed in her eyes, and she began to wring her hands in agitation. He stepped forward and pulled her to him. "Now, my dear," he said, and she could tell that he was fighting to put down his own fears. "Let's not jump to any conclusions. I'm sure there's a reason—"

"What reason?" she cut in, her voice full of panic as she

pushed back from him. "What possible—?"

"I don't know yet, but—"

"She has never been late. This is not like her."

"Perhaps one of her students had an emergency."

It was something to grasp at. She prayed he might be right. But even as he spoke the words, her heart began to doubt again.

"But—she would have let us know—someway. She'd know we'd worry."

"Maybe she had no way to let us know. Maybe—there wasn't time," he continued.

"Come on to the table," she said, brushing at the snow on his coat. "I've got your supper." Her voice sounded weary—dead.

He resisted. "No . . . no, I just came to . . . to let you know . . ." His voice trailed off in an evasive manner. "We—I've spoken to the sheriff—some of the townfolks. We . . . we're going to keep looking. We . . . we'll check out the homes of all the students. Make sure—"

"But it's dark. And the storm—"

"We'll all carry lanterns."

Her next protest caught in her throat, between concern for her husband and worry over her daughter. Silently she nodded her head. "Travel in pairs," she said softly. "Are you dressed warmly enough?"

He nodded.

He reached for her again. Her worry had turned to alarm, and now she felt as though her heart were being squeezed. She allowed herself to be drawn up against him, and the tears spilled out and mixed with the melting snow on his shoulder.

She felt him bend his head and kiss her silvery hair.

"We'll find her," he promised, his voice full of emotion.

She lifted her head and fumbled for her pocket hanky. "You should eat," she tried once more through her sniffles.

"Later."

"Travel in pairs," she reminded him again.

He nodded.

"You should have your heavier mittens," she fussed.

He nodded. "Would you get them, please?" he asked her.

She knew he was trying to distract her, but she brought the mittens and watched as he removed the ones he was wearing and replaced them with the heavy pair.

"I'll be praying," she said and lifted her hanky to wipe tears again.

He again held out his arms to her and she quickly took refuge. He was her minister now as well as her husband, and together they bowed their heads while he led them in fervent prayer. Then with one final kiss on her forehead he released her and turned back into the night.

⁂

The search continued until it was impossible to carry on. Every home that had a student in the local school was called upon. The response was always the same. The children were shocked and bewildered. "She was still there when we left—same as always," came the reply to the question.

Little girls cried and young boys shuffled in agitation. It just wasn't like their teacher—to just disappear. Something awful must have happened.

At last the tired, hungry searchers returned to their homes, chilled by the cold winds and hampered by blowing snow. There simply was no logic in searching on through the darkness.

⁂

In spite of the continued blowing snow, the next morning the sheriff organized a posse of town citizens to fan out into the surrounding hills and even beyond to the plains. An intense search was made along the creek bank, in the fear that Ariana might have slipped and fallen while crossing the footbridge. No sign of her was found.

Bernard Dikerson asked his father to post reward money for her safe return, and the man responded. As the day wore on and the searchers drifted back with no news, the whole town was stricken.

Nothing—not a trace of the missing girl was found. The doors of the school were closed, and folks of the town huddled in whispering groups, shocked and saddened by the tragic and mysterious disappearance of the beloved schoolteacher.

In the parsonage, the fear and grief filled every room. The Bensons clung to each other. They prayed, they cried, they reminded themselves that they had a sovereign God, then they prayed and cried some more.

"Surely God . . . surely God knows where she is and . . . and can preserve her," insisted Pastor Benson. With her handkerchief clutched in her hand and tears on her cheeks, Mrs. Benson shakily nodded her head in agreement.

Ariana could not tell if it was day or night when she was roused from sleep by the nudge of a well-worn boot. The big man stood over her, staring down into her face.

"Time to ride," he ordered.

Ariana struggled to stand. She moved nearer the fireplace, brushing futilely at her wrinkled skirts. The door opened and Sam came in. He was shivering from the cold and muttering words of profanity.

"Fool weather fer anyone to be out," she heard him grumble.

"Where's yer coat, ya dumb ox?" demanded the big man, no sympathy in his tone.

"Didn't think I'd need it jest to get the horses ready," Sam replied, not looking up from the coffee he was pouring.

Ariana's eyes dropped to her feet. Sam's heavy coat had been her bed for the night. She felt her cheeks warming with the thought that he had chosen to face the bitter cold rather than awaken her. It both embarrassed her and gave her reason to hope. Perhaps the man was not all bad.

"How're the horses?" asked the big man between gulps of coffee.

Sam nodded. "Near froze to death, I'm thinkin'. Anxious to be movin' so's their blood'll flow agin."

"Then let's git movin'," said the big man, and he drained his cup of the last swallow of coffee.

"Girl ain't et yet," remarked Sam.

The big man turned to Ariana and scowled. "Best grab ya a biscuit or two. Won't be stoppin' fer no teatime."

Ariana moved forward. Every bone in her body protested. First the ride through the cold. Then the night on the crude bed on the floor. Her entire being hurt.

She reached for a biscuit, but the pain in her wrist brought a sharp intake of breath. For a moment she felt faint and fought to stay upright.

Sam made a motion as if to move toward her, but then stopped. Neither made comment.

As soon as the room came back into focus, Ariana reached out with her left hand and claimed one of the biscuits lying on the table. She switched it to her right hand so she could accept the cup of coffee Sam held out to her.

The biscuit was hard. The hardest thing Ariana had ever tried to chew. Hesitantly she dipped one edge into her coffee and chewed off the softened portion. It was not pleasant—but at least it was edible.

Ariana did not have to be encouraged to take full advantage of all of the warmth she was offered. She accepted the heavy mittens, the blanket, along with the moth-eaten beaver hat for her head. Even with this, she still shivered against the cold.

She could hardly tell if it was day or night. The snow continued to fall, obliterating the sun—if indeed it was somewhere up above. The swirling whiteness wiped out all landmarks. All sign of the world around them. Ariana wondered if the two men really knew where they were going or were simply wandering on through the storm. She dared not ask any questions.

After what seemed hours and hours of stumbling their way along the hidden trail, the big man pulled up his horse and the other horses stopped in line behind him.

"Snow's deep," he said when Sam pushed up beside him. "Think it might be wise to camp here tonight."

"I was sure hoping to git on home to my own bed," said Sam.

"It's been slow goin'. Don't think we'll make it home tonight. A bit too risky on thet ridge."

Sam nodded. He didn't seem about to argue on that score.

"There's a cave mouth in there somewhere," said the big man, motioning vaguely. "See iffen ya can find it."

Sam moved off cursing. "Jest hope no big bear found it first," Ariana heard him say.

The big man turned to her. "Git on down," he said, not offering her any assistance. Ariana wasn't sure if her legs would hold her, but she moved stiffly to obey.

It was as she had feared. Even though she clung to the horse for support, she could not stand upright. Her legs gave way and she found herself in a heap in the deep snow.

"Women," groused the big man to accompanying curses. "Don't got no more starch in their backbone then a snake."

Ariana quite expected to remain in the snow until she could find the strength to move—unless Sam took mercy on her. But to her surprise the big man reached down and roughly scooped her up. He carried her easily to the side of the trail and deposited her unceremoniously on a tree stump without bothering to brush off its cap of snow.

Ariana sat silently, willing herself to hold her tears at bay. They would only freeze on her frosted cheeks, making her even more miserable than she already was.

Sam returned after some moments and announced he had found the cave—and it was uninhabited.

Sam moved the horses toward it. Ariana managed to get one foot to proceed the other. With great difficulty she followed the trail broken by Sam and the mounts. The big man brought up the rear.

They gathered in the cave. Sam built a fire, and to Ariana's surprise it was warmer than the cabin had been. But soon swirling gray smoke filled the cave and made Ariana's eyes sting. She moved back into the farthest corner, even though she longed to take advantage of the heat that radiated from the beckoning flames. Sam made the coffee, and along with more hardtack and pemmican, they shared the simple supper. Ariana was only too willing to curl up on spruce boughs and Sam's buffalo robe. She was exhausted. Besides, it was only in sleep that she could shut out the horror of her present experience—even if only for a few hours of time.

Chapter Six

Arrival

As they traveled the next day, Ariana grieved as each hour took her farther and farther away from her family and home. She ached for her father and mother. If only she had some way to communicate with them. To let them know she had not been harmed—at least not yet. She worried about her students. What would they do? What would they think of her, failing to show up for classes?

She prayed and worried by turn. Frantic mental searching for ways of escape, followed by clinging to the one word, *trust*. "Surely God knows where I am, even if I don't," she would remind herself, and then turn right back to worrying again.

Stop it, she scolded herself. *I can't trust and worry at the same time—can I?*

It was so difficult to obey her own admonition.

The blinding snow still swirled around her. Her tired pony stumbled on and on. Her bones ached. Her flesh felt numb with cold. She sometimes wondered if she was more dead than alive—but they traveled on through the blank whiteness.

Guessing it to be afternoon, she had a strange sense that more than falling snow obliterated the pathway. She looked around but could make out little of the landscape. At times she knew she was very close to brushing up against something on one side or the other. She caught brief glimpses of solid rock. *Is it some sort of passageway?* she wondered. But she could not see well enough for her question to be answered.

She was slumped in her saddle, eyes half closed, when she felt the steps of her horse quicken. Then she heard a neigh from the big black that the man ahead was riding. Sam's horse pushed at hers from behind.

From the near distance came an answering whinny. Ariana felt a new stirring of the animals and the two men who guided her. Before her eyes buildings began to take shape. She could not see them clearly through the snow, nor could she count them. Was it a town? But no, they all looked poorly kept. Ramshackle. And then she heard the big man say "Whoa" in his loud raspy voice, and the four horses stopped as one.

Ariana did not move. She was aware that someone stood near her. She wondered if she would be lifted down or left to fall off her mount.

"Git her to the south shack. I'll have one of the boys take care of the horses," the big man's voice instructed, and she was moving off again, her horse being led away by Sam.

There was no way she could have made it into the building on her own. Sam half supported, half carried her. Once inside, he helped her to a wooden bunk in the corner.

"I'll git a fire goin'," he announced. "It'll soon be almost livable in here."

Ariana did not respond.

She heard the man moving about the cabin and sensed that the fire had been started. But she didn't care. Didn't care about any of it. She was cold clear through and weary beyond belief. Her swollen wrist did not hurt any more than the rest of her. She closed her eyes and almost immediately fell into a deep sleep.

Ariana woke up stiff and sore and in a strange place with no idea how long she had slept.

Her first conscious thought was that the sun was now shining. She could see its faint light through the cracked, dirty window. She breathed a prayer of thanks for the sun. Now someone would be looking for her. Now there was some hope she would be found.

Her next awareness was that she was not alone. She felt a moment of panic and her eyes quickly scanned the room.

Sam sat on his log stool with his back against the cabin wall. He was tilted back so his feet could extend to be propped up on a rough table.

"Mornin'," he said lazily when their gaze met.

Ariana groaned in response. It brought a little chuckle.

"Little stiff?" he asked good-naturedly.

Ariana struggled to get her feet off the bed and under her. Every movement hurt.

"You'll git yer bones shook out—all in good time," Sam commented, cutting himself a chew of tobacco.

Ariana concentrated hard on standing to her feet.

"Brung ya the things ya be needin'," went on Sam, and he dropped his heavy-booted feet to the floor with a clunk.

Ariana looked about her. The room was small. It had a potbellied stove, the rough wood table, two log stools, and the bunk in the corner on which she had slept. Over by the door, a simple shelf held a dented basin and a sickly green, chipped enamel pitcher. On the floor stood a pail with water. A second pail stood near. Sam nodded at it now.

"Yer slops," he explained. "Winder is nailed shut so's ya'll jest have to wait 'til we come to dump 'em."

Ariana noticed her schoolbag on the table. She was comforted to see even that little bit of home.

Sam stood to his feet. "Reckon ya'd like to get washed up. Water's hot in the kettle."

Ariana had missed the kettle that sat near the back of the stove.

"I'll brung ya over some vittles."

Sam shuffled toward the door.

Ariana moved as though to follow. She wanted to call after the unshaven man. She had so many questions. Where were they? Is this where she would stay? For how long? Why? *Why?*

Before she could get her voice to work, he had gone. She heard the thunk of a heavy bar falling into place over the outside of the door. She was locked in.

❦ ❦ ❦

Ariana spent most of the first two days in her captive cabin in tears of fear and frustration. She was locked in. Solidly and securely. She didn't know where she was or why she was there. The most frightening thought was that she didn't know what her captors intended.

There was no way out. She had already pushed with all her might on the door and clawed at the window until the tips of her fingers bled. There was nothing she could do. Nothing but weep and pray.

On the third day, Ariana awakened from a troubled sleep and took a fresh look at her situation. So far, nothing too terrible had happened to her. She was a prisoner, yes, but other than that first encounter with the two men and her damaged wrist, she had not been hurt or mistreated, at least so far. Only Sam had been to the cabin—though she had heard other voices outside and other footsteps on the path. She should thank God for each day of safety. Her father—and the townsfolk—would be looking for her, led by the sheriff and his men. Maybe they were closing in even at the moment. She just had to be patient. Be calm. Trust. Really trust in her heavenly Father. Her fighting and agitation and tears were getting her nowhere. Ariana wiped her eyes and decided that those tears would be her last.

❦ ❦ ❦

"Well, ya got her here—now what?"

Sam spit at the fire and turned back to eye his boss. The big man said nothing. He seemed to be thinking.

At last he stirred and turned to Sam. "So far—plan's worked jest fine," he said with satisfaction. "Ya picked a good one. Pretty an'—well, she oughta race the blood of any man. Even one as cool and calculating as the Kid."

He stopped and laughed, not a pleasant sound. Sam shifted nervously on his wooden block.

"The storm did jest what we wanted it to," went on Will Russell, then stopped to curse and spit on the floor. "Not even an Injun could track us through all thet."

Sam shivered at the thought of the storm. There had been more than once when he'd thought they would all end up frozen in the saddle.

"So now—" prompted Sam.

The big man scowled. "What ya frettin' on now?" he growled.

"Ain't frettin'," responded Sam, unruffled. "Jest wonderin' how long I'm gonna be playin' nursemaid to the little schoolmarm."

Will stomped across the room and looked out the window at the sunny day. The snow lay in shimmering drifts across the floor of the canyon. The buildings all wore big fluffy caps of winter snow, and the trees bowed down with the weight of the whiteness. It was a pretty world.

But Sam could tell his thoughts were on other things. "'Bout time to have us a meetin'," Will said, and he grinned an ugly grin that showed his stained teeth and highlighted the jagged scar crossing his cheek.

He turned back to Sam. "Tell the fellas we want to have them all in here followin' supper. Who's on guard duty?"

Sam thought for a moment. "Right now—James. Then Curly. First night shift—McDuff."

"Good," said the big man. "I wanna be sure that Skidder is here fer this meetin'. And the Kid. Make sure the Kid's here."

Will Russell began as usual, spitting on the floor, then clearing his throat. His son watched as the big man's eyes scanned the group of rough and rugged men, a motley crew, to be sure.

"Ya all know thet we got us a guest," was his opening statement. He paused. There was no response.

"Now this here guest is—special. I can't give ya none of the particulars—jest want to say thet the keepin' is important. Thet's all thet's necessary to say. Iffen anything should happen to—our guest—thet is anything thet would lend itself to—leavin'—well, I wouldn't take a bit kindly to thet."

He paused again and his eyes swept the room, stopping to bear down on each of the occupants in personal challenge.

"Ya git my meanin'?" he growled.

No one moved. Laramie knew that each man understood. The prisoner was not to escape.

"Thet means thet we gotta have extry guard duty."

He let the words hang heavy in the air, and then turned slightly to look at his son. Laramie forced himself not to flinch.

"Kid," he said, "thet's you."

The young man's face purposely showed no change of emotion. He did not even nod. There was no need to agree to the assignment. It was understood that he would.

"From now on, yer off the usual sentry duty. Yer full duty will be to guard thet cabin."

The father looked at the son. Their eyes locked for a moment. The Kid had never been shown favoritism by the big man. He expected none now. Yet it didn't seem fair that he was to be given the sole responsibility for guarding the man in the south shack. Who did his father have in there, anyway? Some bank president? A wealthy rancher? Some politician? Or was it an Indian chief? And what was the game? Some huge ransom? Laramie didn't like it. Didn't like it at all. He had sensed—had known—that something strange was going on. He just hoped the whole camp didn't live to regret it. If they lived at all.

"Like I said," continued his father, his dark beard and dark eyes making his scowling face appear even more menacing, "I won't be happy iffen anything should happen—no matter who allows it."

The meaning was clear to Laramie. He was guarding the prisoner at the risk of his own life.

"Please," said Ariana as Sam opened the door a crack and handed her in a plate of unsavory food. "Please—can't . . . can't you wait a minute? I really need to . . . to talk."

Sam looked about the camp. No one was in sight. Uneasily he shifted his weight from one foot to the other. Then he pushed the door open farther and slipped into the room.

"I . . . I . . ." Ariana looked down at her rumpled garments. "I really do need to . . . to freshen up," she ventured. "I've been in these same clothes for . . . days." She had not counted the days. She truly had lost track of time.

For a moment Sam looked sympathetic, then he shrugged thin shoulders. "Missy," he said, "iffen ya didn't notice, there ain't 'xactly a ladies' shop nearby."

"But surely . . . surely there is some way for me to . . . to bathe. To wash my . . . my hair and my . . . garments," protested Ariana. "I . . . I'm filthy."

The man shrugged again. "I'll see what I can do," he promised as he turned to go, but he quickly added, "But don't ya go expectin' much. I've no notion where we gonna find any—bathtub."

"Thank you," breathed Ariana as he left.

She had been living one day at a time since arriving. She spent most of her hours reading her cherished Bible. It was the only way she could survive the uncertainty and tedium. Then Sam came. Only to bring her a supply of wood and fresh water. He emptied her slop pail and brought her a plate of food. Other than Sam, she saw no one.

Her one window faced away from the camp into the woods. There was a small window on the camp side—but it had been covered over on the outside, so Ariana still had no idea where she was. She prayed for release. She thanked the Lord for daily safety. But she felt as though something needed to happen—soon—or she would lose her sanity. How long had it been? Six days? A week? More? She wasn't sure. But each day seemed like an eternity.

She was pushing the food around on the plate—the fork had a broken tine—when she heard someone at the door again. It was Sam who poked in his head.

"You found one," she exclaimed, jumping to her feet.

He waved her words aside.

"Ain't even had time to look," he quickly informed her. "Jest thought of somethin' else."

Ariana sat back down.

Sam entered the room again and his voice lowered as though he feared someone might overhear their conversation.

"Jest thought ya oughta know," he said in a raspy whisper, "things have changed. I won't be comin' anymore. Boss has assigned—"

Terror gripped Ariana, and she stood shakily to her feet and reached out her hand to him.

"Please. Please," she pleaded. "Please don't let him change. I . . . I don't want anyone—"

"Now calm down some," Sam said with a measure of irritation. "It won't be all thet bad. The Kid will be takin' care of ya. Ya jest . . . jest mind yer manners an'—"

"Who's . . . the Kid?" asked Ariana, her eyes wide with fright.

"Aw, he ain't so bad. It's the boss's son."

Ariana's mind filled with an image of the man Sam called the Boss. She hadn't seen him well. There had always been the storm—or the darkness of the cabin or cave, lit only by the light from the open fire. But she knew enough to fear him. To feel terror at the very thought of his nearness. Unconsciously she reached her left hand to rub her right wrist. Though it was improving, Ariana well remembered the searing pain. Sam's boss was some kind of madman. And now—she was to be guarded by *his son.* Her whole body began to tremble.

Sam turned back to the door. "Jest thought ya oughta know," he said as he exited the room and pulled the door shut behind him. Ariana heard the bar fall into place.

There was little sleep for Ariana that night. She forgot about her unkempt hair. Her rumpled clothes. She even forgot to throw more fuel into the heavy iron stove. Hour after hour she lay shivering in the darkness. Shivering with terror.

She tried to pray. Tried to trust, but every time she shut her eyes she saw the dark, brooding face of the man they called the Boss. What was to happen to her now? Ariana found herself wishing she had perished in the storm.

Ariana stirred from her sleep to thumping on her door. Sam must be bringing her breakfast. But then she became fully conscious and remembered Sam had said he would not be coming anymore. That she would now be cared for by the boss's son.

Ariana frantically cast her eyes about the room, looking for a place to hide. Even as she acknowledged that there was none, the door pushed open.

A tall young man ducked his head to enter. She saw his hand on his pistol as his eyes swept the room quickly. When they lit on her, he froze. She saw the confused, shocked expression that momentarily transformed his face.

Chapter Seven

The Dilemma

He stood where he was, staring at her. The food in his left hand threatened to spill from the forgotten, tilting plate. His eyes quickly scanned the room again as though he must have missed something, then came back to her.

She stared back with eyes wide and frightened. She clasped the tattered blanket in both hands, holding it up against her like a protective shield. Her breath caught in her throat in a little gasp.

The sound seemed to jerk him back to reality. The gun hand lifted to push his Stetson up a little on his head. From the way his hand moved, she guessed it to be a nervous gesture on his part. Yet he looked so calm. So composed. She still had not risen to her feet but sat on the edge of the crude bunk, as though poised for flight.

He nodded silently and moved into the room.

Without a word he set the plate of food on the table. His eyes moved over the room once more. She could see a steeliness in his face and instinctively knew she would never wish to challenge this young man. She noticed the hard set of his jaw—as though something had deeply disturbed him. He looked almost angry—yet what had she done?

He cast a glance toward her iron stove and without a word proceeded to build a fire. Then he picked up her water pail, filled the kettle and set it on the stove, then poured the remainder of the water into the empty basin.

He still had not spoken, and Ariana had not moved toward the plate of food. He did not look her way again, but left, the water pail in his hand.

Ariana heard the thunk of the wooden bar across her door. She heard the steps crunching on the new snow of the path. And then he was gone—as quickly and as silently as he had come.

Ariana shivered anew. She felt all trembly inside, further frightened—but she knew not why.

Whoever had entered her cabin had not looked *vicious.* He had not looked at all like the man Sam called the Boss. While that man was dark and heavyset, this man was tall and lithe. He was much fairer, too. His eyes were blue rather than almost black.

But the memory of those piercing blue eyes made her shiver again. She longed for the return of Sam. It was frightening enough to be held captive, but to have to face a new guard. . . .

Ariana shook her shoulders slightly and wrapped her arms close to try to hold at bay the fear that had overtaken her being. This new guard had brought food. She must eat if she were to keep up her strength. Surely the day would come when she would find some way to escape from her prison. She must be ready.

In spite of her fear and her lack of interest in the bland plate of food, her stomach growled. She forced herself to her feet and moved toward the shelf with its basin.

She splashed the fresh water over her face and washed her hands as best as she could. Without soap, she always felt she hadn't really washed—simply rinsed. Still it felt refreshing, if nothing else.

She dumped the used water into the pail beside her feet. It was full.

He hadn't emptied the slop pail.

Laramie had never felt so disturbed in all his life. First of all, the secrecy of his father's plans and mission had bothered him. Then the strict orders on the importance of guarding the prisoner, leading the whole camp to believe they had some—some armed desperado or high-ranking official in the south cabin. And now this. A girl. A mere girl. A girl did not belong in a camp of men. Any camp of men. And certainly not in their camp of men. He shook with anger. He had never questioned his father before—but he was going to demand some answers now.

He had to calm himself. He was in no condition for either a confrontation with his father or another visit with the prisoner. He took the path through the woods to the spring where they got their water, glad for the pail in his hand that gave him a good excuse.

Not calmed down by the time he reached his destination, Laramie stared at the spring. The small pool had frozen over again during the night, and he picked up the axe, relieved to be able to expend some of his anger in strenuous activity.

He made a hole large enough to dip in the pail and still kept chopping. The silver slivers of ice flew with each swing of the axe, sprinkling the new blanket of snow that lay on the surface.

Why had his father done it? Why? What was behind this fool scheme? Surely this bit of a girl was worth nothing to the gang. Or was she? Was she some wealthy rancher's daughter? Was there a large ransom on her head? If so, he hoped that it quickly would be paid so she could be returned to wherever she belonged.

He knew nothing of women, but he didn't like the thought of one in the camp. Instinctively he knew that this eventually would mean trouble.

He finally laid aside the axe and dipped the pail. But he was not prepared to see her again. Not yet. He was still shaking from the last encounter. She was so young. So—so delicate. And her hair hung about her shoulders like—

He shivered and pushed away the memory. He didn't want to even think about it. He emptied the pail back into the pool and hung it on a tree limb. He'd care for his horses first. Maybe by then he'd have himself back under control.

"I'd like to talk."

Laramie stood before his father in the main cabin that the gang shared during the daylight hours. All the men were there except for Shadow, who was taking the morning watch. Seven pairs of eyes lifted at the simple words. There was something different in the voice.

"Alone," he added.

Will Russell did not look up from his game of solitaire, simply nodded. The men, without question or further orders, began to rise from wherever they sat and leave whatever they were doing, to file from the room, grabbing needed wraps from the pegs by the door.

At another nod from his boss, Sam took his log seat again. Laramie made no objection.

A few of the men dared to curse under their breath as they went. The day was not warm even though it was sunny, and some had been in the middle of a game of cards. McDuff was grumbling along with the curses. "Jest when I had me a good hand," Laramie heard him mutter. They could not take the game along with them like Curly was doing with his whiskey bottle.

The door closed and the room became silent. Will Russell continued his game. Sam shuffled uneasily, then pulled his plug of tobacco from his shirt pocket and began to cut off a large chew.

"What's on yer mind?" Will growled, still not lifting his eyes.

Laramie took a deep breath to control his emotions—his voice.

"I've got a feelin' thet ya know," he responded.

They had never played games with each other. The father looked up now and met the steely eyes of his son.

"The girl?" he asked simply.

Laramie nodded.

Silence hung heavy in the room. Will played a few cards.

"What's she doin' here?" asked Laramie, his voice controlled and hard.

Will looked up quickly. "You questionin' me, boy?" asked the man, his black eyes growing darker.

Sam shifted on his log seat again.

"Jest askin' fer a little information—man to man," Laramie replied coolly.

The father appeared to calm himself. He returned to his cards, laying a ten of diamonds on a jack of spades.

"Pa?" Laramie prompted.

Will shoved back from his card game and looked up at the tall young man. He nodded toward another log section that stood upright near the table, and Laramie knew he was to take a seat. Obediently he pulled the log forward and straddled it.

"We gotta git us some more chairs," growled the big man.

"The girl," reminded Laramie.

"Pretty little thing, ain't she?" said the father, and Laramie felt his cheeks grow hot. It was a new experience for him to flush with anger. His father misunderstood the reddened cheeks and haw-hawed heartily, slapping Laramie on the back and making ogling eyes at Sam.

Laramie's flush deepened. So this was how it would be with a girl in camp.

He fought for calm. He had to remain cool and levelheaded.

"She's pretty," he agreed so as to distract his father, but he tried hard not to think of the head of tumbling curls, the frightened eyes.

"How long she gonna be here?" asked Laramie.

Will looked up and exchanged glances with Sam. "Well,

now," he drawled in his raspy voice. "That there depends."

"What's she here for?" asked Laramie.

"Boy—you sure are full of questions, now ain't ya?" said the big man. He was beginning to sound irritated. Laramie knew better than to make his father angry.

"I jest figure—bein' part of the gang—"

"I don't need to talk things over with the gang," cut in his father.

Laramie paused. He was inclined to rise and walk out the door. His father was not being at all cooperative.

Yet he needed some answers. He took a deep breath to steady his nerves and decided on another approach.

"Well—bein' yer son—"

He had never done that before—never inferred that he should be treated differently from any other gang member simply because he was the boss's son.

His father did not take kindly to the words now. His dark eyes lifted, and a scowl deepened the creases on his cheeks above the line of his dark beard. "An' I say," he thundered, his fist coming down on the table and making his cards dance, "when the time comes fer you to be given privileges, it'll be because I give 'em to ya. Ya hear?"

"Yes sir," answered Laramie, and he touched his hat in unconscious subservience.

"Now git out there an' follow yer orders," barked the big man.

Laramie nodded and left the room, more troubled than ever.

"Ya really think this is gonna work?" asked Sam as he poured them both a cup of strong coffee after the boss had calmed down some.

The big man looked up and his eyes began to twinkle. "'Course it's gonna work," he growled pleasantly. "He's riled up already."

It was midmorning before Laramie felt in control enough to take the fresh pail of water to the south cabin. He deliberately made plenty of noise with the bar on the door to give her lots of warning that he was coming.

She was at the table, sitting on the log stool that had been provided. An open book was spread out before her, and she nervously looked up from it as he pushed open the door.

Her hair was no longer spilling about her shoulders but had been pinned up behind her head. It made her face look even smaller, her eyes larger. They were dark blue and as open as her book. She looked both scared and confused. Laramie looked away quickly, feeling that he was looking into her very soul and thus invading her privacy.

"Brung yer water," he said for something to break the silence, even though he knew it was quite evident what he had brought.

The plate was on the table. Some of the food had been eaten—but not as much as should have been. He supposed that, under the circumstances, she found it hard to have much of an appetite.

He checked the fire but found that she had recently added wood. At least she could take care of herself, he thought.

He wanted to check to see if she had other needs, but he knew he had to get out of there quickly. He was most self-conscious in her presence. She sat there watching him, saying nothing—just looking alone and scared and out of place.

He was at the door before she spoke. Her voice was low and soft—and trembly.

"The slop pail," she reminded him.

He stopped in his tracks and looked at her. Her voice had surprised him. He was used to male voices that were little more than dark growls.

"The slop pail is almost full," she explained. "It is all I have for—"

She stopped and looked down in embarrassment. Her

cheeks flushed. "For . . . everything," she finished softly.

He nodded and lifted the pail.

His anger flamed again as he carried the pail down the path to the edge of the bush and dumped it. "What a way for sech a little bit of a thing to live," he exploded. "It's jest plumb crazy."

❧ ❧ ❧

He had to renew her wood supply. He was glad for the chore—it gave him reason to swing the axe in his frustration. He cut far more than he needed. By the time he was done he was sweating in spite of the cold winter day. He put down the axe and pulled his sleeve across his brow, knocking his Stetson into the snow. He had forgotten it was up there. With soft curses he reached down and retrieved his hat, whipping it against his knee to shake off the snow.

He still hadn't figured anything out. He had gotten no answers from his father. Nor was he likely to. He didn't know why she was there or how long she was expected to stay. He only knew that they had a girl in camp and that he was expected to guard her. She was living in deplorable conditions. Even a man would hate the bareness, the crudeness of the cabin, the isolation.

Then an unfamiliar idea crossed his mind and caused him to flush slightly. Was that why he was riled? If it had been a man in there, he wouldn't have given him a thought—except to watch him carefully and guard his own back. But a girl. It wasn't a case of just guarding her; he had to somehow—care for her. And he had no idea how to go about it.

❧ ❧ ❧

Ariana paced back and forth across the squeaky boards of the cabin, trying to sort through her troubled thoughts.

On the one hand she felt terror. On the other hand she dared hope. For what? She wasn't sure. But the young man, though hardly to be considered friendly, had not really been menacing.

But he was the boss's son. He was her prison guard.

He was strangely quiet. Hardly seeming to acknowledge her presence. She had the impression he did not care much for his assignment. Did not want her in the camp any more than she wanted to be there.

Ariana trembled slightly. No, it was not realistic. Sam might have been persuaded to be an ally, to help her—but not this cool, distracted young man with the steely blue eyes.

She shivered again at the very thought of the silent, cold look that he had turned upon her, and a tear trickled down her cheek.

She was helpless and at his mercy. At the mercy of the entire camp of loud, offensive men. She still had no idea why they had taken her, but she prayed as she paced that the awful ordeal might soon end.

Chapter Eight

Guardian

Laramie stacked enough wood against the wall of the cabin to keep the fire stoked for many days—even if the temperature continued to drop. Cautiously he surveyed the room with each trip he made. He noticed that the girl had very little in material comforts.

She had rinsed out the scrap of towel in the basin and hung it to dry by the iron stove. She must have brought a comb with her in that little bit of a cloth bag, for one lay on the shelf by the pitcher. There was no soap, no mirror, no garments, except for the heavy coat hanging on the peg, hat and gloves tucked up beside it. On the floor was a pair of fur moccasins. He was sure they were much too big for the small feet tucked under the table.

Apart from that, the room was bare. Bare and miserably dirty. His own stark quarters were in better shape. At least he could sweep them out and chase down the cobwebs with the broom.

For the rest of the day Laramie watched for an opportunity to speak with Sam alone. He would get no answers from his father—he knew that now—but Sam might be another matter.

He thought of Sam as a reasonable man, and had always been on good terms with him. It was Sam who had taught

Laramie his basic letters and sums. Laramie figured that Sam was likely the only one in camp who could have done so.

No, that wasn't true. Laramie remembered being surprised one time to find Shadow reading fluently. Who knew what other secrets the men of the camp might have? No one ever asked them to share about their past.

But Sam, as his father's right hand, might have some valuable information. If Laramie could just ease it from him.

It was almost sundown before Laramie found himself alone with the little man. They were both in the crude barn, preferring the company of their mounts to the company of the men in the smoke-filled, smelly cabin.

Laramie let his eyes travel around the dark enclosure to be sure they were alone.

"Sam," he began, choosing his words carefully, "ya know I got me this here new duty."

Sam nodded and rubbed the curry comb over his horse's withers.

"Well—I don't rightly know how to take it on," went on Laramie.

He waited. There was no response.

"I don't know nothin' 'bout lookin' after . . . after a woman," he added. "Know far more about carin' fer a horse."

Sam chuckled, then said, straight-faced, "Reckon there's not much difference."

Laramie waited.

"Ya gotta feed 'em an' keep 'em warm and healthy," commented Sam.

Laramie stopped his brushing. "But—it's the healthy part what gets me," he observed in a soft drawl.

"Meanin'?" asked Sam, not missing a stroke.

"Well—fer starters—how long ya think she's gonna be here? Thet might have a heap to do with what she be needin' to stay healthy and all."

It didn't look as though Sam was going to be drawn in. He shook his head to indicate he had no information, or else would give none.

"Well, it seems to me thet she's needin' more'n a basin and a slop pail," argued Laramie.

Sam chewed on his mustache.

"Well—she did ask me fer a tub of some kind," he replied with little concern or emotion.

"A tub?"

"She wanted to bathe—wash her hair an' her clothes, she said. Womenfolk do thet. Right in the dead of winter," Sam noted with some astonishment.

Laramie nodded. He led the brush over the chest of his horse and on down the left front leg.

"Where we gonna git a tub?" he asked.

Sam shrugged. "I've no idee," he answered.

"But thet was what she asked fer—a tub?"

Sam nodded and spit into the straw at his feet.

"Then I guess I'll jest have to ride on out and find us a tub," mused Laramie to himself.

Sam's head came up. "Ya can't do thet," he exclaimed. "Yer pa'd have yer hide."

"He told me to take care of her," said Laramie, his hand continuing the even strokes with the brush.

"He said to guard her," growled Sam. "Not—fuss."

Laramie let Sam's words drift into the air of the steamy barn, and then he turned to the older man.

"I really don't see much difference," Laramie said softly, "her being a woman. Ya can't do the one without the other."

Mrs. Benson rose from her knees and wiped her eyes one more time. One day had slowly passed into another, day after day, and still there was no trace of Ariana.

She had grieved and hoped and wept and fretted and prayed. She had tried with all of her heart to trust. She had pleaded with God. Had begged for His intervention. She had even bargained—offering her own life in the place of her daughter. Still, the searchers returned empty.

But this morning as she wept before the Lord, a strange peace had entered her aching heart. She couldn't explain it. Wasn't even yet sure if she could fully trust it. But something seemed to be assuring her that Ariana, wherever she was, was in God's care. Her mind had told her that ever since that first dreadful night, but now her heart was answering yes.

"God," she whispered softly into the quiet of the room, "help me to trust. Help me to go on with life. Help me to forgive those who have tried to find her and have now gone back to minding stores and caring for businesses. They tried, Lord. They tried everything they knew. They couldn't go on searching forever. They have lives—families of their own—to tend to. Help me to leave Ariana . . . in your hands."

She blew her nose and straightened bent shoulders. Somehow she would find the strength to go on. She knew that strength must come from God.

"Where'd ya git thet thing?" asked Sam, his eyes round with amazement.

Laramie reined in his horse, bringing the pack horse to a halt as well. The tin tub bumped up against the outstretched boughs of a spruce tree, and Laramie pulled the lead to ease the horse over so there would be no chance of damage to his important cargo.

"Found it," he said simply as he swung lightly down from the saddle.

Sam lifted his hat and scratched his balding head.

"Yer gonna take a heap of teasin' iffen the fellas see ya with thet," he observed.

Laramie simply shrugged his wide shoulders and busied himself with untying the ropes that held the tub in place.

Sam chuckled. "Ain't seen nothin' like thet since I was a kid," he observed as he ran his hand over the cold metal.

"Can't figure how one carries it when it's full of water,"

mused Laramie as he lowered the tub to the snow. "It's heavy as is."

"Ya don't," explained Sam patiently. "Ya put it where ya want it an' then pour the water in."

Laramie looked surprised. "How do ya git the water outta it?" he asked innocently. "Thing ain't got no drain spout."

"Ya dip it out," Sam answered.

Laramie stood to his full height and rubbed the back of his hand across his brow.

"Seems like I got me a powerful amount of work here," he said softly. "Sure hope she don't count on using it too often."

Then he turned back to his saddlebags. "Got a few other things, too," he informed Sam in conspiratorial tones.

"Like?" asked Sam.

"Some soap. Couple towels. This here—what ya call it—wash towel."

"Washcloth," Sam corrected.

"Some hair soap."

"Where'd ya git all thet stuff?" asked Sam again.

Laramie gave the older man a smile. "You got yer secrets—I got mine," was all he would say.

"Seems ta me yer taking yer guardin' duties awful serious-like," muttered Sam.

Laramie made no comment.

Ariana was both surprised and delighted when the tub arrived—without comment—in her small room and was deposited close to the big iron stove. Silently she watched as Laramie filled both the kettle and the basin and placed them on the stove. Then he emptied a saddlebag of its contents, spreading the small items on the table.

"Thank you," said Ariana softly.

Laramie picked up the pail to go for more water, outwardly calm, though inwardly in turmoil. He had never been thanked before in his life. Her words caught him off guard.

He nodded his head toward her but did not look her way. "I'll git more water," was his only comment.

After he left, Ariana moved to look at what he had left behind on the table. Soap, a hand mirror, towels, a couple of washcloths, a bottle of shampoo advertised to make "one's tresses silky and perfumed," and a pair of ivory-tipped manicure scissors. In spite of her circumstances, Ariana had to smile. At least these few things would help to make her feel more human.

On the other hand, the simple items brought new worry to her already troubled heart. It looked as though they were expecting her to occupy the cabin for some time to come. The very thought made Ariana want to put her head in her arms and weep. Instead, she stiffened her back and tried to turn her thoughts to other things.

While Laramie was hauling and heating the water for her bath, Ariana was looking for some way to hang one of the towels over the fully exposed window. Even though the pane was so dirty one could hardly see out of it, she didn't want to take any chances with someone seeing in.

But there were no nails, no pegs, no way of assuring any privacy. She still stood there, a frown on her face and the towel in her hands, when Laramie rattled the door again. Along with the pail of water, he carried another dented kettle and a big pot. He added these items to the stove top and filled them from the pail. The little stove was now so crowded that Ariana feared to move any of the pots lest she send one of them tumbling to the floor.

He turned to leave again, water pail in hand.

"I . . ." dared Ariana, her voice tight with nervousness. "I was wondering . . ."

He turned back to her.

She pushed aside her fear with grim determination. "The window," she said, pointing to it, "is there . . . can we . . . it needs to be covered . . . someway. If I had a hammer and some nails . . ." She held up the towel in her hands.

He made no reply but seemed to understand her faltering words of concern. He nodded and left again.

When he returned he not only had another pail of water but a hammer and some rusty nails. He set the pail on the small shelf and proceeded to the window, where he pounded the nails into the dust-covered logs. Ariana watched silently. When he had completed the task, she handed him the towel, which he hooked in place, making a makeshift but workable curtain for her window. He stepped back and eyed it carefully; then seeming satisfied he nodded his head.

"I'll be back to put the water in the tub," he said as he was about to leave.

"I can do it," Ariana was quick to inform him.

He looked at the stove and then back to her. He nodded in agreement and turned to go.

"But—" Ariana's voice stopped him.

"Somethin' else?" he asked as he turned to her.

Ariana looked nervously from the young man to the door and back again.

"Could you . . . could you . . . knock . . . before coming in next time?" she asked timidly, and her chin lifted just a bit to bolster her courage.

It took a moment for the meaning of the words to register. Then his face flushed.

"Miss," he said, his hand raising unconsciously to tip back his Stetson, "I'll be knockin' every time."

Then he was gone.

⁂

As much as she longed to linger in the warm, soapy water, Ariana hurried with her bath. It didn't seem quite safe to remain in the tub in spite of his promise to announce his coming.

She yearned to wash her filthy garments but had nothing

to change into. She thought of wrapping herself in the coarse blanket while her clothing dried, but under the circumstances it didn't seem like a good idea.

Reluctantly she put on the same skirt and shirtwaist that she had laid aside. They smelled of woodsmoke and room dust. She was glad the weather hadn't been such to cause perspiration odor as well.

Then she set about washing her hair. It felt so good to give her scalp a good scrubbing. The shampoo lived up to its boast. As her dark brown curls began to dry, they did feel silky again, and they did have a delightful scent—even in the dust and dirt of the dank cabin.

When he came with her evening meal, her hair still had not dried completely and hung about her shoulders like a soft mantle. He could smell the perfume of it as he set the tin plate on the bare table. He moved quickly away.

"Yer done with the tub?" he asked, for something to say.

"Yes—thank you," she responded.

He was surprised that she had dipped out most of the water. The slop pail was full, as were the basins and big pot he had brought. As far as her circumstances allowed, she was independent. He liked that, though he really couldn't have said why. He set about finishing emptying the bath water while she toyed with her supper.

He was carrying out the tub and its last bit of water when she spoke again. "Is that . . . is that someone else's tub?"

He looked at her, wondering just what she was asking.

"No," he said curtly.

"Then . . . do you mind . . . bringing it back in?" she asked him.

He stopped short. Surely she wasn't going to bathe again—so soon.

"It'll get very cold if it's left out . . . out in the elements," she explained. "When it's cold it cools the water too quickly."

He understood then and nodded his assent.

He brought the tub back into the room. He had to kick some clutter aside in order to make room for it against one wall of the cabin. He swore beneath his breath, ending his words with "filthy place."

"If I had some sort of broom I could sweep it out," she offered from where she sat.

He felt embarrassed that she had overheard him.

When he reached the door he hesitated. "Anything else?" he asked.

It was almost a smile she gave him—though it was checked and guarded. "You've been most helpful," she said quietly. "I appreciate it. Thank you."

Her words made him squirm with discomfort. A prisoner—voicing thanks.

He nodded and turned quickly to go. He could stand no more—niceness or womanliness or whatever it was. But he promised himself that the next time he came to the cabin, he'd bring his stub of a broom and sweep out the place.

"I bin thinkin'," said Sam, throwing a card on the pile between him and the boss. "Haven't we still got us a trunk 'round here somewheres with woman clothes?"

Will looked up and squinted his dark eyes at his card partner. "Why ya askin'?"

"Jest thinkin'," Sam replied and studied the cards in his hand.

Will took a long drink from the bottle at his elbow.

"Been thinkin'," Sam went on slowly, "thet there little gal be in the same batch of clothes ever since we brung her in."

"So—?" responded the big man. "I ain't changed mine neither."

"Well—you an' me is a little different," Sam followed slowly. Then he added, "We wear 'em 'til they fall off—or crawl away." He chuckled softly at his own joke.

They played on in silence for several minutes. Sam waited. Would Will refuse to give consent—or even consideration to his casual remark?

"Ya think those clothes would fit her?" Will finally asked when Sam had about given up.

Sam shrugged. "No idee," he responded, "but guess ya could mention 'em to the Kid an' see iffen he wants a look at 'em."

The big man nodded. "Ya can dig 'em up and show 'im," he said.

The dim glow of the kerosene lamp did not give away the sparkle in Sam's eyes.

Chapter Nine

Early Trouble

"Where'd ya git this stuff?" Laramie asked Sam as the two of them ran rough hands over the soft garments.

Sam said nothing—just watched the young man sort idly through the clothes. What was he to say—and just how much?

"Yer pa thought the gal might be able to use something. Git herself cleaned up," Sam said instead.

"Where'd it come from?" Laramie insisted.

"Been here a long time," Sam answered.

"Some raid?" asked Laramie. He lifted another calico gown and laid it aside. Then his eyes opened wide and he reached again into the trunk. "This here's a baby—somethin'," he said, disbelief in his voice.

Sam nodded. He looked off into the distance, thinking back in time. He hadn't expected the trunk of laid-aside things to affect him so deeply.

"Sam!" prompted Laramie. "What are these clothes?" He lifted up the tiny soft nightgown and stared at the smallness of it in his man-sized hand.

Sam spit into the dust on the floor.

"Well, boy," he said when he could trust his voice. "Yers, I reckon."

Laramie stared. "Mine?"

"Yessir."

"You mean—?" Laramie turned back to the trunk of feminine attire. "You mean—this was my ma's trunk?"

Sam nodded again.

"You mean she—? Did she live here? Was—?"

Sam raised a hand. "Look, Kid," he said and his eyes had grown dark, "I've said all I intend to say. This was yer ma's trunk of things. That was yer baby do-dad. I—yer pa thought this here gal might use some of the"—Sam reached down a hand and lifted one of the garments and let it fall back into the trunk again—"fancies—an' thet's *thet* an' thet's all I'm gonna say."

He lifted himself awkwardly from his kneeling position on the floor and turned to stalk away.

"Ya do what ya wanna do," he flung back over his shoulder with a wave of his hand, indicating that he had washed his hands of the whole business.

Laramie lingered over the trunk, staring at the tiny garments—his. And the other soft, feminine things—his mother's. Nothing—nothing in his life had ever given him cause to think about the fact that he'd had a mother. A mother. What had she been like? Who was she, anyway? How had she come to connect up with his father? The items in the trunk looked totally foreign to the world he knew.

He again lifted the small baby garment and looked at it long and hard. His. Made undoubtedly by the hands of his mother.

Laramie couldn't have said why, but after carefully returning the clothing to the trunk, he kept out the one small soft item and tucked it inside his shirt.

The next morning he had Sam help him take the trunk to the south cabin. "Thought there might be somethin' in here ya could use," was his only explanation.

As the trunk lid was lifted back to expose the contents,

he saw the girl's eyes light up. It gave him strange, unexpected pleasure.

"I wonder . . ." mused Ariana as she went through the trunk, carefully lifting out item by item and examining them.

What she found was clothing that had belonged to a woman about her size—but they had been worn during a previous time. Styles had changed a bit, but she couldn't fault the material. Whoever had claimed ownership had been a woman of some means. Ariana could tell that by the soft cottons and fine linens.

They were not party clothes, not silks and satins—they were sensible, everyday, workable clothes, though of the best fabrics available. Ariana's puzzled frown deepened with each garment she drew out. "Who was she?" she kept asking herself.

Then another question brought a new frown. What had happened to this woman? Had she also been brought to the camp as a prisoner? Why was her clothing left behind? What had become of this woman of mystery?

Ariana had no answer to any of her questions.

She came upon a blanket, folded neatly as though making a division of the contents of the trunk. She lifted it and saw carefully folded baby garments comprising the bottom layer. She could tell at a glance they were not new items, but carefully laundered and folded.

She stared, openmouthed. Did Sam and . . . and that other man know the trunk held baby items as well? Who was this woman? This woman who obviously had prepared garments to welcome a baby. Had the baby arrived? What had become of the woman and her infant?

There was a great mystery hidden here somewhere.

Ariana left the folded baby things and let the blanket fall back into position. She did not wish to intrude further on the privacy of this unknown woman—but thankfully she would wear some of the fine garments her unknown benefactor had left behind.

❧ ❧ ❧

Laramie pulled his horse up in the shadow of the tall spruce and slipped silently to the ground. He left his mount ground-tied and moved stealthily through the trees. It would be impossible to hide his tracks in the snow—but he knew the area well. No outsider ever came to the hidden springs, and his own gang members were presently more interested in staying by the warm fire than venturing out.

He was in no danger. But the party he had plans to meet had to be a bit more cautious. He would not be welcomed should he be spotted by any of the other members of the camp, or by the sentry on duty. For that reason, Laramie hoped they would not be seen.

He was early—had planned it that way. He would just find a comfortable, hidden spot and wait.

He chose his place of concealment carefully, brushed the snow from the stump with the brim of his Stetson, and took a seat. He had no sooner settled himself than he heard a soft chuckle.

"You make noise like moose," came the soft, familiar voice.

Laramie whipped around. White Eagle stood a few feet away, grinning, his arms folded across his chest.

"Yer here," said Laramie, rising to his feet again.

White Eagle, the amused look still on his face, made no comment but crossed to where Laramie now stood.

"We meet here—no?"

It was Laramie's turn to smile. He reached out, and the two young men shook hands firmly.

"Yes, we were to meet here," he agreed. "It's been a long time," he continued, placing a hand on the young Indian's shoulder.

"Long," agreed White Eagle. He nodded his head to the stump Laramie had vacated and eased himself to the ground. Laramie returned to his seat.

For some minutes the two friends sat silently, their eyes traveling out over the expanse of the valley beneath them. White Eagle broke the stillness. "You call," he said simply, and Laramie understood his implied question.

He removed his hat and ran a finger through shaggy, heavy hair. "Yeah," Laramie admitted. "I had to talk to someone."

"Trouble?"

"Not . . . not really trouble. Jest . . ."

Laramie stopped and White Eagle waited for him to go on. It was some time before Laramie continued.

"My pa brought this here girl to the camp," he said, feeling that the spoken words sounded pretty silly.

White Eagle nodded solemnly. "Trouble!" he said softly.

"Well—no trouble yet," Laramie hurried to explain. "I mean she's just a . . . a young . . . not a troublemaker or anything like thet. She's off in a cabin all alone. The fellas don't even know she's there."

White Eagle waited.

"Pa gave me the . . . the chore of . . . of guardin' her," went on Laramie.

"Nice—chore," White Eagle said, his eyes glinting with amusement.

"No—it's not," quickly cut in Laramie. "She's . . . she's . . . it's not a nice job—at all."

"She mean squaw?" asked the Indian.

"No," Laramie said quickly. "Nothin' like thet. She's young an' she's scared an' I have no idea what she's there for. I mean—I don't know what Pa plans. I asked—an' he got mad. Wouldn't say nothin'. Jest says I gotta guard her."

White Eagle shrugged his shoulders and spread his palms upright as if to say that there was nothing he could do to help the situation.

"It's jest . . . well, I mean . . . you've lived in camp—with women—all yer life. I . . . I don't know a thing about women. What . . . what am I supposed to . . . how am I supposed to. . . ?"

White Eagle smiled. Yes, he knew about women. Elderly ones who, because of their years and wisdom, were the mothers of the tribe, wives of hunters who tanned the hides of the game the men brought in and tended the cooking pots. Younger women, eyes soft with love for their newborn papooses, maidens who modestly lowered their eyes when the young braves walked by, and then stole covert glances beneath long, dark lashes. Even the frolicking, playful little ones—on their way to "becoming." He knew about life surrounded by women.

"But," he went on to explain, "I have visited the white man's fort—a few times. The women there are different—very different—from the Indian women in my camp."

He shrugged again. "I know nothing—of white squaws," he said, and spread his hands again.

"But—"

White Eagle shrugged again. "Not same," he said as though that was final.

Laramie was agitated. White Eagle stared at him, looking both surprised and confused. Finally he asked, "Why such little bit of woman trouble so much?"

Laramie couldn't answer the question.

"What you do for her?" White Eagle asked, his tone indicating he was genuinely trying to help his friend.

"I jest . . . jest bring her wood an' water an' food an'—"

"Why she not get own wood and water?" questioned White Eagle.

"She's our prisoner," responded Laramie.

White Eagle nodded. Then he frowned. "White man not make prisoner work?" he asked.

"She's locked up," said Laramie.

White Eagle nodded again.

"So you not like . . . chore?" asked the young brave.

Laramie stood to his feet and began to pace. He reached

up to push his hat back a trace. "No," he said. "No, I don't like it. She shouldn't be there. Shouldn't be in the camp. It's gonna mean trouble. I can feel it in my bones."

"Maybe she . . . escape," observed the Indian with a knowing look.

"She'd never make it. She'd die—or be killed—or taken," declared Laramie. He continued to pace, his jaw set firmly, his blue eyes darkening.

"You . . . not want that?"

Laramie whirled around to face the young brave. He did not even offer an answer. Of course he did not want that.

"So . . . you not like . . . care for . . . but you want . . . keep," White Eagle continued, as though carefully sorting through Laramie's problem.

Laramie did speak then. "I don't want to keep—I jest want to—"

He broke off. How could he explain to the Pawnee what he was feeling? That it was all wrong to take another captive. That his father had broken some moral code in bringing the young girl into camp. That he knew, deep down inside, that this was totally against everything that a real man should stand for.

"I want her . . . back . . . where she belongs," he stumbled on awkwardly. "Only . . . I have no way to get her there . . . so . . . so I have to do my best to take care of her and I don't—"

"You got trouble," agreed the young Indian again. "Plenty trouble."

Laramie stopped his walking and stared out over the valley. Down below he could see the ramshackle buildings of the camp. From the high vantage point the crude shacks looked fairly organized, almost attractive. In the far distance he could see the rising smoke of a campfire. By the way the small column drifted, he guessed it to be an Indian hunting party who sat around its warmth.

"Yer men?" he asked White Eagle, nodding his head eastward.

"Three," said White Eagle in reply.

"Hope they got something," mused Laramie.

White Eagle nodded. "They did. Snow deep. Stop to roast meat for strength on home trail."

"I think I'll do a little huntin'," said Laramie. "We could do with some fresh meat."

The young Indian brave stood to his feet, his movements catlike with grace and strength.

He did not brush the snow from his leather garments but pulled down a branch of the spruce and brushed it back and forth across the ground where he had reclined, removing all trace that he had been there. At its release, the branch sprang back into position.

"Fresh meat," he echoed Laramie. "Make strong. If girl ever . . . escape . . . she need eat. Be strong."

The two young men looked at each other. A silent message passed between them. Even as the idea crossed Laramie's mind, he discarded it as preposterous.

"You make signal," said White Eagle, and Laramie understood the brief words as a promise that he would be there. He nodded.

Before his very eyes the young brave seemed to melt into the shadows of the forest.

"You should get some fresh air," said Laramie after he had knocked, then brought in the plate of food to his charge the next morning.

Ariana glanced at the heavy wooden door.

"After you've finished yer breakfast we'll go fer a walk," Laramie continued. He had done a lot of thinking throughout the night. White Eagle was right. He had to try to keep her strong. Keep her healthy. Who knew what the future might hold?

She nodded silently, but he thought he saw a little sparkle come to her eyes. Was it fear—or anticipation?

When he returned later he was surprised to see she had

eaten more than usual of what was on the plate. She stood, dressed in one of the calico gowns from the trunk, staring out of the window.

"It's rather cold," he observed. "You'll need all the warm clothes ya got." He hesitated, then pointed to the corner. "I would suggest thet ya wear those moccasins 'stead of those shoes."

She changed footwear quickly, her back to him. He walked to the window and stood looking out so she wouldn't be embarrassed by his presence.

She was soon bundled in her heavy coat, her hat firmly in place over her pinned-up curls. He knew the flimsy bit of felt and ribbon would be absolutely no protection against the elements, but he didn't say so.

He pushed the heavy door open and proceeded her out into the wintery sunshine. Though it was weak in warmth, it was bright as it reflected off the whiteness of the snow. He saw her squint against it and remembered it had been some time since she had seen the full light of day.

They had taken only a few steps when the door of the big cabin burst open and three of the gang members stepped out into the light and headed for the barn.

Instinctively Laramie glanced around for cover. There was none. There would be no way to avoid a meeting.

Laramie heard the rough words, the coarse laughs, and then three heads came up and three pairs of astonished eyes stared in his direction.

"Well I'll be—" exclaimed James and followed his comment with a muttered curse.

Curly, a bottle dangling from his limp hand, could only stare, openmouthed.

But it was Skidder who drew the attention of Laramie. After his initial shock, his eyes narrowed and an evil grin began to spread over his face. "A 'prisoner'?" he guffawed. He spilled out a stream of profanity. "Prisoner, ya call thet? I'd bet my Winchester thet Daddy done gone and got his boy a pretty little filly."

He hooted again and slapped his thigh.

Laramie felt the heat rushing to his face.

All three of the men grinned, James fidgeting nervously and Curly twisting his near-empty bottle in bare hands.

Laramie chided himself for his carelessness. He had stepped out of the cabin right into a nest of hornets. He glanced in silent apology at Ariana's downcast eyes and burning cheeks. Skidder, who was known to be drawn to women, was bound to make an issue over a girl being in camp. But how big an issue? Would he be smart enough to back off? Or would he force Laramie into unwanted action?

For the first time in his life Laramie felt his fingers itching for the security of the cold butt of his forty-four.

Chapter Ten

What Now?

Laramie had heard the girl's sharp intake of breath and sensed her stiffen at the crude comments of the men before them. It was all he could do to hold himself steady. Inwardly he willed Skidder to keep his head and just move on. What would he do if the rough outlaw decided to push further?

"Reckon you boys got business at the barn," Laramie drawled softly. But his hands hung loosely and his stance had changed.

For a few moments the whole winter world seemed to hold its breath. Skidder stood poised as though deciding whether to have a bit more fun at Laramie's expense, or get himself out of the area in one piece. Common sense finally won and he nodded, still leering, and moved off toward the barn.

Laramie waited until the three were several steps away before he relaxed, nodded to the girl, and motioned for her to continue.

Her face had blanched white; her large eyes had widened. He could see that she trembled slightly, and he knew she was fully aware of the danger that had just passed.

"I . . . I'm not sure . . ." she began in a trembling voice.

"He won't be back," he said with more confidence than he felt.

She looked unconvinced.

"I think I'd just like to stay in," she managed hesitantly.

He nodded. He would not argue further. It was unfortunate that they had been spotted. He should have been more cautious. Now the others knew there was a girl in the camp. Now there would be no rest—and sure trouble.

Secretly he wondered if she would even be safe in the cabin—but he didn't mention that to her as he led her back down the snowy trail.

He would do what he could.

⁂

Ariana was surprised later in the day when the young man returned and brought with him a hammer and a large hook and eye. He spoke not a word as he nailed the two pieces firmly in place. She watched from her spot at the table, her book open before her, but she said nothing.

When he had finished he lifted his eyes to hers. "Keep it locked," he said simply. "Don't ever open it—'less it's me—or Sam."

Ariana nodded at another reminder that she was constantly in danger.

She let her eyes fall back to the pages before her. "Trust in the Lord," she read—then reread—and it brought her a measure of comfort.

She had been going through the Bible since her time of captivity, selecting all the passages that confirmed that truth. She was amazed at how often she found them—and at the heartrending circumstances in which they were spoken. She was excited to read how God acted on the behalf of those folks long ago. Surely she had great reason to trust such a powerful and merciful God.

⁂

"What's yer name?"

The question surprised Ariana. The young man often came and went without any conversation taking place between the two of them. Now he was stacking an armload of wood inside her cabin. He wasn't even looking her direction.

"Ariana," she said after hesitating.

"Ariana," he repeated, and Ariana was surprised at how her name sounded on his tongue.

He continued to stack the logs by the cabin wall.

"And yours?" she dared to ask.

"Call me Laramie," he replied.

Ariana did not repeat his name aloud but she did mentally. In some strange way it seemed to suit him.

She watched the even flow of his movements as he tucked the logs in place. He looked ordinary—yet she could not forget the change she had seen—had felt—when they had been confronted on the trail. Here was a kind of man she knew absolutely nothing about. So different from those she knew in her own small town. The very thought made her tremble.

Mrs. Benson put another check mark on the wall calender before she loosed her braid and shook the silvering hair out to spill down her back. How long had it been? Thirty-one days. Thirty-one days and no word—nothing. She knew everyone in town had already given up. She wondered if her husband had joined their ranks. But no—not yet. He still included his petition for the safety of their girl in each of his spoken prayers. And how many times each day, like she, did he send up silent but fervent petitions? They both still clung to hope.

Hope in a sovereign God—that was all they had.

But surely—that was enough.

"You must be tired of reading the same book," Laramie

casually observed as he set the extra pail of water on the shelf for her weekly bath.

Ariana looked up. His words surprised her. He so seldom spoke to her—and she never initiated a conversation.

"It's the Bible," she said.

"The Bible?"

"One can read it over and over and over—and still never stop learning or run out of fresh truths," she dared to continue, sensing that he was puzzled by her answer.

"I see," he said, looking at her, but she felt that he really didn't.

He changed the topic with, "I'll bring yer supper. Ya want it after yer bath—or before?"

Ariana thought of the tasteless food. She took a deep breath, then dared to bring up what had been on her mind for the past several days. "If I had a couple of pots—and some supplies—I could do my own cooking and you wouldn't need to bother—"

"No bother," he cut in quickly.

She felt disappointment seep through her at her unsuccessful bid to prepare her own meals. She was sick of the sloppy beans and tasteless biscuits.

He seemed to reconsider.

" 'Course—iffen you'd like to do yer own cookin'—guess it wouldn't hurt none," he said tentatively.

Ariana almost smiled in her delight.

"Make out a list of what yer needin'," he invited.

Ariana was perplexed. "I . . . I don't have a pencil or . . ."

It was his turn to look frustrated.

"Reckon there ain't one in camp," he confessed. Then he shrugged broad shoulders. "Suppose ya need the usual grub stake. I've picked thet up plenty of times. I can git it for ya."

Ariana let her eyes travel to the trunk against the wall. "You don't suppose there is anything like . . . a pencil . . . in there?" she mused, nodding her head in its direction.

"Thought you'd looked."

Ariana shook her head. "No, not at everything. I . . . I felt like I was . . . intruding. I just looked partway and then I . . . I found . . . I felt that I . . . that it was . . . private."

He nodded, seeming to be pleased at her respect for privacy.

He crossed to the trunk and lifted up the lid. "Maybe we should look," he said. Ariana joined him as he began to lift out some of the dresses. "Never seen ya wear this one," he said of a blue check. "It looks kinda pretty," he added, almost to himself.

"No," said Ariana in a voice not much above a whisper. "I just took one . . . change of clothes. I . . . I use them . . . and my own, and wash them turn by turn. I . . . I . . . appreciate the chance to . . . change . . . but I didn't think that I should . . . use all her clothes."

He looked surprised but made no immediate comment.

"These were—my ma's, I'm told," he said frankly. He stopped in some confusion, then said, "She's gone an' won't be needin' 'em."

"I'm . . . so sorry," breathed Ariana.

He came to the blanket, lifted it up, and deposited it on the floor beside him. But Ariana could sense his surprise at the sight of all the baby garments.

Then rather roughly he began to lift out the tiny things and lay them on the floor beside the blanket. He stopped short again after lifting up another handful of small clothing.

He peered into the trunk. A little chest lay on the bottom, and beside it a book with a black cover.

"Look!" Ariana exclaimed excitedly. "A Bible."

But Laramie was looking at the chest.

Carefully he lifted it up and opened the lid. In it were a number of small items. Brooches—hankies with lace trim yellowed with age—a tintype—buttons—lace—little bits of this and that which he did not take time to sort. He closed the lid again.

"The little chest . . . it must have been . . . your mother's," she said softly. "You should . . . keep it. It's a treasure. . . ."

He looked uncomfortable. He abruptly put the box down on the floor by his knee.

"Didn't see any pencil or paper in there," he said gruffly. "Guess it's not much good to you."

She reached down into the trunk. Almost tenderly she lifted up the Bible. She could tell from the covers that it had been well used, but she did not open it.

"You must take this, too," she said in a whispery voice. "I know your mother would want you to have it."

He did not argue but watched as she placed the Bible on top of the little chest. She had known as soon as the chest appeared that he would take it—would need to take it.

Quickly he rummaged through the rest of the belongings, but there was nothing else among the baby garments. An impatience seemed to have taken hold of him.

Ariana understood his mood. She stepped back. "I'll put the things back," she offered. She was sure he couldn't wait to carefully study each item from the chest in private.

He nodded and picked up the newly discovered items, clearly anxious to be on his way.

Laramie did not forget about the supplies. Sam brought her meal the next morning—thumping on the door and calling out in a louder than necessary voice to identify himself.

When she unhooked the latch to let him enter, he came in growling.

"Day not fit fer man or beast, yet he decides he has to run off. He'll freeze hisself to death, thet's what. You'd think there was a train of gold or a—"

He stopped and looked nervously toward the young girl as if he had said too much.

"Said he needed supplies," continued the man with another growl. "Don't know what he's needin' thet wouldn't wait."

He cast a glance at her and Ariana felt embarrassed. Was

he blaming her that Laramie had ridden off in the cold? Maybe he was right. She hadn't given any thought to the weather when she had made her request. She had been selfish. She'd had no idea that the food staples would not be obtainable in the camp.

"Yer breakfast," said Sam more softly.

"Thank you," replied Ariana.

"Don't know why you'd thank me fer it," Sam said. "Thet stuff ain't hardly fit to eat. Ole Rawley ain't much of a cook. Beans an' biscuits. Beans an' biscuits. Thet's all we ever git—an' they ain't even good biscuits."

He set the plate on the table with a grimace and turned toward her. "See yer still readin' thet book. Must have it near worn out by now," he observed in a lighter tone.

Ariana managed a wobbly smile. "The pages—maybe," she said, "but the message—no."

"Message. Thet some secret code?"

Ariana smiled fully now. "Code? Not to a believer, it's not."

The old man frowned.

"It's the Bible," explained Ariana. When there was no response she continued. "God's words to His people."

"I know what the Bible is," the old man retorted sharply. "My ma—" He shuffled uncomfortably and said no more about it. "Well—ya jest et up—thet—poor excuse fer breakfast," said the man, "an' I'll be back fer the plate. How's yer firewood?"

He turned to study the pile. "Look's like the Kid got ya enough firewood to last 'til a week from Christmas," he noted, and Ariana thought he looked relieved. "Guess ya need some fresh water, though."

Then he looked at Ariana with some alarm. "Ya ain't plannin' on bathin' today, are ya?"

"No—not today," she replied, shaking her head.

"Good," he said with feeling. "I sure weren't anxious to do all thet haulin'."

He left with the pail, and Ariana crossed to latch her door before turning to the food.

As determined as she had been to keep her strength up, she found it difficult to make herself eat the tasteless fare.

⁂

It wasn't until the next afternoon that Laramie knocked on her door and identified himself.

Ariana hastened to answer. She was relieved to hear his voice and prayed as she lifted the hook that he wouldn't have suffered from the ride in the elements.

He looked fine. She sighed with relief.

He carried a burlap bag in each hand. "Hope I got what ya needed," he said matter-of-factly, " 'cause I don't think I'll be welcomed back fer a while."

Ariana frowned at the words but couldn't sort out his meaning. He deposited both bags on the table.

"Got a couple pots and this here thing," he said, drawing a strange piece of metal from the closest bag. "It's a reflector of some kind. Supposed to make biscuits without an oven."

Ariana had never seen one before. She had no idea how to use it but determined to give it a try.

He had brought a nice selection of basic supplies. There wasn't much in the line of spices or flavorings, but at least she would be able to do her own cooking. Ariana was thankful.

"Now—if I just had some meat . . ." she mused.

"I'll git some," he promised simply and later kept his word, appearing at her door with some venison steak just before the winter sun dipped behind the nearby hills.

⁂

Ariana could not believe how good the stew tasted after her weeks of unsavory beans. She even enjoyed a second helping.

The biscuits hadn't done well. They were burned in spots—and undercooked in others. She would need to practice with the new reflector. Even so, they were definitely better than what she had been served from the gang's kitchen. Perhaps now she could regain some of the weight she knew she had lost and have more strength when the time came for her to escape from her captors.

For Ariana lived for the day when the weather would improve, and she would find a way to slip away from the four log walls that held her captive.

Chapter Eleven

An Ally

In the privacy of the small cabin he called his own, Laramie lifted the small items from the chest, one by one, and laid them on the rough board table. According to Sam, these were his mother's things. He felt a strange connection with them—a longing to know more about this woman he had never known. He appreciated Ariana's reluctance to disturb the contents of the trunk any more than necessary for her own survival.

The pin he studied was a cameo. It looked fragile and delicate—the white profile surrounded with intricate filigree. It seemed out of place in a rough camp of lawless men. Did she really wear it here? Had she truly ever been in residence in the camp? Laramie found it hard to believe, yet her trunk—her things—were in camp. It puzzled him.

He withdrew one of the lace hankies. The cloth was soft to his touch—fine and smooth. He had never handled such fabric before. It was embroidered with a little pattern in delicate work, and as he looked closer he could make out letters. *L-A-L.* He put the letters together and whispered them softly. "Lal." They spelled nothing as far as he knew. Yet he felt they held a secret. Lal. It was a strange word.

He tenderly lifted the other handkerchiefs and placed them all in a neat little pile.

Another pin. This one small, with a blue stone in the middle that caught the afternoon light.

Another hankie—then an oval on a long gold chain. He turned it this way and that as he surveyed it carefully. He noticed a little clasp. Carefully he pressed on it and it opened. It held a small lock of downy hair. Whose hair? Why had his mother carried it in this strange little oval? He studied it for a long time before he closed it and laid it aside.

A scrap of lace. He turned it over in his hands, discovering no purpose for the bit of cloth. Yet he did not discard it—but put it gently on the growing pile. Another hankie, elaborately embroidered. It looked like a pair of intertwining rings. What had that meant?

And then he was lifting the tintype. He turned it to catch all advantage of the light. It showed a woman. A woman whose face still shone out at him in spite of the fading of the years—whose eyes were turned lovingly upon a baby boy she held in her arms. Could it be him—with his mother?

Her face was so sweet—so gentle. He had never seen such an expression before. For long moments he studied the picture. Something about the woman's likeness reminded him of the girl in the cabin. What was it? Was it the expression? The features? Maybe the eyes.

Carefully he placed the tintype on the bottom of the small chest and began to return the other items. Then he went to the corner shelf, lifted up the tiny gown that Sam had said was his, and gently added it to the other items in the chest.

His whole being was shaken by the experience. And yet he knew so little. He understood even less. Who was his mother? What had happened to her? If she had remained with him, would his life have been different? Somehow he felt it would have been, even though he wasn't sure just how.

He closed the lid of the little box and turned his attention to the Bible. He opened the cover and read of one King James, who had authorized the version. It meant nothing to him. He continued to turn the pages.

He came to a page with a list of names, entered in precise

and careful penmanship. His eyes quickly scanned the contents. It looked like a family record of some kind. He checked the heading at the top of the page and saw that it was titled *Births.* He skimmed down the page and read the last few lines.

Tilford James Bradley, 1812–1816
Margaret Rose Bradley, 1814–1842
Weyburn Oliver Bradley, 1817
Mary Louise Bradley, 1820–1820
Lavina Ann Bradley, 1822
Conrad Timothy Bradley, 1823–1824
Ethan David Bradley, 1826

There was a space and then the line announcing,

Burke Timothy Lawrence, August 10, 1860

Laramie wondered about the last entry. Why so much later? Why a different name?

Laramie turned thc page. The headline at the top announced *Marriages.*

Margaret Rose Bradley & Thomas Cullen Roberts, 1833
Lavina Ann Bradley & Turner Donair Lawrence III, 1840
Weyburn Oliver Bradley & Jane Titford Gray, 1841

Laramie flipped another page. This one was labeled *Deaths*, and he quickly let his eyes scan down the page, noting the names he had read previously, now with little notations behind the dates. Died of natural causes—in childbirth—whooping cough—pneumonia. It seemed that his forebears, if indeed that was the record he held in his hands, had more than a little difficulty.

He turned the page again and found a table of contents and then on into the printed pages of the book. But the pages held more than print. Here and there he found, in the same careful handwriting, brief notations or comments about passages. The truth dawned. The same person who had recorded the births, marriages, and deaths was the owner of the Bible. His mother? It was among her things. If he was to believe Sam, then this Bible had belonged to his mother and her name might appear in the book he held.

But it didn't add up. His name was Russell. Laramie Russell. His pa's name was Will Russell.

Then Laramie smiled a cynical smile. It would seem his pa had seen fit to change his name. Perhaps more than once. There was nothing new about that. Laramie supposed there wasn't a man in camp who went by his given name.

Was there a chance his pa had once answered to one of those other names?

"So he was once Bradley or Roberts or Lawrence or maybe Gray," he mused aloud. "Quite a different handle than Russell."

Laramie slowly closed the book and promised himself that he'd do some more investigating into what it held as soon as he had the time. His horses needed to be fed and rubbed down. He'd have to satisfy his profound curiosity later.

Carefully he picked up the well-worn volume and the chest. His eyes scanned the room quickly. Then he walked to his wooden bunk, lifted it over a way, and knelt on the floor. With a small amount of coaxing, one floorboard groaned reluctantly upward. He slipped his treasure into the hole beneath, beside his money poke and extra Colt. It wasn't safe. There was nothing safe in the camp. But it was the safest place he knew.

He moved the bunk back into position and picked up his Stetson, anxious to get his chores out of the way.

* * *

Laramie had finished with the horses and would have returned to his cabin and lit the kerosene lamp, but hunger drove him toward the main bunkhouse.

As he passed the south cabin the smell of cooking food caused him to stop midstride. He decided to check on Ariana to see how she was managing with the provisions he had brought her. Perhaps there had been something he'd forgotten.

He knocked, then called out and heard her move to the door and unlatch the hook.

She looked surprised, since Laramie never came in the evening except to bring her plate of food—and now the arrangement was for her to make her own meals.

"Jest came to see how ya made out with the cookin'," he quickly explained.

"Fine," she responded, indicating the empty plate she had just left to answer the door.

He moved past her and into the room. "Smells good," he observed.

"Just stew," said Ariana, her heart thumping with uncertainty. What did he want? She saw his eyes wander to the biscuits still on the cooking sheet.

"They didn't turn out too well," Ariana confessed. "I need to practice with the reflector."

"They look a heap better than Rawley's," he observed.

Ariana noticed the slight twitch of his nose.

"Help yourself," she offered.

He did, without hesitation or apology.

"There's a little stew left—"

"Do ya mind?" he asked and glanced at the plate on the table.

"I'm sorry," she offered quickly. "I only have the one plate, but I'll wash it—"

"No need. I've et off worse things," he responded and picked up the plate. He moved to the stove, where the stew still simmered, and dished out the remainder of the contents.

Ariana stood mute as she watched him squat on the floor, his back up against the door.

“You can sit at the table,” she said quickly. “I’ll—I’m finished.”

But he shook his head. “I’m used to sittin’ most anywhere.”

Ariana had never seen a man eat so hungrily. She found herself wondering when he had last had a decent meal. She roused herself and moved to rinse the one cup so she could pour him a cup of coffee.

“Thank you,” he said, looking a little embarrassed at the unfamiliar courtesy.

“I’m sorry I didn’t make more,” Ariana apologized as he cleaned up the plate with a biscuit. “I didn’t—I was trying to—to not use the supplies—”

“I can git more,” he stated briefly.

“But you said—” began Ariana.

He smiled. A lazy, good-natured smile. “True,” he replied, “but there are other stores.”

Ariana still didn’t understand his meaning, yet she couldn’t help but wonder if the food had been obtained with the help of a pistol rather than a gold piece.

He set aside the emptied plate. Ariana supposed that he must still be hungry. She had eaten two servings herself.

“Do you want those other two biscuits?” she inquired.

He nodded and moved to get up, but she brought the biscuits to him. He washed them down with great gulps of coffee.

The warm food seemed to relax his usually tense body. He even lifted off the Stetson and placed it on the floor beside him. Ariana noticed that his hair was curly. He was also in need of a good haircut. Then her eyes noticed a scar on his forehead—just at his hairline. She was wondering about it when his words drew her attention.

“What does lal mean?” he asked her suddenly.

“Lal?” she echoed.

“Lal. Jest like thet. L-A-L.”

“Where did you see it?” She was forgetting some of her caution.

"On one of them hankies in thet little box."

"Oh," said Ariana, "then it likely was a monogram."

"A monogram?" He sounded puzzled.

"One's initials."

The frown still puckered his brow.

"The first letters of your names," went on Ariana. "Mine would be AYB. Ariana Yvonne Benson."

He seemed to be pondering.

"You mean, the hankie has my ma's—what'd ya say—initials on it?"

"If it was truly your mother's hankie—then, yes," said Ariana.

"So her name was like thet. LAL?"

"That would be my guess," responded Ariana.

He stood suddenly. "Thet's right interestin'," he said as he picked up his hat with one hand, the empty plate with the other. "Want me to clean this off in the snow?" he asked her as he looked down at the plate and cup he held.

"No, no—I'll take care of it," she quickly answered.

He handed it to her. "Mighty obliged, miss," he said as he placed his hat back on his head. "Been a long time since I had something other than beans."

"I—would you—I mean, I could make a little extra tomorrow if . . ."

He smiled again and with his finger pushed back his hat. "Well, now," he said, "I'd like thet jest fine—but I'm not sure I'd be too smart—me comin' here to et. 'Course iffen I could come up with some plate, might be I could sneak a little out."

Ariana let her gaze travel to the room's one window.

"I'll see what I can do to free it up tomorrow," he said, reading her thoughts.

She nodded.

He left then. She heard the beam fall across the door, which meant she was again locked in. Then his voice reached her through the heavy timber. "Don't fergit to lock yer door."

Ariana reached up and slipped the hook quietly into the eye.

⁂

Another week passed slowly by. Ariana continued to make stews and potpies. She practiced with the reflector in various positions, and her biscuits improved each time she made a batch. Laramie consumed them with unbelievable ease.

He had surreptitiously removed the nails from the window frame and replaced them with hooks so it now locked on both the inside and the outside. Each night he brought his plate around to the window and held it while Ariana filled it. Then he took it, along with biscuits and coffee, and hastened off toward his own tumbledown cabin.

He had been giving full attention to his mother's Bible. He didn't pretend to understand much of it, but the little notations in the margins often shed some light on what he was reading. Still, he had so many questions and he had no one to ask.

He had also found a name that matched the initials. LAL. Lavina Ann Lawrence. Was that his mother? Laramie wanted to believe it was. Somehow it gave him a strange connection with the woman in the picture, an identity he previously had not had. He looked at the picture night after night until he felt—something—for the unknown woman. Something he had never felt before.

⁂

"Seems ya don't eat much anymore," observed Will as Laramie stepped inside the communal cabin. "Ya been dippin' in someone else's pot?"

The words brought loud guffaws from the men lounging about the room. By now everyone knew the prisoner was doing her own cooking. At times the fragrant smells coming from her cabin made stomachs growl in protest.

Laramie made no answer.

"Maybe he don't need to eat," snarled Skidder. "Maybe he lives on love."

More loud laughter.

"Ya ain't been round much a'tall lately," Will went on.

Laramie got the strange feeling his father was trying to start something.

"Been in my own cabin," he said offhandedly.

"Alone?" asked McDuff, and the whole group of men hooted in response.

"I sure know I wouldn't be iffen . . ." said Skidder with a knowing look, leaving his comment dangling.

There were more nods and hoots in general agreement.

Laramie felt the back of his neck crawl. He didn't like the talk. Didn't like the crude insinuations. "Anybody want a game of cards?" he asked, hoping to turn the attention of the cabin to other things.

His invitation was quickly accepted, and a group of the men pulled their log stools close to the rough-hewed table.

Laramie shuffled the cards, let Shadow cut, then began to deal.

"What say we up the ante," said Skidder with a leer. "Winner gits to guard the prisoner."

All eyes turned toward Laramie to catch his reaction. He never flinched. Never moved a muscle except for the ones needed to distribute the cards. Even his deep eyes did not betray him.

He nodded slowly. " 'Bout time someone else took a turn—but assignments are up to the boss. He decides who does what," he answered easily.

"Ya wanna gamble the girl—thet's yer doin'," responded Will in his gravelly voice, "long as she stays in camp."

Laramie nodded his consent without giving his true feelings away. He studied the cards in his hand. He wished he hadn't gotten himself cornered. Now he was in deep, for sure. What would happen if—? No, he wouldn't even think about it. This was one card game he had no intention of losing—the stakes were too high.

"Ya really think this is gonna work?" asked Sam after the cabin had cleared of all but him and his boss.

Will's chuckle was not a pleasant sound. "Ya saw 'im," he snorted. "He acted like he couldn'ta cared less—but I'm thinkin' thet if someone else had won thet card game, there'da been gunplay."

Sam was surprised. "An' you'd—you'd welcome thet?" he asked, dumbfounded.

"It wouldn'ta been the Kid we'd carried out," said Will simply.

"No—but it mighta been a good man. An' we got a little trip to make 'afore long, to my recollection."

The boss nodded.

"I want this here thing settled before we make the next raid," he said, scowling. "It's drug on far too long already."

Sam nodded. "The boys have been more patient then I woulda expected," he agreed.

"Mighta worked out a lot sooner iffen he didn't keep her hidden away in thet cabin," growled the big man. "No one even gits to see what she looks like."

"Tell 'im. Tell 'im. Yer the boss."

"Yeah, but what do I tell 'im? I told 'im to take care of her. The weather's been mean as a rattlesnake. What reason could I dream up for 'im to make her come out in the cold?"

"Well, the weather should be on the upturn anytime now. Been winter far too long," observed Sam.

"Hope so," exclaimed the boss. "I'm sick an' tired of these here beans."

Sam stopped chewing on his plug of tobacco long enough to give that some thought. "Ya reckon he eats with the girl?" he asked at last.

"I've watched him comin' an' goin'. He don't hang around there long enough to eat," growled Will. "He's in an' out like he was plumb scared of her or somethin'."

"Well—he don't seem to be losin' no weight," observed Sam. "Funny, ain't it?"

* * *

"I've got to get her out of there," Laramie told White Eagle.

His tone of voice and eyes gave away his intense feelings, even though he worked to keep his face expressionless.

"Something wrong?" asked the young brave.

"Yeah . . . yeah, things are . . . are . . . I don't know. I can jest feel the tension mountin'. I . . . I can't keep her safe . . . there anymore. Even the lock . . ."

He began to pace again.

It wasn't just the banter of the boys. Something had been happening since Laramie had been spending his days and nights reading his mother's Bible. Something he didn't understand. It was just there—deep within him. He was beginning to see that this life of his—this way of living was all wrong. And bringing her to the camp and keeping her there against her will—that was about as far wrong as they could get.

"How?" asked White Eagle, his simple question forcing Laramie back to the present.

He stopped his pacing. "I'll need yer help," he said, looking straight into the eyes of his friend.

"White Brother have my help," promised the Indian solemnly.

"Look, White Eagle. This will be dangerous. I know that. You must know that. My pa—he'd shoot to kill. He said so. In front of the whole gang. He'd not hesitate—"

White Eagle nodded. "You have gun," he interjected.

Laramie was shocked. "But I couldn't use it—couldn't shoot my own pa," he said quickly.

White Eagle looked thoughtful. Then he nodded again. "You more Indian than White," he told Laramie. "Have honor."

But Laramie brushed aside the words. He was deeply sorry about the fact that White Eagle felt as he did about the white race, but perhaps some of the animosity had been deserved. He wished things had been different.

He took a deep breath. "I'm not asking you to risk your life," he continued.

"I owe White Brother," replied the brave.

"No. No," responded Laramie. "You don't owe me. Sure I helped you out—"

"You save my life."

"Okay—I saved yer life—but thet doesn't mean—"

"White Eagle owe," the brave said firmly.

Laramie thought on his words, then accepted them with a silent nod. He had to allow White Eagle his Indian ways. Had to give him an opportunity to repay whatever debt he felt he owed.

"I won't pretend I'm not grateful," he responded. "I don't think I could manage it alone."

White Eagle made no comment, but the expression in his eyes as they met Laramie's was as good as a covenant signed in blood.

Chapter Twelve

Explosion

Laramie was in a race against time. He could sense that whenever he entered the main cabin with its quarrelsome occupants. There was a tension in the air—a feeling of agitation. Perhaps it could be chalked up to the length of the winter and the fact that the men had been virtually prisoners together for such a long period of time. Tempers flared. Patience had run out. Intolerance was evident. Snarls and complaints filled the air along with dark curses. Something was about to happen. Someone was going to snap.

But Laramie said nothing of his forebodings. Not even to Ariana. Nor did he tell her of his plans to remove her from the premises before the "explosion" took place.

He was sure White Eagle was working on his part in the escape plan. The hidden cave would be prepared for Ariana by the time she needed its safety. When Laramie gave Ariana her instructions, he wanted every detail to be in place.

It was a fairly simple plot. White Eagle would wait just beyond the cabin for Ariana. Laramie would ease her out of the cabin's window and send her through the darkness to the young brave. White Eagle, with his Indian cunning, would spirit Ariana to the hidden cave and leave her, protected and sequestered, until such time as Laramie was able to come for her.

In the meantime, Laramie was to lay a false trail. Riding his buckskin and leading his big bay and the little roan, he would take off through the valley, following the banks of the frozen river. He would travel dangerously close to the Indian encampment, a fact that would cause the gang some concern. It would pose no threat to Laramie. White Eagle had enlisted the help of his father, Chief Half Moon, and the braves were told to ignore the lone white man. Those orders had not been extended to any men who might follow.

At the edge of the Indian camp the saddles were to be slipped off Laramie's horses and transferred to the backs of new mounts. This too was part of arrangements made by White Eagle. Then Laramie would send his own horses on without a rider. He hoped it would be some time before the trackers would discover that the horses were traveling alone. Laramie was counting on the big bay—stolen from a local ranch—deciding to return to its home.

With the gang off on a false trail, Laramie planned to double back, pick up Ariana, and head out in the opposite direction. With all his heart he hoped that the plan would work and that it would buy him enough time to make an escape.

"If I don't make it," he had told White Eagle reluctantly, "try to take the girl back to your camp. Better she be the captive wife of one man than to be left at the mercy of the gang."

White Eagle nodded.

The two friends shook hands solemnly. Both knew the explosive nature of what they were attempting to do.

"You could die, my friend," said White Eagle.

Laramie nodded.

"That may be necessary," he said without emotion, then added thoughtfully, "But I plan to stay alive. A dead man won't be of much help to her."

White Eagle said nothing.

"I think all is ready," Laramie concluded.

"Must be soon," said White Eagle. "Spring stirring. Soon snow go. Ground go soft. Travel be hard."

"Three risings of the sun," agreed Laramie. "We should

have everything in place by then. Three days. I'll have her come to you."

"She wear buckskins."

"I'll be sure. I'll git to her the things you provided."

"Three sun risings."

Laramie agreed and the two friends parted.

Only two of those sun risings had passed when Laramie's worst fears were upon him. It all started innocently enough. The men had just lined up in the chow line to fill their plates with Rawley's beans and biscuits, and Skidder took a sniff of the mess and turned up his nose.

Laramie, who was eating again with the men so as not to draw undue attention, saw the scowling face but thought little of it. The men often complained about the fare.

But Rawley was in no mood to have his food insulted.

"What's the matter," he snapped, "ya expecting ham hock and sweet taters?"

"Well—iffen I was, I sure ain't now," said Skidder with a snarl.

"Iffen ya think ya can do better, why don't you fix the food—"

"Food?" snorted Skidder. "Ya call this food? Pig wouldn't et this slop."

"Pig? Guess it would too. You've been ettin' it fer a fair piece now."

Laramie saw Skidder's face and knew that trouble was coming. The others saw it too. There was a changing of positions as everyone eased out of the line of fire.

Will intervened. "You fellas have a burr under yer saddle, take it outside," was all he said.

Skidder, the plate of food still in his hand and a mean look on his face, nodded his head toward the door.

Laramie hoped Rawley would let it pass. Would just turn his back on the testy gun-toter. Everyone in the room knew that Rawley was no match for Skidder.

But Rawley was not looking for a way to back off. With one quick flick of his hand he upended the extended plate, splashing its contents over Skidder's face and down the front of his leather vest.

The fight did not make it outside. A hand flashed, Skidder's gun flamed, and Rawley fell forward, clutching his chest. A movement in the corner brought Skidder spinning around just as James, Rawley's sidekick, cleared the gun from his holster.

It was too slow. Skidder's second shot caught the man in the abdomen before he could even pull the trigger.

"Drop it," roared Will, his chair falling to the floor with a crash as he leaped to his feet.

Skidder let his gun hand lower to his side. But the defiance did not leave his eyes.

"I don't take kindly to a man shootin' up my quarters," the boss said, menace in his voice. "An' I don't take kindly to losin' two good men jest before a planned job. Seems to me ya coulda et yer beans an' kept yer mouth shut—like the rest of us. Now wipe 'em off yer face and tend to those men."

Will picked up his chair, swore when he saw the broken leg, and jerked forward a log stool.

"Broke the only chair in the place," he mumbled angrily, still glaring at Skidder.

From the corner of the room, Laramie heard a groan. He pushed his way through the cluster of milling men and bent over James. The man was still breathing, but he had been hit hard.

"Help me git this man to my cabin," he said to Curly.

Curly's hands shook as he set aside his bottle of whiskey and bent to help lift the man.

All through the evening hours Laramie tried to stop the bleeding. Outside he could hear the scrape of the shovel in frozen ground. Skidder had been given the job of digging the grave for Rawley. Laramie hoped there wouldn't be one needed for James as well. Once he thought of going for Ariana. Maybe she could at least say a prayer for the dying man.

But Laramie decided against it. It wouldn't be safe. Besides, a girl like Ariana shouldn't have to be exposed to such horrors. The men in the camp were used to seeing men die—it would be a totally new thing for the young girl. One that could fill her sleep with nightmares—like those kinds of events had done for Laramie when he was a kid.

He made James as comfortable as he could and hoped that the man would make it to see another morning. Then Laramie thought of his mother's Bible. Carefully he took it from its hiding place and thumbed through the pages. He found a spot heavily marked in his mother's handwriting and began to read, his voice low but clear.

The passage had nothing to do with death or dying—or of preparing oneself for the possibility. It was the story of Jesus calling the fishermen away from their nets. "Follow me," He had said, and his mother had, sometime in the past, written carefully beside the passage, "I have decided to follow Him, too. It has brought such peace and joy to my being."

After Laramie finished the story he read on, page after page. He didn't know if the man lying on his bed could hear the words, but he himself needed them, even if James did not.

This life, this way of living made no sense. No sense at all. He had always had questions about it. Now he was more sure than ever. He would have wanted out even if the girl hadn't come into the camp. He had always wanted out. He realized that now. He had never really fit. There was something that had always held him back.

A sudden idea occurred to him, making his spine tingle with the thought. Could it possibly be that this mother—this unknown person in his background—had somehow influenced his life? But how? Was this unseen, unknown God of hers holding him in check? He did not know. He wished he knew. He wished he knew more about this God. He was sure that Ariana had some of the answers, but he dared not go to her. He was sure to be watched. Everyone would be watched.

The whole camp was like a powder keg—about to explode. Given time they would all destroy one another—and the girl too.

Laramie turned back to the Book in his hand. It was the only thing that seemed to make any sense.

Along about midnight he heard footsteps on the path. He recognized Sam's step; then there was a bump at the door and Sam pushed his way in. Laramie was glad to see him. He welcomed the man's company.

"How's he doin'?" Sam asked simply.

Laramie nodded toward the man, whose breathing was becoming more shallow. He made no comment. Sam could see for himself.

Sam pulled up a stool and sat down.

Laramie let his gaze settle back on the man occupying his bed. "Was James his first name—or his last?" he asked quietly.

Sam shrugged. "I dunno," he replied—then gave a little snort. "Most likely weren't neither," he said. "Coulda took it jest 'cause he liked it. Maybe borrowed it offa Jesse. Mighta made him feel big."

Laramie looked back at the man. They really knew very little about him—except that he wasn't fast enough with a gun.

Silence.

"Ya been to see the girl?" asked Sam.

Laramie looked up in surprise and shook his head.

"Figure she might be scared blue," went on Sam. "Bound to have heard the shots."

"She'll be sleepin' now," remarked Laramie.

"Iffen she is, she's in better shape then the rest of us," replied Sam, reaching for his wad of chewing tobacco.

"Would ya mind lookin' in on her?" asked Laramie.

"Why don't you go?"

Laramie was silent for a number of minutes.

"Don't want to drag her in on this," he said finally. "Skidder's been lookin' fer a chance to draw on me fer months."

Sam chewed and spit.

"Yer faster," he said at last, avoiding Laramie's gaze.

His eyes narrowed. Was that the way Sam reasoned too? That a man, even a man like Skidder, had no value? That a snuffed-out life was nothing more than another grave to dig?

The thought troubled Laramie. He got up from his place by the bed and began to restlessly pace the cabin.

At last he wheeled to face the man he had known since he was old enough to recall anything at all.

"Is thet what this is all about?" he asked frankly. "Was thet girl brought in here to force a showdown 'tween Skidder an' me?"

Sam said nothing.

"Was it, Sam?" Laramie demanded. "Tell me. Was it?"

"Yer pa was jest anxious fer ya to . . . to act a man," replied Sam, and he spit into the corner.

Laramie's face blanched white. Then a red stain of anger began to flush his cheeks.

"Thet's 'bout the lowest thing I ever heard," he muttered angrily. "The lowest. To bring a girl—why didn't he jest call me out hisself?"

"Now, Kid—yer pa jest wanted ya to use yer gun 'cause he didn't want some low-liver shootin' ya in the back."

"Why? Why? Am I any better than—than Rawley—or James? Is my life worth more than—?"

"Don't go gittin' all in a knot. No harm—"

"No harm? What do you think this little scheme has done to her? Holed up all these months in the camp of—of no-good desperadoes? What do ya—?"

"Ya could have shortened it some," said Sam with no apologies.

Laramie just stood and stared.

"By killin' a man?" he demanded, his voice like steel. "I could have freed her up iffen I'd jest—pulled my Colt and killed a man? And what would thet have accomplished. Kill one—then there'd be another—an' another."

He lifted a hand and pushed his Stetson back in agitation.

Sam shrugged. "It gits easier," he said casually. "Jest the first one thet bothers a man much."

Laramie stared, anger making his eyes glitter.

"Yer pa was jest thinkin' of you. Didn't want ya leavin' a string of one-arm gunslingers to track ya down—"

"So I shoot 'em all?"

The words were spoken in vehemence. Sam did not respond. The silence hung heavy in the log cabin.

"I don't think so, Sam," Laramie finally went on evenly, his control back again. "I don't think so. I . . . I'm at the place where . . . I'd be willin' to die fer her, but I . . . I haven't come to the place where I'd be willin' to kill in cold blood fer her. An' the more I read in thet Bible, the more sure I am of thet fact."

Sam's eyes widened. It was clear to Laramie that the words surprised and shocked him. "Thet girl been fillin' ya with Bible talk?" he asked, and Laramie could tell he was upset.

"Not a'tall," he drawled. "Been readin' it fer myself—an' fer James here."

"Where'd you git a Bible?"

"You gave it to me."

Sam looked about to explode. "I never did no sech thing an' you know—"

"Sure you did," replied Laramie. "In thet trunk—of my ma's."

"Yer ma's Bible?"

Laramie only nodded.

Sam chewed on his mustache, then spit in the corner.

"So what can you tell me about her, Sam?" Laramie asked quietly.

Sam's head jerked up. "Oh no," he said with a wave of his hand. "I got nothin' to say. Nothin'. Ain't no business of mine. It's yer pa's place to—" He stopped, looked at Laramie, then spit again.

There was further silence as Sam continued working on his chaw of tobacco. At length he looked up. "So yer holdin' yer position?" he asked frankly.

Laramie nodded again, his eyes thoughtful, his jaw set.

"Well, Kid," Sam said as he slowly lifted himself from the chunk of log. "I wouldn't give her much chance of gittin' back to life as she knew it, then. Yer pa's 'bout got his mind made up—an' it's 'bout like a rusty steel trap. Once shut—never git it open."

A slight moan from the corner cot caught their attention. Even as Laramie moved toward the bed he saw that the wounded man had taken his last breath.

Laramie stood over him, feeling helpless and sick at his stomach. He never had been able to accept the sight of a man who'd died because of a bullet in his stomach.

He turned away from the bed, one hand raised to slowly tip back the brim of his Stetson. His knees felt weak, his thoughts were jumbled in anger and confusion. It was so senseless. So brutal.

He heard the sound of scraping as Sam pushed himself up from his block seat and onto his feet. Laramie wondered if the sight of the wasted man was making Sam feel sick inside also.

When he turned to look at the older man, Sam was already moving slowly toward the door. Just before he exited the cabin he turned and spit into the corner. "Guess I'd better tell Skidder to git his shovel out agin," he said. He left the room without further comment.

Laramie longed to go to Ariana. Was she awake? Had she indeed heard the shouting and the shots? Surely she was frightened and filled with questions.

And he was the reason. He was the cause of her being dragged off from home and family to this terrible bandit outpost. He, unknowingly, had brought about this awful deed.

He buried his head in his hands and tried to address a God whom he did not know.

And then a new thought brought some peace to his heart. Ariana knew this God. He had seen the quiet confidence in her eyes as she spread the Book out before her. Even in the midst of her fear, she had shown unbelievable courage. It wasn't her own doing, he was sure of that now. It was because she had faith in the unseen God she trusted.

Chapter Thirteen

Escape

Laramie brought the wood earlier than usual the next morning. Ariana had washed herself in the basin and dressed in her own garments. She was spending time in early morning prayer. The events of the night before had upset her, so she had not been able to sleep. She had heard the angry shouts, the gunshots, and then the scraping of the shovel against the frozen ground and rocky soil. Something terrible had happened. She was sure of it. It brought her added terror. She had spent most of the night in prayer.

She had hoped that Laramie or Sam would come to her cabin and assure her that everything was all right—but at the same time she knew better. Never had she clung so tenaciously to the promises of God as she had through those long night hours.

When the little rap came on her door, she recognized it as Laramie's signal. Without understanding her intense relief that he hadn't been the one who was buried, she crossed to the door and quickly lifted the sturdy hook. As the door swung open she looked from his armload of wood to the stack against the wall. She was not in need of more firewood.

"Close the door," he whispered, and Ariana hastened to obey. Instinctively she knew something had changed—and not for the better. Her face paled. Her hands knotted against her calico front.

Laramie walked directly to the stack of wood and dropped his pile of logs. As he did so a package tumbled out and fell to the floor. Ariana stared.

"Come here," whispered Laramie, and Ariana woodenly obeyed.

"I haven't time to talk," said the man as he began to stack the firewood, making an unusual amount of noise as he did so.

"I'm gittin' you outta here. Sh-h. We might be spied on. I can't stay long enough to give ya all the details. But I've some things fer you to do."

He glanced around the room again and proceeded to lift stacked logs and bang them against one another as he restacked them by the wall.

"First—make a big batch of biscuits—all ya can—an' wrap 'em up—in two different bundles—maybe in those towels. Don't worry none about crushin'. Thet won't hurt 'em.

"Then, after supper—pack the things ya want to take—in as tight a bundle as ya can. I'll pick 'em up. Put on the clothes from this bundle and wait. Light yer lamp—as usual. Keep the big towel over the winda. I'll knock three little raps—then agin three—on yer winda, not yer door. You be ready." More logs crashed against the wall.

"I'll take ya to a friend of mine. He's Pawnee. He'll take ya where ya'll be safe. Trust 'im."

He stood and moved to the fire.

"Ya need more water?" he asked in a normal voice.

Ariana stood mute, staring at him. It was too much to take in all at once. She blinked. Her mouth opened but no words came. His hand gave her a little signal, and she swallowed hard and found her voice.

"Yes," she answered in as even a voice as she could manage. "Yes . . . I'd like some extra . . . if you have time. It's . . . it's the day for my bath."

He smiled softly and nodded his head as though to compliment her on her control. Then he went to fill the kettle and the basin from the pail and left the cabin with the empty bucket in his hand. Ariana put the hook firmly in place. Her hand was trembling so uncontrollably she could hardly manage the small task.

Ariana finally had a day that demanded action. Over and over in her mind she sorted through those things she was to do. She really did take a bath, thinking that it might well be her last one for some time to come. Then she got out her food supplies and baked biscuits as she had been ordered, until she had a large stack of them on her wooden table.

By the time she had finished her baking the sun was moving lower in the sky.

Ariana began to gather the things she planned to take with her. She was glad she had dressed in her own garments that morning so the things that had belonged to Laramie's mother could be freshly washed. They now hung on the hook on the wall. She crossed the small room, lifted down each item, and folded it carefully. It was the first time she had opened the lid of the trunk since Laramie himself had removed the small chest and worn Bible.

"I wonder if he ever reads?" she mused as she placed the items of clothing back on the top of the pile.

" 'Laramie's Mama,' " she whispered to the unknown woman, "I don't know anything about you . . . whether you are alive . . . or dead . . . but I do thank you . . . whoever you are, for the use of your things. I have tried to . . . to return them to you in the same condition . . . ."

Ariana let the words trail off. It did seem awfully silly to be talking to someone who was not there.

She closed the lid quietly, letting her hand rest upon it for several moments as she looked down at the metal top, the stained leather straps.

"If only you could talk," she whispered to the trunk. "I'm

sure you'd have secrets to share."

Then she turned her attention back to the task at hand. She had to be prepared, small bundle and baked biscuits wrapped securely for whatever lay ahead.

❧ ❧ ❧

As darkness fell, Ariana lit the kerosene lamp as she had been told and sat down in the unfamiliar buckskin clothing on the log stool by her table. Normally she would have spent her evening hours reading or memorizing from her Bible—but tonight her Bible, along with her few other possessions, was wrapped securely in the little bundle and waiting on the floor close to the room's window, along with the two packages of biscuits.

Ariana had also made up another small bundle with additional food supplies that could be carried on a pack animal. She had no idea how long the trip might take to get back home. The trip through the storm had seemed to take forever—but if she remembered correctly, they had made it in four days of travel.

More and more throughout the day, the truth of her circumstances had begun to sink in. This was no pleasure trip through the beauties of the woods. She was not going to be released—set free. She had been smuggled into the camp of lawless men—and she was to be smuggled out. Laramie had made that plain with his secrecy and carefully laid plans. It was going to be a dangerous mission. Not just for her, she surmised, but for the young man as well.

"Would they really kill one of their own?" she asked herself.

After the events of the night before—still unexplained to Ariana—she had no doubt of the answer. Yes. Laramie could be killed in his effort to free her from the camp and get her back to her own hometown.

Over and over Ariana offered intense little prayers.

And she waited—her whole body feeling rigid and trembly, her hands clasped in front of her on the wooden boards of the table, the simple buckskin garments feeling strange on her skin.

The tension within her grew and grew as the night hours moved slowly by. Had Laramie forgotten? No, surely not. Had something happened to him? That thought brought her to near panic. *Pray,* she ordered herself sternly. *Pray—and trust.*

Ariana tried hard to fight the waves of fear that swept through her. She had to be calm. She had to be in control. Her flight depended upon it. Without control she might make some very foolish mistake.

And then she heard the gentle rap at her window. Three times. She waited. A repeat of another three. Ariana rose from her seat and moved quickly to the window. Even in her excitement, she noted the silence of the moccasins that had been provided.

She lifted back the towel curtain and could just make out the dim outline of Laramie's face. He motioned for her to open the window, and she did so as quietly as she could.

Without a word, she passed the bundles out the window to his waiting hands, then climbed on the log stool that she had placed below the window earlier in the day.

Without a sound Laramie helped ease her body through the small opening and lowered her noiselessly to the ground. Taking her by the hand he began to lead her through the darkness. Ariana wondered how he could even find his way through the heavy growth of trees, but she followed wordlessly.

Before long they came to a small clearing. Three horses stood, stirring restlessly, anxious to be back in their warm stalls. A late spring storm was bringing snow, icy hard flakes, driven by a biting wind. Ariana felt a sick feeling in the pit of her stomach. Was this a repeat of the whole horrible nightmare?

As if born of the night, another man was suddenly beside her. He spoke not a word, just reached for her hand. The Indian Laramie had told her about.

At the same time the young brave took her left hand, Laramie released her right. She was being led off into the darkness without even a final word.

She looked back once and stumbled slightly. Laramie was tying the bundles she had given him to the pack saddle on one of the animals. All except for one of the towel-wrapped batches of biscuits. The young brave carried that in his other hand.

⁂

"You safe here."

It was the first the Indian had spoken. Wordlessly he had led Ariana across the valley, through the deep darkness of the woods and into the hills. Now they were entering a cave. Ariana could not restrain a shudder. She hated caves. Was afraid of them. Had always been afraid of them—even as a young child.

And now she was to enter one. She did not like the idea. But perhaps—perhaps it was a little better than being in a camp of outlaws.

She steeled herself, took a deep breath, and followed her guide into the opening.

The man was leading her deeper and deeper into the cave. She wondered how he could possibly know where he was going. He stopped and used a flint to light a small lantern that must have been waiting for their arrival. Then they traveled on, winding this way and that, squeezing through small openings in the rocks, crawling through short tunnels, pushing their way through rubble.

Ariana stifled a scream that pressed at the back of her throat. She feared she would suffocate. She frantically wondered just how much more she could stand—and then they passed through a narrow opening and came out into a larger space. Ariana was faintly aware of the sound of dripping water.

"You safe here," the young brave said again.

Ariana let her gaze travel over the cave floor. Someone lived here. There were robes and blankets and supplies. Someone. . . . Who? The Indian? Surely she wasn't expected to share the dwelling with—

"It dry—safe," the young man said again. Ariana still did not move.

"You light candle—one," he ordered.

Ariana stiffly bent to pick up a candle. She noticed that there was a rather large pile of them on the floor. She held the candle to the wick of the lantern he held out to her. The candle sputtered, then raised a tiny, flickering flame. He set the bundle of biscuits on the floor by the other stores.

"You eat—one—each time you light new candle," he commanded her in his soft voice. Ariana nodded dumbly.

"Sleep," he said and pointed to the pile of skins and blankets in the corner.

Ariana nodded again and moved to place her candle in the wooden holder that had been left for it.

He stared at her candle for a long moment with an expression she could not read.

"Don't let candle die," he cautioned. "No more light."

Ariana's eyes widened. Being in this deep, dark cave was bad enough—but with no light. The very thought sent waves of panic through her.

"I not bring another," and he indicated the flint in his hand with some apology in his tone. "I need at front of cave for return." She stared dumbly at him.

"I go," announced the man and moved away before Ariana could respond. She was afraid he would fade into the very rocks of the walls.

"Wait," she cried after him.

He turned back. The flicker of the lantern he held cast eerie shadows on his bronze cheeks. His black eyes seemed to reflect the dancing light.

"Wait," Ariana implored again, reaching out a trembling hand.

He stood silently while she tried to untangle her thoughts and get them in order for expression.

"I . . . I need to know . . . I mean . . . Laramie said you'd tell me what I'm to do," she managed.

He nodded. "You wait," he said simply.

"But . . . in here . . . alone . . . for who . . . how long?" Her questions seemed to tumble over one another.

He came a step closer and set his lantern on the hard rock of the cave floor. Then he surprised her by lowering himself to a cross-legged sitting position. Ariana waited.

He nodded to her, and she understood that she was also to sit—on the pile in the corner that was meant for her bed.

Obediently she sat.

"Alone—here—yes," he began. "Do not leave—ever. We come."

He seemed to feel that was settled. She was to wait here—alone—until someone came for her.

"How many suns? Not know," he continued.

"But . . . who will come? Laramie said—"

"Laramie come," he nodded in assurance, and Ariana's troubled mind grasped at that promise.

But her sense of relief was short-lived.

"Maybe yes—maybe no," he went on calmly, making her heart race again.

"If not—I come," he finished, then sat quietly as though waiting to see if she had any more questions.

She sat trembling, looking down at her folded hands.

"Food," he said, pointing at the supply against the rock wall. "Water," he continued and pointed to the opposite wall and up against the ceiling. It was the first Ariana had noticed the little ledge and the small clay pot that sat on it. From somewhere above, water continued to drip, drip into the container. That was her water supply.

"Sleep," he said again, and he rose like a shadow and turned away from her again.

She knew better than to call a second time. She was alone in a deep, dark cave, somewhere in the bowels of the earth.

And she was to wait—just wait—silently—patiently—until someone came for her. Ariana felt terror rise in her throat until she felt she wouldn't be able to breathe.

All through the night Laramie pressed his mount forward, the two animals on their tethers following obediently at his heels.

At times he hid his trail by traveling along the sheltered rock shelves; at others he left deliberate little clues as to which way he was heading.

He was glad for the snow. By morning, and the discovery that they were gone, much of the trail would be covered—just as it had been when his pa and Sam had brought the girl to the camp.

Laramie smiled. It seemed rather ironic. A snowstorm had kept her would-be rescuers from finding her—and a snowstorm might also defeat her enemies.

Laramie pulled his hat down over his face to protect himself from the bite of the whirling ice crystals and urged the rangy buckskin on.

Chapter Fourteen

Waiting

"Lord, it's been seventy-two days," Laura Benson reminded God in a quiet conversation with Him as she rolled crusts for an apple pie. "Seventy-two days—without any word."

She blinked away tears that welled up in her eyes. "I've tried to be patient, Lord. Tried to trust . . . but sometimes . . . it gets so hard."

The tears refused to stay in check and squeezed out from under her blinking lids and rolled down her wrinkled cheeks. She reached for the hankie in her apron pocket and quickly dispensed with the telltale marks of weeping.

"They say no news is good news, Lord," she continued. "Help me to really believe that."

Ariana huddled in her corner. She was thankful for the warm furs beneath her and the woolen blankets she could wrap her body in. She wasn't sure if she shook from the cold, dank interior of the cave or from sheer terror, but she trembled just the same.

"If only I had my Bible," she said to herself for the twentieth time.

But you do, an inner voice prompted. *Haven't you been busy with memorization for the past weeks? You have much of the Bible within you.*

With a start of surprise, Ariana realized it was so. She had memorized many sections of Scripture during her days of confinement. Perhaps the long stay in the small cabin would not be for nought.

She pulled the blanket more closely about her shoulders. "Where should I start?" she asked herself. "Well . . . why not at the beginning? I'll gradually work my way through the Bible, recalling every portion I have learned."

"Genesis, chapter one. In the beginning God . . ."

Ariana stopped. The few words had given her much to think about.

"In the beginning *God* . . ." she repeated slowly. The words seemed to echo off the dark walls of rock.

Ariana spoke them again. At least her own voice was something with which to fill the stillness.

"God . . . in the beginning . . . and always," she mused to herself. "Well . . . if He has always been—and I fully believe He has—then I guess He must know all there is to know about what's going on. Even now. Even in this cave."

The thought brought comfort to Ariana.

She reached down one hand to feel the softness of her bed. Someone had taken a good deal of trouble to prepare it for her. Spruce and pine branches intertwined to make a soft layer beneath her. Soft moss covered the boughs. Then the thick fur—likely buffalo, Ariana guessed—and then the warm, though scratchy, blankets of wool.

Yes, she could not complain about her bed. It was much more comfortable than the rough wood bunk in the cabin.

Ariana let her gaze travel to the little stock of supplies. Here again her needs had been met. True, it was not especially tasty food that had been stored in the cave. But it was palatable—and nourishing. Pemmican. Dried berries and fish. And her own biscuits—which would soon be as dry as the berries, she thought wryly.

And water. She had a good supply of water—though at first the constant drip, drip had threatened to drive her mad. But the water was cold and fresh, and she had no trouble convincing herself to drink straight from the small earthen pot.

Ariana looked at the little stack of candles. So far she had relit a new candle from the old one seven times. She had no idea how long one candle burned. She had no idea whether it was now day or night in the outside world. She had even less of an idea how many hours had crawled by since she had been brought to the cave. She only knew that it seemed like a very long time.

And now her thoughts turned again from the cave and back to the Scripture.

"In the beginning God . . ." she said again and smiled to herself. "And in the end, God as well," she went on. "And in the middle, and in the past, and in the future—God. For always and ever—what a wonderful truth."

"In the beginning God created. . . ." She stopped again and let her eyes drift over the eerie walls of the cave. The flickering candlelight cast funny dancing shapes over the roughness of the rock.

"You did this," she spoke to the God she knew shared her abode. "You made this. Why? Why this strange little room way back in the rocks? Did you know—even then—that someday. . . ?" Ariana let her voice fade. It was too big an idea to even think about.

Suddenly the cave no longer seemed menacing. It did not even seem as cold and clammy as before. Ariana had the comforting knowledge that she was not alone.

The severity of the storm made travel more and more difficult for Laramie. At the same time, it would make his trail harder to follow. He began to wonder if he shouldn't change his plans and head straight for the cave and Ariana.

At length he decided against it. He and White Eagle had laid their plans carefully. To change now might mean a disruption that could be costly—even deadly.

Laramie pulled the collar of his heavy coat up more closely to his chin and nudged the buckskin with a blunted spur.

He lifted his face to try to judge the time of day. It was hard to tell with the sky so overcast. He turned his thoughts back to the camp behind him. Had they discovered his absence? How had his pa responded? Laramie could easily guess. Were they already on his trail?

Then his thoughts turned to Ariana. He had no reason to think that White Eagle would have had any trouble getting the girl to the safety of the hidden cave. The sentry posted on the ledge would not have been able to see the brave and the girl, and certainly would not have heard them creeping through the cover of darkness. The rest of the gang members would pose no threat. They much preferred their bunks or the card table during the hours of night.

It seemed to Laramie that the first part of the mission had gone as planned. The hardest part was still to come. He had to backtrack and lead the girl from the cave to further safety. That would mean getting her out almost beneath the noses of the gang, and they were bound to be stirring about like a nest of disturbed hornets.

Laramie set his jaw and pushed on. If only the second part of the plan worked as well as the first.

Laramie watched as White Eagle separated himself from the overhanging spruce and moved forward. Without a word to the waiting brave, Laramie swung out of the saddle. Three ponies stood ground-tethered in the shadows. The horses exchanged whinnied greetings and stomped in impatience.

White Eagle began to undo the girth of the pack saddle even as Laramie began to uncinch the belly straps of the riding saddle, still warm from his body.

"Any signs?" asked White Eagle.

Laramie shook his head. "Didn't see a soul," he replied. "The storm made sight and sound nigh impossible."

"They follow," White Eagle informed him. "Five." He pointed his hand straight up, and Laramie understood that he was saying the five men had not ridden out of the camp until near noon. That had given him even more time than he had counted on. For one moment he wished his plans had not included the trip to the cave. He should have just taken the girl and headed right out. But how could he have known that a spring storm would move in? How could he have known that the camp would not stir and discover the missing horses, then the girl's empty cabin, until noon? No, it was better that they had played it safe. But now—?

"What do you think, White Eagle?" he asked his friend. "Do you think it is safe to keep on riding, or should we change horses as planned and wait?"

White Eagle looked at the clear sky overhead. Laramie followed his glance and knew what his friend was thinking. The storm was over. Now there would be no advantage of being hidden by a winter storm or of having the trail covered by falling snow. There would only be drifts of whiteness on the ground. It would be impossible to cover one's tracks.

"Wait," said the young brave. "Send horses. Wait."

In spite of his similar assessment, Laramie wanted to argue. He had hoped White Eagle would assure him that it would be days before the men at his back would be able to sort out his trail. After all, they would not be expecting him to head straight to the Indian village.

And he had hoped—had just hoped—that he might not have to lose his buckskin. He had a great deal of affection for the animal. He would have liked to have left the saddle on the horse's back and just ridden out of the encampment the way he had ridden in.

Besides—things looked good right now. But what if something happened they had not anticipated? It could mean a long delay. Ariana was waiting. She would be restless, fearful. Wondering.

He hated to wait.

"I watch," White Eagle spoke again. "I take you to hiding place. Then I watch."

"Do yer people know I'm here?" asked Laramie.

"They know," said White Eagle solemnly. "My father say, 'Leave to White Eagle white brother.' They know. You safe. But for other men—my people not like white man."

Laramie knew that to be an understatement. There had been bad blood between the little pockets of outlaws and the Indian people. Raids—especially of horses—took place back and forth and often resulted in bloodshed.

"What if someone else—from another tribe—discovers me?" he asked his friend.

White Eagle shook his head. "I take you to sacred mountain," he said in a conspiratorial tone. "No Indian go there. Afraid."

Laramie nodded and removed the bridle from the buckskin. Without comment he ran his hand over the soft neck, the sleek back of the horse. He sure would miss him. He hated to let him go.

"Take care, partner," he whispered under his breath, and then he gave the surprised mount a slap on the rump with the flat of his hand. The startled animal leaped forward at the same time as the big bay who had been turned loose by White Eagle. Both animals started off at a gallop, the little roan fast on their heels. The Indian ponies stamped in impatience, their heads tossed high, their nostrils flaring, and pulled against their tethers.

The two men stood and watched the driven horses gallop on through the woods.

"He go back to ranch?" asked the Indian about the big bay, who had quickly taken the lead.

"I shore do hope so. He's tried to head thet direction each time I take him out," replied Laramie.

"Maybe he go," nodded White Eagle.

As the three horses disappeared from sight, the two men turned their attention to the other mounts.

"These fellas broke to saddle?" inquired Laramie as he carried his saddle toward them.

For the first time, White Eagle laughed. "We see," was his response, and Laramie guessed they might have a bit of a rodeo show in store.

Ariana had worked her way through Genesis. When she came to portions that she had not memorized, she filled in accounts with her own version of events. Then she moved on to Exodus—easily recalling many of the stories and even quoting some of the scriptures. She reviewed each of the Ten Commandments, studying thoughtfully each one in a way that she had not troubled to do in the past. On to Leviticus. She found she had a difficult time untangling the laws and rules for living, worship, and sacrifice. Numbers. Deuteronomy. "I'm going to have to study those books more," she chided. "I haven't paid close enough attention."

She began her mental journey through Joshua, marveling how God led His people to victory time after time—whenever they were walking in obedience.

Occasionally she stopped to wonder how many days had passed. How many more meals the little store would provide. How long her supply of candles would last. At times fear gripped her and she wanted to scream against the confines of her quarters. Was her present circumstance really that much better than her former state had been? At least in the cabin she had had the blessing of seeing daylight. At least she had known whether it was day or night.

Then she would determinedly force her thoughts to other things. It would not do for her to get despondent. To give up. She must keep fighting for survival. She must eat her daily rations—must light her candle. And she must fight the urge to stumble her way out of the dark cave and into the sunlight. Her very life depended upon it.

Laramie chafed with the delay. It wasn't that he feared for his own safety. White Eagle had led him to a well-hidden spot close to the Indian settlement. It was not likely that the men from the gang would search for him here, and White Eagle had assured him that Indian braves stayed well away from the "place of the angry gods."

Still he paced restlessly. Shouldn't he be on the trail? Shouldn't he have picked up Ariana and galloped off while the men searched for him in the other direction? What was keeping White Eagle? Had something happened to the young brave?

It was all Laramie could do to hold his post. His agitation seemed to take hold of his very being. He had never been so troubled before.

Would Ariana be facing the same doubts? Would she be as restless? As irritated? Would her impatience drive her to do something foolish?

Laramie had to hold himself in check. He felt it would be easier to face a herd of stampeding buffalo—a nest of rattlers—than just to sit and wait. At least then he would feel that his destiny, to some measure, was in his own hands.

Just as he was about to explode from the tension, White Eagle slipped quietly into the little camp.

Chapter Fifteen

Terror

Laramie moved eagerly forward to meet the young Pawnee. "What's the news?" he asked impatiently.

White Eagle shook his head, and Laramie feared the word was not good.

"Red horse not go," he answered evenly.

Laramie stopped midstride. "Did they find 'im?" was his next question.

White Eagle nodded in reply.

Laramie licked his lips. He felt confused—betrayed by the animal.

"What happened?" he asked.

"They backtrack—close to village," responded White Eagle.

"They think yer people captured us?"

"Maybe yes," said White Eagle. "Maybe no."

Laramie waited. He was sure White Eagle had more to report.

"They know Indian not let horse go," said White Eagle simply.

Laramie thought on that and then nodded. It was true. The Indians would not have released the horses.

"So they know it's a false trail," he admitted aloud.

"They wait—just outside village—in draw."

"Are they still there?" asked Laramie.

"Had to tell Father to stop young braves," went on White Eagle. "They want to raid. Like horses. They wait now."

Laramie nodded.

There was silence as the young men pondered their situation.

White Eagle spoke. "You want braves attack?" he asked simply.

Laramie shook his head. He could not utter the order that would surely send the gang members to their death—including his own father. Nor did he wish to cause danger to the Indian braves—though he imagined the chief was having difficulty holding his men in check. They would have welcomed an opportunity to attack the little camp of desperadoes and plunder their supplies and their horses.

"No. No, don't attack. We'll wait."

But at the same time he still hated the thought of waiting.

"One thing more," said White Eagle thoughtfully.

Laramie turned to him.

"One sentry. One. He sits by big rock on hill."

Laramie waited.

"Leaning Tree, brave man. He like big red horse."

Laramie still waited patiently.

At last White Eagle continued. "Leaning Tree will silence sentry. Me take horses."

Laramie's eyes grew serious. "Kill the sentry?" he asked. He wanted no part of killing if there was another way out.

"Maybe yes. Maybe no," said White Eagle.

"Tell him no," said Laramie. "Take his guns. Leave him tied if you have to."

White Eagle looked dubious but nodded. "Leaning Tree not like this. . . ." He shrugged his shoulders when Laramie did not change his mind.

White Eagle spoke again. "Leaning Tree get big red horse. You—buckskin. Me—rest."

Laramie nodded. It would make White Eagle a very

wealthy young brave. He would be able to pick from all the maidens of the village.

"Wait," said Laramie, raising his hand to show that the deal had not been completed.

White Eagle watched his face closely.

"I get back the buckskin—and the roan," said Laramie, remembering the excitement when he first had put his saddle on the Indian pony White Eagle had provided. "You git yer mustangs back."

White Eagle looked amused. Then nodded in agreement. "Come," he said simply. "I take you to girl."

"Now?" Laramie was both surprised and excited.

"Now. You must be ready to ride tomorrow when horses come."

Laramie nodded. It sounded reasonable. After all, the whole gang that sought his hiding place would then be on foot.

Ariana paced the small hideout. She told herself she had to keep limber—but in truth she knew she was just restless.

She had been in this hole in the rocks for such a long time. She didn't know how much longer she could endure it. Even the reciting of scriptures failed to quiet her troubled spirit.

She walked back and forth—back and forth.

Now and then her eyes traveled to her little stack of supplies. She had already eaten all the biscuits and the dried fruit. Only pemmican remained. Ariana was not sure just how long she could stretch it out. She was drinking more and more water in order to keep her stomach from gnawing with hunger.

Her pile of candles was being quickly used up too. Ariana would not let herself think about being left in the dark. She simply would not be able to endure it. She would bolt for sure. But did she know her way out? The young Indian had turned this way and that, selecting one tunnel over another—and he had a lantern. She would get lost in the labyrinth for sure without any light. She might wander forever and never find her way to daylight. The mere idea was more than she could bear.

"Sleep," she told herself. "Sleep. Time will pass more quickly. Surely he will come soon. Surely . . ."

She checked the candle to make sure it had plenty of burning time left and eased onto the bed of fur. She tucked the blanket firmly about her and closed her eyes. The constant dripping of water distracted her, but she fought against it. She found a hymn whose beat kept time with the dripping and sang it over in her mind. Over and over—until it was almost hypnotic. Finally she drifted off into a troubled sleep.

Ariana awoke, fighting for full consciousness. Something was wrong. She knew it—but in her state of drowsiness she was unable to reason it through.

She listened, straining to hear in the darkness. Nothing. Nothing but the soft drip of the seeping water.

Then if a noise had not disturbed her—what had?

She groped to pull the blanket more closely about her chin. Something was wrong. She could feel it.

And then the truth hit her full force. There was no light! Her candle was no longer burning. What had happened? What had put out the flicker of light?

It took several minutes before Ariana could gather enough courage to reach out in the darkness. The place where the candle had been was just a sticky spot on the wooden holder. She had slept too long. Her candle had burned out.

"Oh no," she cried out. "No." Her voice echoed around her.

Panic nearly suffocated her. She would never be able to stand it alone in the dark. Never. She wouldn't be able to find her food. Her water. She'd die. She'd surely die.

A feeling of total desperation overtook her. She found herself praying that she might die quickly. Then Ariana buried her face in the warm fur, and for the first time since the early days of her capture, she wept uncontrollably.

"Ya sure we won't be spotted?" Laramie asked as he followed White Eagle along an unmarked trail.

"Leaning Tree watch," replied the brave.

The answer satisfied Laramie and he picked up the pace. Each man led one of the mustangs, saddles again in place after a struggle to get the horses to accept them. But White Eagle insisted it would be safer for them to walk through the trees rather than to ride. The horses had now quieted to the saddle, but accepting a rider in the saddle would start the battle all over again. They had no time to lose.

As it was, it was getting dark by the time White Eagle pushed aside a small bramble bush and motioned Laramie into the mouth of a hidden cave.

They had moved in a short distance when White Eagle stopped and lifted a lantern from a hidden place in the rocks. Silently he lit it and then moved stealthily on.

Deeper and deeper into the cavern they went, winding first one way and then angling back another. Laramie was counting on his friend to eventually get them to the right place—and to make sure they would find their way out again.

They had walked what seemed to be a long way when White Eagle stopped and put a hand to Laramie's chest.

"What is it?" Laramie whispered, the hair on the back of his neck lifting eerily.

"No light," responded White Eagle.

"No light?"

"No candle," repeated White Eagle.

Laramie felt his whole body tremble. Had something happened to Ariana? Was the whole effort in vain? He closed his eyes and willed strength back into his body. White Eagle began to move forward again.

They pushed their way through one last opening and entered a wider hole in the rocks. Laramie could see the pile of furs and blankets in the corner. Were they too late?

Then the blankets shifted. And she was looking at him, her eyes wide and terrified, pale cheeks stained from the cave dust mingled with her tears. Her hair hung about her shoulders in a tangled mass of uncombed curls, and her face looked gaunt.

"My candle went out," she gasped, then with a look like a wild thing, she turned her face back into the furs and began to weep again, her whole body shaking.

"I had to crawl about in the dark to—" she continued along with the sobs. "I had to—"

But she could not go on. The two men exchanged glances. One felt as helpless as the other. What could they do to comfort her? How did one reassure a distraught woman? What unspeakable terrors had she experienced in the darkness of the cave?

It was White Eagle who moved forward, handing the lantern to a stunned Laramie.

He knelt on the rock floor beside her bed and reached out one hand to her shaking shoulder. "It's over," he crooned softly. "Over. Soon you go. Soon. You safe now. Alone no more. Safe now."

As he talked he patted her shoulder rather clumsily and pushed back her hair. It reminded Laramie of one gentling a terror-stricken horse. Gradually the words and the human contact brought calm to the frightened girl. The sobs lessened. The shoulders stopped their shaking. Ariana began to fight for control.

"We light two candles," offered White Eagle. "Three candles. We light whole cave."

Ariana giggled—somewhat giddily—accompanied by hiccups. She forced her way up from the blankets and furs and dabbed at her face with a corner of the woolen throw.

"I was so scared," she admitted, apologetically, without looking up. "I had waited so long—I didn't know the way out—I thought you'd never come. Never."

"We come," said White Eagle—and he lit a fourth candle for good measure. "Tomorrow you go."

Ariana seemed to ponder his statement. For the first time she lifted her eyes to Laramie. Her face was still pale, her cheeks smeared, her hair in tangles. "Is it true?" she asked simply.

He nodded. He was still afraid to speak. He had never seen anyone look so desperate before.

Self-consciously she pushed hair away from her face. For the first time she seemed to realize her present state of disarray.

"I can't believe it," she said at last, her hands fluttering nervously. "I . . . I thought I'd never see the light of day again."

Laramie finally found his legs—and his voice. He moved forward with the lantern and set it on a small ledge of rock. The light spilled out in fanciful splashes, joining with the candles in lighting up the rock walls of the cave, making deeper shadows where the light did not reach.

"We'll leave in the morning," he promised her.

She fidgeted nervously and cast her eyes about the cave.

"I . . . I guess I can stand . . . one more night," she finally managed and swallowed hard.

"I'll stay," said Laramie quickly, though he had intended to guard the cave's mouth and watch for signals from the valley.

White Eagle nodded. He seemed to understand.

"Both sleep," he said. "Long ride with new sun."

White Eagle gathered his lantern and left them, admonishing them again to get a good sleep in preparation for the next day's hard riding.

Laramie had nodded in agreement, but he wondered just how much sleep they would manage.

"When did you eat last?" he asked her.

Ariana looked puzzled. "I'm not sure," she replied honestly. "I . . . I lose track of time."

He nodded, then crossed to the food supply. It was almost gone.

"You'd better eat," he said and handed her a piece of the pemmican, then went for the little pot of water.

She appeared calm now. He marveled at the difference in her as he watched her dutifully chew away at the tough meat.

"I'm sorry it took so long," he began. "It didn't work like we'd planned."

She sat silently.

"It must have been . . ." He couldn't finish the thought. He didn't really know what to say.

She looked up then. Her big eyes had lost their terror.

"I was fine until the candle went out," she informed him. "At least . . . pretty good. I . . . I recited Scripture and prayed. I even sang . . . a little bit. But . . . after I lost the light . . ."

She shuddered and did not finish the comment.

"I'm sorry," he said softly.

They sat silently. She was the first to speak.

"I can't believe it . . . after all this time," she began. "I can't believe that I'm going home."

He began to say something and then quickly closed his mouth.

"My mama will be so . . . so . . ." She lifted her head, framed by her tangled hair. In the near darkness her eyes looked deep and shining. She pulled up her knees and wrapped both arms around them. The candlelight caught her face, making her eyes sparkle. Her soft buckskin clothing blended into the shadows of the walls. She could have been an Indian princess as she sat regally on her bed of furs.

Laramie cleared his throat. He hated to break the spell. Wasn't quite sure what he should say and how he should say it.

At last he took a deep breath and spoke with all of the gentleness he possessed.

"Ariana?"

It was the first time anyone had spoken her name in such a long time. She turned her full attention on his face.

He swallowed again.

"We won't be going home," he managed.

He winced at the look that came into her eyes.

Chapter Sixteen

At Last!

"*What do you mean?*" The words seemed to break as they rushed from her lips.

Laramie wanted to go to her—as White Eagle had done—but he did not stir. He was not sure he could have moved. Her eyes seemed to pin him to the spot.

"We can't," he managed, his own voice hoarse with emotion.

"But I thought—"

"I know, I know," he quickly cut in, "an' I wish it was thet way but—"

He did move then—but not toward her. He could not bear the look on her face. He turned his back slightly, his hand stealing up to push at the Stetson. When he had better control he turned back to face her again.

"I wouldn't dare take ya home," he said evenly. "Thet is the first place they'll look. And they will continue to watch an' wait for many days to come. I know—"

"But . . . what about . . . my folks?" Her voice still quivered.

"Once we're out we'll git word to them," he said simply.

He thought he saw tears slide down her cheeks in the light of the fluttering candles, but he wasn't sure.

She drew her knees closer to her chest and hugged them

to her. Her head lowered toward them until he could no longer see her face. The tangled hair spilled about her, providing her with privacy in her deep hurt at his words.

"I'm sorry," he managed.

He saw her shoulders tremble as she sat in silence—and then she seemed to give her shoulders a little shake. Her head came up again, and though he was sure now that he saw tears on her cheeks, her eyes looked at him frankly.

"What is the plan?" she asked. Her inner strength had returned.

Laramie felt more confused by her calm than he had been by her agitation.

What was the plan? Beyond the fact that he needed to get her out—away from the band that had confined her—what then? Edginess suddenly took hold of him. He had been so busy preparing for the escape that he had not thought much further.

"Is there anywhere—anyone else—that you know?" The idea came to him suddenly. He would have to take her to someone. He couldn't just free her from her prisoners and leave her alone in a hostile world.

She seemed to give his question deep consideration. At length she answered, hesitantly at first, and then the words poured out.

"An uncle—my father's brother—and his wife. I'm not sure—I've never met them—but Papa spoke of them. In Montana. Farmers. They live near a little town called . . . oh, dear . . . what is it now . . . Preston? Princeton? Oh, dear. It'll come to me . . . I just—"

"Montana," Laramie repeated. "Thet's a fair piece away."

Ariana looked apologetic. "They're the only ones I can think of. I—"

He cut in quickly so she wouldn't feel he had vetoed her suggestion. "Montana. Might be a good place to start over."

The silence stretched out between them for several minutes. It was not an awkward moment. Each was busy with personal thoughts. The other was content to let it be so.

Laramie spoke again. "You should git some sleep. It'll be a long day tomorrow."

Ariana stirred.

She let her eyes travel around the small cave. Three tunnels led off from it. One had been the entrance through which the Indian had brought her in. One was simply a closet-sized addition to the room she used now. She had made use of it over the days of her confinement. She had no idea about the third opening. Perhaps it led to a bigger cave. Perhaps it wound this way and that, twisting deeper into the rocks of the mountain. Maybe it ended abruptly, going nowhere.

"You need sleep too," she answered simply. "Here, take some of the bedding."

She stood to her feet and began to separate the furs and blankets. He started to protest and then realized how tired he was. Besides, it was easy to see that White Eagle had done his job well. The stack in the corner would serve more than one bed.

"This is plenty," he said as he lifted a heavy buffalo robe.

"Take this blanket too," she insisted, so he did.

He placed the robe on the rock floor and lowered himself to it. It really wasn't much harder than the wood bunk he was used to. He pulled the blanket firmly about himself and settled for the night.

He heard her stirring and turned so he could look at her. She was lighting a fresh candle.

He was awakened by a touch on his shoulder. White Eagle bent over him, his lantern held high in his other hand.

"You sleep like old bear," he said with a glint in his eyes.

Laramie stirred, chiding himself that he had not heard White Eagle approach. He quickly laid aside the self-incrimination. White Eagle moved like a shadow. No mortal man would have heard him enter the cavern.

His eyes asked the question that he did not voice. White Eagle responded.

"You have horse," he said simply.

Relief swept through Laramie's whole body. He freed himself of the blanket and sat up. "Then I guess I have a trip to take," he replied.

In the corner Ariana began to stir. Sleepily she opened her eyes and then quickly jerked to full wakefulness. "Did it work?" she asked before she even had time to stir from her blankets.

Laramie could not hide his smile. She was like a small child in her eagerness. "It worked," he replied, and Ariana began to push the blanket back as she unwound herself from the bedding and sleep.

"We must hurry," she exclaimed excitedly, and set about gathering together the last of the supplies in a little heap on her deserted bed.

Laramie and White Eagle exchanged glances. Their plan was working. They would get her out.

Will Russell was in a sour mood. First, his well-laid strategy had not worked out right. Instead of the girl bringing about the change in Laramie he had desired, she had been the final straw in breaking Laramie from the gang completely. Will's sense of loss was exceeded only by his great rage. Sam's knowing looks and mumbled pronouncements had not helped to appease his anger.

When the discovery had not been made until noon, Will knew Laramie had worked it out so that he had a long head start. With the snow falling, it had been hard to pick up the trail, but Will knew the direction that must be taken to get the girl back home.

He'd had the boys saddle up and they rode out, leaving only Skidder behind to guard the camp. Will had not wanted Skidder in their little posse. He knew the man would use any possible excuse to put a bullet in Laramie's back.

At first they had ridden hard, direct as the crow flies, toward the small town from which Ariana had been taken. Just before they were forced to make camp for the night, they came upon three horses, feeding casually in a small meadow. Laramie's mounts.

Will's first thought had been that the young man and his prisoner had run headlong into a small band of Pawnee. But that didn't add up. The Indians would have kept the horses. So what had really happened? Will was left scratching his head.

It was clear Laramie had made other plans. But what? Where could he get on foot? Had he changed horses? But why? His own mounts were still fresh. It hadn't appeared that they had been ridden hard. The whole thing had him puzzling.

"Set up camp," Will had growled to his men.

So they set up camp.

The next morning the gang expected an order to break camp, but Will looked in no hurry to leave. Instead, he had sent out scouts to scour the nearby countryside.

"See anything—fire three shots," they had been ordered. At the end of the day they had returned with nothing to report.

"Well—we jest sit here an' wait. He'll hafta crawl out sometime," Will had growled.

In the days that followed, the same procedure was repeated. Sam began to question how long they were to sit and wait—so close to the Indian settlement. Will just growled and said he figured he was still the boss. He'd give the orders.

But a nighttime Indian raid had changed his plans. The braves took all their horses—all the saddles. Even the small grub stake right from the center of the camp, as though to mock the little band of outlaws. Will was glad to be left with his scalp, though he would not have admitted it to his men.

The air was blue with curses directed at the "red savages." But Will knew many of them would have been directed at him had his men been expressing their true feelings.

So they were all on foot, tramping their way home. The warm spring sun turned the trail into slush, and then mud. They slipped and slid their way up the winding trail and forded waist-deep creek water.

No, they were not a happy group of travelers. The next raid had been carefully planned to take place in just three days—and here they were with no mounts except for a couple of scraggly animals back at the corral—and those without saddles for riding. Their supplies, even back at the base camp, were dangerously low.

As Will Russell trudged through the sloppiness of spring thaw, he kept checking over his shoulder. Men had been known to mutiny for less reason. He was glad he could count on Sam—who was dutifully bringing up the rear of the straggling band of reluctant hikers. Sam's loose hand was never far from his gun holster.

"Do you have any idea what day it is?" Ariana asked as she raised a tired hand to push windblown hair back from her face.

"I know we've been ridin' fer eight days," replied Laramie.

"Where are we?"

"We've a good piece to go yet," was his simple answer as they plodded on.

Ariana felt like groaning. Her whole body ached. It felt as though they had spent those entire eight days in the saddle. Laramie had pushed them hard. He was intent on putting as many miles as possible between them and the camp in the hidden valley. He had not even allowed them the comfort of an open fire.

Ariana did groan, just thinking about it. The nights had been cold, and the scant blanket she clutched to her shivering body did very little to keep out the wind.

They had outridden the snow. The late spring storm that had swept through their area, giving them cover for their escape, had been followed by a bright warm sun that melted the small drifts and set the creeks to singing.

Ariana welcomed the feeling of warm rays on her back. At least there was one spot of her that was not still shivering from the cold night.

Ariana was surprised when Laramie reined in the buckskin. As soon as his horse stopped, Ariana's roan pulled up beside it, nuzzling the buckskin's lathered neck with its nose.

Laramie said nothing. Just sat his saddle as though born to it, studying Ariana with intent eyes. Ariana shifted uncomfortably. There were times when she felt he looked into her very soul.

"Little town up ahead—'bout a mile," he offered. "We're in need of some more supplies."

Ariana's eyes widened. "Have you been . . . way up here . . . before?" she asked incredulously.

"No," he answered with a shake of his head.

"Then how. . . ?" she began but didn't finish.

He smiled then, a lazy, easy smile. He nodded his head toward the north. "It's stickin' out—plain as day—on thet hillside."

Ariana flushed and shaded her eyes with her hands so she could stare off into the distance. Sure enough, she could make out buildings against the backdrop of trees and rock.

"We're going to stop?" she asked, hoping the eagerness was not too evident in her voice.

He nodded again. "We'll stop," he promised.

Suddenly Ariana felt she had new strength in her weary bones. She straightened in her saddle and gave her mount a heel. If they were going to be stopping, she was anxious to get there.

The small town had a rooming house, and Laramie ordered a room and a hot bath for Ariana before he went to the stables to arrange for the horses' care. They had pushed the animals hard. Laramie wanted time to check them thoroughly, searching for chipped hooves or sore muscles. He had always made a habit of checking the mounts at the end of each day and had noticed nothing seriously amiss, but the little roan had seemed to have a sensitive spot on her right shoulder. He decided on a little liniment and put on some warm compresses.

By the time Laramie had finished at the stable, the sun was setting. He looked down at his trail-soiled clothes and decided he could sure use a bath himself.

The doors of the town's one store were still open, so Laramie made his way into the building. All sorts of goods lined the shelves and formed stacks of deep piles anywhere the owner could find room.

"Howdy," greeted Laramie.

"Howdy," replied the man, letting his eyes travel up and down the newcomer as if to gather all the information he could in one glance.

"Ridin' through?" he asked casually, but Laramie knew the question was far from casual.

"Thet's right," he replied, his voice just as relaxed and offhanded. He began to finger one of the shirts in a nearby stack.

Both men waited.

"Wouldn't have supposed there'd be call fer this much merchandise in such a small town," observed Laramie. "Business must either be powerful good—or a sight poor."

The man responded with a hard laugh. "Where you been, cowboy?" he answered. "Don't ya know there's gold in them hills?" He jerked his head toward the northwest. "Been pouring through here a dozen a day—an' more on the way. I'm the last store between here an' the strike."

Laramie's head came up. "Ya don't say," he said with interest.

Silence again as Laramie went back to eyeing the merchandise.

"Ya fixin' on minin'?" asked the man, breaking the code of the West to wait until the information was freely given.

"Me?" Laramie's head came up. "Naw—I don't reckon. Had never thought on it." He hesitated a minute while he turned a black Stetson over and over in his hands.

The man looked disappointed. Laramie let him wait.

At last he looked up and gave a bit of a nod. "Do need me a bit of a grub stake, though," he announced. "Takin' my sister on up to stay with our kin."

Even as he spoke the words, his face flushed slightly. He had read in his mother's Bible an account of someone named Abraham making the same false statement regarding his wife Sarah, many, many years ago.

But the man behind the counter did not seem to question the remark. Perhaps his thoughts ran only to the sale.

"You jest pick out what ya want—an' show me hard cash, mister," he replied.

Laramie thought the merchant looked as though he was having a hard time keeping from rubbing his hands together in anticipation.

"Usual grub stake," Laramie said. "I'll be by to pick it up in the mornin'."

He hesitated. He had a bag full of stolen coins in the small saddlebag he kept with him, but he was reluctant to squander any of it. Actually, he was feeling uncomfortable even having the ill-gotten money. Still, they needed food and he did need a change of clothes. "An' you can add this to the list," he went on, selecting the articles of clothing. "Pay ya fer 'em right now."

Laramie felt much better after he'd had a bath and dressed in the clean clothes. He even thought about getting his hair cut but decided against it. He didn't want to scatter too much money about the little town. There was no use starting tongues to wagging.

As soon as he had finished his simple grooming, he placed the new black Stetson on his head and picked up his money bag. He tied it carefully around his body under his shirt and strapped on his guns. Then he set off down the hall to see if Ariana was ready to try to find a place that served up supper.

Ariana waited impatiently, one small foot tapping the worn carpet. She was starved. She had lingered in the hot bath, enjoying the soothing warmth on her aching muscles. Then she had toweled herself dry and dressed in her own clothing from the pack-sack Laramie had left behind for her. The garments had felt strange at first after so many days in the buckskins, and she did deplore the fact of the many wrinkles. Still, she felt a little more herself as she pinned her hair carefully and surveyed her image in the darkened mirror in the room. Now she had been waiting for what seemed hours. Her patience was wearing thin. Had Laramie just dumped her and expected her to fend for herself? Was she to find her own supper—or just do without? He knew she had no money with which to make purchases.

And then a horrid thought raced through Ariana's mind. Did Laramie have money? Were they penniless? Would they need to *steal* their way to Montana—like Laramie had been doing all his life? What if—what if he had been—raiding—and something had gone wrong? He could have been thrown in jail. Been shot and wounded. She might be on her own in this strange little town. Miles from her parents. Miles from the uncle and aunt she did not know.

Ariana felt the panic rising in her chest. Should she go look for him? Should she deny ever having known him, if he'd been caught? Should she seek out a lawman and explain her dilemma?

A lawman? Strange. Ariana had not thought of that. Certainly it would be the reasonable thing to do now that she was in friendly environs. Surely this little town had law of some sort. They would help her. After all, Laramie was—was an outlaw.

Ariana hated to think of him in that fashion. But it was true. True. He was an outlaw. Why had she felt she could trust him?

She began to tremble. Her face paled. Her eyes widened with fear and concern. "Oh, God," she prayed, covering her face with her shaking hands. "What do I do? Should I . . . it would be proper to . . . escape . . . wouldn't it?"

Chapter Seventeen

End of Journey

Ariana rose shakily to her feet. She lifted her chin and looked about her. The room held very few of her personal items, but she carefully gathered them and bundled them into her little pack. Then she pinned her crushed hat carefully in place on her upswept hair and reached for her wrinkled coat and winter gloves. She would do it. It was the only reasonable thing to do.

She lifted her pack. It felt lighter now that she had emptied it of extra clothing and the heavy coat. There really wasn't much in it at all. Her few personal grooming aids. Her Bible. She let her eyes scan the room again to be sure she had missed nothing. The travel-worn buckskins were folded neatly and left on the chair, the moccasins placed on top of them.

Ariana took a deep breath to give herself courage and reached for the door handle. A sharp knock made her gasp and draw back quickly.

"Ariana," came Laramie's voice. "Ya ready?"

Ariana could not have said whether the intense feelings that passed through her were of regret or relief. Quietly she laid her little bundle on the floor behind the door, took a deep breath to calm herself, and reached to undo the lock.

Laramie stood there, clean-shaven and polished until he

fairly shone, his shirt still stiff with newness. Even the worn, droopy Stetson had been replaced. Ariana's little gasp caught in her throat. If he had been raiding it seemed he had covered a lot of ground in a big hurry.

He stood looking at her. Ariana looked down at her own faded, wrinkled garments. When she looked back up he gave her a slight nod as though to express his approval.

"Thought ya might be nigh starved," was his comment.

She swallowed and shifted uneasily. "Yes . . . yes, I am," she stammered. "I . . . I was beginning to think . . ."

But Ariana did not finish the statement. She wasn't sure how much she should say.

They left the town bright and early the next morning. Ariana was surprised when she went down to join Laramie that he had added another horse to the number. Bulging packs were secured to the pack saddle.

"Don't worry," he drawled, as though reading her mind. "It's all paid fer."

He did not explain how he had come by the money that paid the accounts.

Ariana was back in her buckskins, her dress repacked in the bundle she handed to Laramie. She noticed a slicker tied behind each saddle. His eyes followed hers. "Keeps out some of the wind and rain," he offered.

Laramie settled the bill with the woman who kept the rooming house, and he held Ariana's horse while she mounted, and they were on the trail once again.

It was almost a pleasant day. Ariana tried not to think of the little town they had left behind. She tried not to scold herself for not having attempted to find a lawman. She tried not to wonder if Laramie could really be trusted to deliver her to the home of her uncle in Montana. She pushed all of the troubling thoughts as far into the back of her mind as she could and tried to concentrate on prayer, even as she swayed slightly in the saddle.

Laramie was still pressing the mounts forward at a fast pace. Ariana had thought he would relax a bit. The spring sun was high in the sky before he took the first break. Ariana climbed down stiffly.

"Sorry to keep pushin'," he said in apology as he watched her dismount.

"I . . . just thought that . . . that we'd be . . . rather safe . . . now," she suggested.

He was squinting into the sunlight, studying every direction from their vantage point. At last he turned to her.

"Should be far enough ahead of . . . Pa," he conceded. "Don't s'pose he's on our tail but . . ." He let the words hang on the stillness of the spring day. Ariana waited.

"I've no idee who shares these hills," he finished at last.

That was a new and frightening thought to Ariana. Were they never to be out of danger?

"You mean. . . ?" she began but couldn't finish.

"Crow. Blackfoot. I don't know who ranges here." He hesitated for a few more moments and then went on soberly. "An' those hills yonder—bound to welcome stray pockets of malcontents."

So they had left one nest of robbers to be threatened by others. The thought was not a pleasant one.

"No need to tighten up," went on Laramie offhandedly, using an expression Ariana had not heard before. "Jest pays to keep a sharp eye—'specially at one's back—take stock now an' then."

Ariana nodded, but the fear that constricted her throat was not so easy to dismiss.

Gradually Ariana was beginning to think of Laramie not as her captor but as her deliverer. Without realizing why, she was able to relax in his company. She was learning to trust again.

When they stopped to make camp in the evenings, she was at ease enough to discuss little happenings from the day, to offer to share in camp chores, or to relate small events from her past.

Laramie responded in his easygoing way, even though she felt he never totally gave up his vigilance. He answered her questions, added comments to her chatter, and gladly shared the duties of preparing an evening meal and setting up camp.

"You know," said Ariana one evening as they cleaned up the tin dishes at a small stream trickling past their campsite, "I've totally lost track of time. I don't even know what day it is."

Laramie thought on her words and then drawled, "Does it matter?"

Ariana lifted her head, then laughed softly. "Guess not," she agreed. "Only it would be nice to know. If I were home . . ." She did not finish. If she were home it would be important for her to keep track of every passing day. To know school days and weekends, Saturdays and Sundays, holidays and birthdays. Yes, it would matter. It did matter.

"I don't even know if . . . if my mama's birthday is past," she went on wistfully.

"When's her birthday?" asked Laramie.

"May the second."

Laramie looked at the evening sun just dipping behind the distant hills.

"I don't think we're into May yet," he answered.

For some reason Ariana felt relieved. She would like to be home. . . . She let her thoughts drift. She wasn't going home. Well, she'd like to be at her aunt Molly's before her mother's birthday.

"When is your birthday?" she asked, turning her attention back to Laramie, who was rinsing the frying pan.

He shrugged.

"You don't know?" she asked candidly.

"I've no idee." He turned slightly toward her. "Never stopped to think about it, I guess. Maybe never cared. Should I?"

"Well . . . yes. Sort of. I mean . . . I'd want to know. Don't you?"

"Never thought on it," said Laramie as he swung the pan back and forth to dry it in the breeze.

"Didn't your father tell you?" asked Ariana.

Laramie let his eyes look out over the hills wrapped comfortably in gathering twilight. "Birthdays don't mean much in the camp," he said casually.

"Do you. . . ?" Ariana spoke hesitantly now. "Do you know . . . how old you are?"

Laramie turned back to her with seeming indifference. "I dunno. Somewhere around twenty, I guess."

He seemed totally unconcerned.

Ariana found it hard to accept his attitude. She was about to speak again when Laramie turned his face toward the west.

"Looks like it could blow in a bit of a storm," he observed. "We'll need to be sure things are rainproof tonight."

"There's an outcroppin' of rock up ahead. We'll let the horses graze here and take our meal up there."

Ariana welcomed the opportunity. The view would be spectacular. Inwardly she knew it was not the view that interested Laramie. He saw the rocks as a lookout point.

They ate slowly, savoring the intensity of the sun, allowing its fingers of warmth to ease the aches from wearied muscles. Ariana began to feel drowsy. She wished she could stretch out and sleep—maybe forever.

Laramie seemed content to let her rest. The horses needed a break as much as their riders. He leaned against the rock at his back and pulled his old Stetson downward over his eyes. The new one rode proudly on the slicker behind his saddle.

But along with her sleepiness, Ariana also felt restless. They were getter closer and closer to their destination. She felt both excitement and reluctance. She could not unscramble her own thoughts or feelings.

Nor could she untangle her thoughts concerning Laramie. He was an outlaw—yet why had she learned to feel so secure, so safe with him?

She longed to study him, but she did not dare lest her searching eyes cause him to stir in recognition of her interest. She decided instead to rouse herself and take a walk.

She had only taken a few steps when his voice reached her. "Don't go far," he said lazily.

She did not even answer. Just continued to scramble up over the warm surface of the rocks. It was amazing what the sun could do to cold stone.

She found a spot just above him where she could see out over the whole valley. It was a magnificent sight. First the tall timbers of pine and spruce, dotted here and there with patches of birch and aspen just barely unrolling fresh spring leaves. Then the valley floor with its sparkling ribbon of river that curled and twisted through the greenness, being lost time and again in the lushness of the forest. Way beyond was a slim column of smoke. Ariana could not tell if it came from some small cabin's chimney or some wanderer's open fire. It really did not matter. It added something—mysterious—romantic—to the scene before her.

"Should be movin'," came Laramie's soft call.

Ariana breathed deeply, took one more longing look at the vista before her, and began to scramble back down over rocks to join him.

She was almost there when she was startled by a sharp command. "Don't move!"

Ariana jerked to a halt in unquestioned obedience, though she did not understand why.

Before she could even draw a breath, two shots rang out

through the day's stillness. Ariana was frozen to her spot. Only her eyes dared move. Laramie was standing, guns in hand, and they were pointed to the place where she stood. Smoke drifted lazily from each barrel. Laramie's whole body was tensed as though ready for further action.

Ariana became conscious of movement at her feet. She let her gaze drop down and beheld the most hideous sight she had ever seen. A snake was writhing just beyond her moccasined foot. What was left of its head was ragged raw flesh, spurting blood. It splashed on the hem of her leather buckskin as it swished back and forth in the agony of death.

Ariana felt the world spinning round. She wanted to scream. Wished to run—but she could do neither.

"Don't move," came Laramie's voice, but this time it was controlled and gentle, though still urgent. "Where there is one there is often more."

Ariana had no intention of moving. She was vaguely aware that Laramie was moving toward her, the smoking guns still in his hands as his eyes darted back and forth among the rocks.

"Looks okay," he said at her elbow. "I don't see any more."

Ariana closed her eyes and sucked in her breath—but it was too late. The whole world was quickly going black.

Laramie had caught her just before she hit the rocks. Gently he carried the young woman down the slope of the hill toward the waiting horses. He eased her down to the softness of the new spring grass and went for the canteen that hung on his saddle. Taking the bandana from his neck, he wet it and began to sponge her pale face. She was so delicate—so vulnerable. Then again he marveled at her strength. A lesser person would have given in long ago under the horrible captivity, the dreadful wait in the cave, and the pressure of the rigorous ride.

Anger gripped him as he thought of the injustice done to

her. Why had his father come up with such an unthinkable scheme? What had given him the right to so grossly interfere with the life of another?

He wet the kerchief again and ran the dampness over her forehead, smoothing back tendrils of wisping hair.

He had told Sam he would be willing to die for her. As he looked at her now, he knew he had spoken true words. She was something beautiful—precious. He wondered what his mother would have thought of her. Would she have loved her—like he did?

The unbidden acknowledgement startled him. What did he know about love? It was hate he had been raised to recognize and understand. Hate—and bitterness. Envy and greed. Those were the passions he had grown up with.

Yet as he bathed her face and ached for her to return to consciousness, he knew that what he was feeling was far from any of those emotions. Love her? Maybe. Maybe he did. But he had no right to love her—that much he knew. And the secret knowledge that he did was not going to make his job any easier, though it was certainly going to make it more intense.

He was relieved when she began to stir.

Her eyes fluttered open and she looked up at him, seeming puzzled by the fact that he knelt over her, supporting her head with one hand.

"A rattler," he explained to remind her. She looked as though she was about to faint again.

"It's okay," he soothed. "He's gone now."

She shut her eyes tightly against the memory of the headless, writhing snake. He remembered the blood on her buckskin skirt and wished he had thought to try to wash it away.

He eased back from her, but she reached out a trembling hand and clasped the front of his shirt. "Don't leave me," she begged him.

"I won't. I won't," he promised, and he pulled her close and held her until she stopped trembling.

"It was awful," she whispered against him.

"It's gone now," he reminded her.

"Its head—"

"I know. I know."

He patted her shoulder instinctively, pushed back the hair from her face. At last she opened her eyes. Her body still felt limp, but she had stopped shaking.

She pushed gently against him and he reluctantly released her. "We need to go," she said in a trembling voice.

"Not 'til yer ready," he assured her.

The color was returning to her cheeks. She swallowed hard. Then sat up.

"Could I have a drink of water, please?" she asked, her voice still trembling.

He reached for the canteen and held it for her. She drank, then reached a hand to brush a drop from her lips. He noticed the fullness of her mouth. He had never noticed it before.

"I think I'm okay now," she said with a nod, then flushed. "I'm . . . I'm sorry . . . I . . . it just caught me by surprise."

He longed to pull her close and hold her again. Instead, he reached out to help her to her feet. She stood shakily, still weak from the incident. She put out a hand to the trunk of the nearby birch for support. He moved back to hang the canteen on his saddle horn. He had to put some distance between them. He did not trust himself with his newfound knowledge.

"Whenever you feel ready," he said, his voice sounding stiff and forced.

"I'm fine—now," Ariana assured him.

He nodded. Perhaps. Perhaps she was. What about him? Would he ever be fine again?

He allowed the building of a fire when they stopped each evening. He knew they needed to be cautious, but he felt he could not deny her any small comfort that was within his means to provide.

It was homey around the fire. Ariana always got out her Bible and read portions for her evening devotions. Rather hesitantly, he asked if she'd mind reading aloud. She nodded her assent, hoping her rapidly beating heart was not heard in the quiet of the still evening. Inwardly she prayed, over and over, that the words from the Book would be understood. That he might respond to the Gospel as it was given. Carefully she selected the portions for reading, praying that Laramie's heart would be responsive to the message.

As the evenings passed he seemed to be drawn in more and more. If he had questions, he asked, and she was patient as she explained her understanding of the passage. He began to look forward to those evenings and even thought of bringing out his mother's Bible so he might follow along. He wondered if the notations in the margins might be helpful to both of them. But he never had the courage to make the suggestion.

He had never been this intimate with anyone before. Sharing thoughts and feelings—and on occasion wishing he could also share his dreams. But he held them in check, for no matter how he fought against it, he could not envision his future without Ariana—yet that dream was an impossibility.

He was sure Ariana understood nothing of his discomfort. Nothing of the struggle going on within him. But Laramie was very aware of the conflict he felt within. On the one hand he was most anxious to deliver her to the safety of the unknown uncle. On the other hand, once he did, he would have lost her forever. He knew that. It made him somber, moody. Something he had never been.

Ariana did not understand why, but she did notice the difference. She supposed she had inadvertently done something to annoy him. Or was it that he was feeling the break with his father?

She dared to broach the subject one night as they sat

around the open fire listening to the voices of the night creatures.

"What will you do after we get to my uncle's?"

The question brought his head up.

"Will you go back to . . . to. . . ?"

"Back? No . . . I won't go back," he said thoughtfully.

"I've . . . I've spoiled that for you . . . haven't I? I've made . . . a breach between you and your father," she went on, and there was apology in her voice.

At first he looked surprised and then he smiled his slow smile. "I reckon you have," he said frankly, "but not in the way you suppose."

She was puzzled but did not probe deeper.

"Do you miss . . . your . . . father?" she asked after a time of silence, finally getting to the question she had been longing to ask him.

"Miss 'im?" He stared into the fire a moment. "No," he said frankly.

She was sure her astonishment at his answer showed on her face.

"I . . . I think of him . . . wish things could be different . . . but I don't miss him," Laramie explained.

She drew up her knees in a manner he had come to recognize, and hugged them to her. "Oh . . . I miss my papa," she said with deep feeling. "And Mama . . . so much." A tear trickled down her cheek, exposed by the dancing firelight.

He made a move as if to come to her, but instead said, "We need to git some sleep. We got a long ride tomorra."

"I remember," called Ariana with excitement in her voice. "It's Pinewood."

Laramie turned back to look at her, puzzlement on his face.

"Pinewood," she repeated. "That's where Uncle Jake and Aunt Molly are. Near Pinewood."

He turned back to his mount. There—they had it. There would be no excuse to keep her with him now.

"Last name?" he called back to her.

"Benson. Benson—just like my father."

He guided his horse carefully over a fallen log.

"Pinewood," he repeated. "Guess we'd better stop first chance we git an' find out jest where thet is."

* * *

When they finally found a farmstead, they were both amazed to discover how close they were to the little town of Pinewood.

"Happen to know Jake Benson?" Laramie asked the farmer.

"Jake? Sure I know Jake. Don't have many neighbors out here, so ya make it a point to get to know 'em," the man in the worn overalls stated. "Lives other side of town—'bout six hours from here."

Laramie was relieved to hear that they would have to share one more evening campfire, but he didn't say so. Nor did he tell the farmer they would be camping out again. He was afraid the man might, in his friendliness, take Ariana into the family's crowded cabin and offer Laramie the barn loft.

"Thank ya kindly," Laramie said with a tip of his head, and he led Ariana and the pack horse back out onto the dusty track that meant roads and civilization.

"We'll ride on fer an hour or two and then make camp," he said simply. "Shouldn't be much of a ride tomorra."

Ariana could hardly contain her excitement.

* * *

Ariana trembled as she lifted her skirts and moved toward the farmhouse door. They had stopped back a piece, and Laramie had gone for a walk while Ariana took a quick dip in the cold waters of a small creek, then dressed hurriedly in her own clothes. She had not discarded the buckskins. Instead she'd folded them, almost tenderly, and put them in the bundle from which she had withdrawn her rumpled cotton. The buckskins had served her well. Calico or gingham would have worn through long ago on the endless trail.

Ariana looked down at her faded dress. She certainly was not coming to her kin looking pressed and proper. Hesitantly she lifted her hand to rap. Then she cast one more glance back over her shoulder to where Laramie stood holding the horses. The brim of his hat was shading his eyes, so she could not read his expression.

She took a deep breath and knocked on the wood. The door was soon opened by an elderly woman, a dish towel still in her hand.

"Yes?" she said, then blessed Ariana with a smile. "Come in," she welcomed and waved Ariana into the humble home. "You must be new here. Are you from the place down on Cedar Creek?"

"No . . . no . . . I . . ." Ariana took a deep breath. "Molly Benson?" she asked tentatively. "Are you Aunt Molly?"

The woman nodded her agreement but looked puzzled by the question.

"I'm . . . I'm Ariana," the girl managed. "George and Laura's daughter."

For a moment the woman stood silent, her face showing shock. Then with one quick movement she gathered Ariana into her arms, holding her close as she laughed and wept in unison.

"Ariana? Oh, God be praised. We all feared you were dead."

Chapter Eighteen

A Joyous Hello and a Painful Goodbye

"Oh, Aunt Molly," Ariana said through her own tears and laughter, "I was afraid we'd never find you." She realized that her long ordeal was finally over. She was back with those she loved. Her life could go on again.

"What arc you doing here, child? How'd you get here?" the woman quizzed excitedly.

Ariana moved back out to the porch, drawing her Aunt Molly with her. She nodded toward Laramie, who stood with the horses.

"It's a long story—one I promise to tell—someday. It wasn't safe for me to go back home. But we must let Mama know. And Papa. We must."

"You sit right there." The woman pointed at a small bench in the shade of the porch. "I'm going for your uncle." She started off toward a nearby field, removing her apron as she bustled along. Ariana watched as she ran, waving the apron in the air to get the man's attention.

"It seems you've caused quite a stir."

Laramie stood close behind Ariana. She brushed at the tears on her cheeks.

"You know, I don't think I really believed it would happen. Oh . . . I tried to have faith. I prayed. But it . . . it seemed so

. . . so impossible at times. I don't think I really thought that . . . that it would ever end."

He was silent for several minutes as they watched her aunt draw near to her uncle, arms waving, fingers pointing back at the house. Ariana could almost guess her words.

"It's been hard for you," said Laramie simply. "I'm glad it's over."

Ariana turned to him, her eyes brimming, her face flushed. "I . . . I can never thank you enough. Never," she said with conviction. "If it hadn't been for you . . ."

Laramie shuffled uncomfortably. He reached up to push at the brim of his hat. At last his eyes lifted. "If it hadn't been for me you'd still be in your own hometown," he said huskily.

Ariana's eyes clouded. "What do you mean?" she asked him.

He took her elbow and steered her to the porch bench, out of the bright rays of the sun.

"I don't know if you've guessed . . . if you've really understood it all . . . but you were brought to the camp . . . because of me."

Ariana was still confused.

"I . . . I wasn't quite . . . shapin' up . . . like my pa . . . had planned. You see . . ." He hesitated, then swallowed. "I had never . . . killed a man."

"Killed a man?" she whispered. "I don't understand. That . . . is a fault?"

"In Pa's eyes," he said simply.

Ariana shivered.

"But I don't understand. What did that have to do with me?"

He took a deep breath. "Pa figured I'd . . . I'd be forced to . . . to . . . git into a fight over you . . . an' have to use my gun."

"But I—"

"You had nothin' to do with it—directly. Only indirectly. Pa knew thet there'd be other fellas who would . . . anyway, he figured there'd be a showdown—likely with Skidder—"

"Skidder?" said Ariana with a shiver. "Is he the one who said those awful things?"

Laramie nodded.

"But why would Skidder—? Why would you—?"

"Pa thought I'd fall in love with you." He said the words hurriedly as he watched the man and woman scurry up the lane.

She was shocked. "But that's—preposterous," she exclaimed.

He started to say something, then stopped.

Then her eyes softened. "I'm sorry," she whispered to him. "I didn't know. I've been the cause of . . . a lot of trouble between you and your father."

His face showed his surprise at her words.

"But I am glad—and I cannot deny it. Glad—and thankful—that you never . . . never killed. I . . . I just . . . don't think you are that kind of man."

"Ariana, I'm an outlaw," he reminded her.

"Not anymore you're not," she said quickly. "And I don't believe for a moment you ever would have been if you'd been given the choice. I've seen . . . enough . . . to believe that you—you're not like that."

By now the man and woman were rushing into the yard, panting from the hurried trip from the field. The short, private conversation was over. All Laramie could manage was a quiet "thank you."

Then her uncle was rushing toward Ariana, his arms open.

Everything seemed in turmoil after the quiet days on the trail. Jake Benson hitched a team to the wagon and hurried off to town to send a wire to Ariana's parents. Molly fluttered about the kitchen, laughing, praising the Lord, and crying by turn. Ariana, flushed and excited, talked more in a few short hours than she had during the last four months.

Laramie withdrew from all the commotion, not used to the intensity of emotions, the free expressions of love and tenderness between Ariana and her family. He spent his time at the corral tending to the horses.

Slowly he unpacked the pack horse, lifting aside Ariana's small bundle. His job was over. He had delivered her safely to her aunt and uncle. They would take over now.

So what was he going to do? He had not thought about it. He could not turn around and go back. He wouldn't have wanted to, even if that was possible. Yet he had no particular skills—other than with a gun. Had never really worked. He was adrift. Freed from a world he had never felt a part of, to enter a world where he did not fit. What would he do?

He climbed up on the rail of the corral to watch the horses and ponder the question. He'd have to find work—somewhere. Maybe he should go back to the small town on the side of the hill, buy himself a grub stake, and try his hand at finding gold. Maybe he could look up a ranch and hire himself out as a cowpoke. He was good with horses. He might work fine with cattle, too. Maybe he should—

But every idea that came to him brought little inner response. Nothing seemed to connect with him. Yet here he was—for the first time in his life—free to make his own decisions.

He couldn't understand his mood.

"Aw, it's jest the letdown after all the days of tension," he tried to tell himself. But down deep inside he knew the real reason. It was Ariana. Once he left her, he would never see her again. His pa had been right. Loving a girl could nearly ruin a man.

* * *

"Hungry?"

Laramie's head jerked up as Ariana came up beside him.

"Aunt Molly has fixed tea," she announced.

At the look on Laramie's face she began to laugh. A soft,

joyful laugh. It was the first Laramie had heard her laugh so freely in all the months he had known her. It was a reminder of how much they had taken from her in holding her captive in such a degrading way.

"You don't have to drink tea," she said with a sparkle in her eyes. "I'll fix you some coffee."

Laramie supposed he should be hungry, but he really had little appetite.

"It's not the tea," he was quick to inform her, not wanting to be uncivil. "It's just that—" He let his gaze drop to his trail-dusty attire. "I'm not really fit company an' I—"

"Oh, come on," she coaxed. "Uncle Jake and Aunt Molly are just ordinary folk. Farmers. Uncle Jake didn't change out of his dusty overalls."

"It's not just the . . . clothes," he said, still hesitating. "I . . . hardly fit in with . . . proper company. I know little of—what do you call it?"

She smiled again. "Social graces? I promise we won't expect you to use one of those little teacups and eat bite-size sandwiches." Her eyes were twinkling again.

He was still uncomfortable.

"We're going to eat on the back porch," she continued.

He reached up one finger to tip back his new Stetson.

"You have to start sometime," she encouraged. "We won't be eating around a campfire anymore."

She had said "we." Was that just a slip? Surely she wasn't thinking that he intended to hang around.

"Come on. Aunt Molly is anxious to get to know you better. She's worried about letting you sleep in the loft. Says it's not really fixed for guests. I said, after where we've been sleeping—"

He stopped her. "You're not thinkin' I'll be stayin' here, are you?"

Her eyes widened. He could tell from her expression that it was exactly what she had been thinking.

"Where else—?"

"I can't." He shook his head.

The concern in her eyes deepened. She reached out and put a hand on his arm.

"But I thought—I mean, I never dreamed—that you wouldn't stay."

"I can't," he said again.

"But Papa and Mama will want to meet you."

"Your papa and mama? I thought they were back in Smithton."

"They are. But they'll come. Just as soon as they get the wire—they'll come."

He shook his head stubbornly. "I don't think they'll be wantin' to see the likes of me."

"What do you mean?"

"I was the reason . . . remember? I was your . . . prison guard."

She looked annoyed. "Can't you get past that?" she said tersely. "You brought me out. You risked your own life to help me get back to my folks. That's what they will think about and remember. That's what I remember."

He shuffled uncomfortably. She might forgive so easily—but could her parents?

"Come on," she coaxed. "We'll talk about that later. Come—have some sandwiches. Aunt Molly has them ready and Uncle Jake looks like he's about starved."

He was totally aware of the fact that she still had her hand on his arm.

"Sandwiches," he agreed and let her lead him toward the house.

Ariana hummed as she prepared herself for the evening meal. She didn't remember when she had felt so light-hearted. *It is so wonderful to be free,* she exulted inwardly. It almost made her giddy.

But it was more than that. Perhaps it was because she now knew the real difference between imprisonment and freedom—fear and security. Perhaps it was because all the bottled tension of the past months was seeping slowly from her, making room for happiness to spill back in. Perhaps it was the loving welcome that her uncle and aunt had so willingly extended, making her feel so loved and accepted.

Perhaps it was—Laramie.

Ariana blushed, even though she was alone in the room.

What were her feelings concerning Laramie? She didn't know if she could answer the question—even in her own heart. But she did realize that her feelings had gone about a slow change during the days they had traveled to freedom together.

At first he had been her captor, and she had feared him just as she had every aspect of camp life. She was confused and lonely and terribly frightened. He had seemed civil enough. But he was the one guarding her as prisoner, and so she had remained aloof, on guard, watchful for any sign that might show his true colors.

Then he had become her liberator. She knew enough to know it had been daring on his part. Dangerous. His own father would have had no mercy had they been caught. But even in this role, Ariana had been cautious. Guarded. He was, after all, an outlaw. How could she know what strange and warped behavior might lurk beneath the seemingly controlled exterior?

But now something had changed. Ariana felt that it had something to do with the snake incident. She blushed again at the thought of it.

It wasn't that he had killed the snake. No, it was more than that. Something—that she found hard to define. Hard to think through. But it was there—between them. She saw it in his eyes as he bent over her, holding her head, wiping her face with his bandana. There was compassion reflected there. Tenderness. There was nothing evil in those eyes. Had he changed? Or was this what he had always been? Would have been, had his circumstances been different?

Ariana did not know. But in some unexplainable way she

felt in her heart that they were rather on even ground. Laramie had rescued her from her captors—and she, in some strange and unplanned way, had rescued him from his.

And he had listened to her read from the Bible—with such interest. Surely, surely, given a little time, he would understand its message and seek out God's forgiveness for his past. She prayed for that with an impatience and urgency she had never brought to prayer before. And she felt confident her prayer would soon be answered.

So she hummed, her heart light. Life held so much promise. She could hardly wait for what each new day would reveal.

Ariana slipped up beside Laramie as he stood leaning against the corral fence, watching the horses feed from the overflowing manger of hay.

"You look very serious," she said in a teasing tone. "Was it really that hard to sit up to a table with a checkered tablecloth?"

Laramie smiled. "I plumb enjoyed it," he admitted. "Especially the apple pie."

Ariana stood beside him and placed her hands on the top rail. They remained silent for a number of minutes, each deep in thought.

In the distance a coyote howled and the farm dog answered in protest.

"Two different worlds," mused Laramie.

Ariana looked puzzled.

"The coyote and the dog," he explained. "Same family—yet two different worlds."

Ariana gave a slight shrug. "Guess either one of them might adjust—if they had to."

Laramie did not answer.

Silence again. The horses continued to feed, their energetic chewing reaching the ears of the two silent people.

"Which one would find it hardest, do you think?" wondered Ariana.

Laramie looked toward the horses. Ariana wondered if he had already forgotten the conversation of a few moments before.

"The dog—or the coyote?" she reminded him.

He seemed to be thinking on it.

"Would it be hardest for the tame animal to adjust to the wild—or the wild animal to adjust to being tamed?" she persisted.

"I couldn't say," he responded, but his voice sounded wistful.

Ariana waited before she spoke again. "Do you mind if I ask you something?"

He seemed to consider it a moment. At last he nodded. "Go ahead," he invited. "I'll answer, if I can."

"That scar—just at your hairline—how'd you get it? I noticed it before—when you took your hat off in the cave—and when you came in—"

"Now—thet I can't answer," he said with good humor. "It's been there fer as long as I can remember. All I know is thet jest a bit shows—but it reaches back further. Jest can't see it—with all my mane. Gotta find some place to git me a haircut. Surprised yer kin even let me in the house."

Ariana laughed softly. He smiled in response.

They fell silent again.

Then Laramie picked up the thread of the conversation. "I was jest thinkin'—'fore ya came out," he said. "You interested in keepin' thet little roan? Seems ya got on quite well. . . ."

Even in the gathering twilight he could see her eyes darken.

"You're still planning to go . . . aren't you?" she said quietly.

He nodded. He hated to see the hurt look on her face. If only she understood his impossible situation.

"I'm sorry," she whispered into the soft darkness. "I was hoping you'd want to stay."

Her words tore at Laramie's soul.

"Ariana . . . you know . . . I can't," he argued, his voice husky with his emotions. "I can't."

"But—"

"We don't even know for sure . . . who I am," he continued, turning toward her.

"But we do. Your mother's Bible—"

"It might not even be my ma's. We are just goin' on Sam's say-so—an' Sam ain't exactly one ya'd stake yer life on."

"But—"

"I might be thet . . . thet person named there. She might have been my ma . . . but I've still got lots of questions. I mean . . . she . . . she jest don't seem to fit . . . with him. The picture . . . the pretty things . . . the Bible."

"Maybe we can find the answers—together."

He took her by the shoulders and turned her toward him.

"I'm a wanted man," he reminded her.

He could see the tears spring into her eyes and slip unbidden down her cheeks.

"That doesn't matter," she whispered intensely.

For one moment he looked deeply into her eyes. "It does to me," he answered, and his words were spoken with finality. "It matters a whole lot to me. I . . . I'm not a free man. I'm . . ."

A sigh from somewhere deep within him stopped his words. He took another deep breath and contiued.

"I'll be leavin' before sunup." The words sounded blunt. Harsh.

She looked hurt—and angry. She pushed his hands off her shoulders. "Go then—go if you must."

She took two steps back from him and stood silently. He could see her shoulders lift and fall.

When she lifted her face the tears were falling freely. Her chin quivered. But her voice was now soft.

"I'm sorry," she apologized. "I had no right . . . I had hoped that . . . you'd wish to . . ."

She lifted her head and stared into his face, her eyes pleading.

"What I want has nothin'—" he began quickly, but he couldn't finish. The unvoiced thoughts seemed to tear at his very being.

Ariana stood before him, paying no heed to the tears that wet her cheeks. "Nothing will change your mind, will it?" she managed to say barely above a whisper. "Please, please—just promise me one thing," she implored. "When you've sorted it out—please—come back."

And then she was gone—and a big part of Laramie went with her.

Chapter Nineteen

Adjustments

When Ariana opened her eyes the next morning, her first thought was of Laramie. Did he really mean to do what he had insisted on the night before? Surely—surely he had changed his mind. He wouldn't just ride out of her life. Leaving her—alone again.

She scrambled from the bed and crossed quickly to the window, lifting back the curtain and peering out. Her heart was racing as she looked toward the corrals. "Please, God—" she whispered, but even before she could finish her prayer her eyes fell on the little roan, his head extended over the top rail of the corral fence as he gazed off down the rutted country road toward the distant hills. He had been left alone. The buckskin and the black pack animal were gone. With them had gone Laramie.

Ariana felt like the pony. Deserted. Alone. She returned to the bed, where she threw herself down and wept.

Laramie rode all day. He wasn't sure where he was going. Wasn't sure what he would do when he got there, but he knew one thing. He had to put some miles between himself and Ariana. Had to be sure that he couldn't give in to impulse—to turn around and head back to her. He had no right. No right to love such a girl. He wasn't sure just who he was, but he was a wanted man. He knew that. Raids. Robbery. Rustling. He didn't know what the penalty might be for his crimes. He had even shot a few men. True, one could argue self-defense—and he'd never shot to kill. But he'd used his gun. What would that mean? Imprisonment? Hanging? He had no idea. But he was sure he'd better stay well away from any lawmen—and Ariana.

His life looked bleak. He was a man on the run.

Ariana moved woodenly through the days. She spent hours with the little roan. They had been left, but they were together. Now they needed to start to rebuild their lives.

The fact that Ariana's father and mother were coming helped her to look forward. Each day she checked off one more day on the calendar. But she was restless. Cut adrift. She couldn't slip back into the same comfortable rut—nor did she seem to be able to slide into a new one. It was difficult.

If I could have gone back home, it would have been different, she told herself. *I could have gone back to my teaching . . . to the church . . . and life could have picked up where it left off. But this . . . I don't know where I fit. Don't know how I should fit. I'm floundering.*

Ariana busied herself with helping her aunt Molly. She even ran errands for her uncle Jake. They were soon declaring they didn't know how they'd ever gotten on without her. Still, she was restless and agitated.

Daily her thoughts went to Laramie. Where was he? Was he all right? Was he still looking for answers? Had he found at least some of them?

"Oh, God," she prayed over and over. "May he realize that you have the important answers. That you can forgive. That you love him, too."

Wisely, she turned to her Bible. Back to the wisdom and comfort of its pages. *I need to look up all those verses on trust again,* she told herself. *I thought I had learned that lesson . . . but I guess I need to start all over.*

So Ariana began again to explore the Scriptures.

The day finally arrived when the incoming stage brought the Bensons. Ariana's excitement was easily matched by her parents'. It was so wonderful to be held in her father's firm embrace, to hear his whispered words of love. Her mother's tears of joy, the familiar fussing over her, made them all laugh and cry and thank God together. Then they turned to having a good visit with Jake and Molly.

They had brought all of Ariana's things. "It wouldn't be safe for you to come home—not yet," Ariana's mother insisted, wiping away tears as she spoke.

"Who'll teach my students?" asked Ariana.

"They are looking for a new teacher for the fall," was the reply. "The children have already lost half the term."

"Why don't you teach here?" Aunt Molly asked.

"They need a teacher at a local school?"

"Well, we don't have a local school—yet—but we do have young'uns in the area," added Uncle Jake.

"Jake, why don't you talk to the neighbors at the next community gatherin'?" Aunt Molly went on, then she turned to her brother-in-law. "We don't have a church yet, but we meet for Bible lessons once a month—turnabout—in one of the neighbor's homes."

"Papa," cried Ariana, "why don't you start a church?"

Four pairs of eyes turned on George Benson. They all looked eager. Anxious.

He shook his head slowly. "I'd have to do a lot of praying about that," he said slowly. "God hasn't shown me that my work in Smithton is finished yet."

There were looks of disappointment, followed by nods of

assent. Certainly he had to follow the will of God.

"But we do need a school," went on Aunt Molly. "Jake, you talk to the neighbors."

Jake nodded. There was no harm in discussing it.

"I can't believe you brought—*everything*," Ariana said to her mother as she carefully unpacked her belongings and stacked them in the chest of drawers Aunt Molly had provided.

"I didn't know when you . . . might be . . . home again," said her mother slowly. "I didn't want to put you in jeopardy."

"I really don't think they'd ever . . . take me again," said Ariana thoughtfully. "I mean . . . their reason is gone now."

"Reason—what was the reason? I never have understood it."

Ariana sat down, her eyes misty. She patted the bed beside her for her mother to join her.

"It's a long story," she managed. "You really want to hear it?"

Her mother nodded and took the seat on the bed.

"Well . . ." Ariana took a deep breath. She was finally going to get to tell her mother about Laramie. She welcomed the opportunity. They had always shared secrets. She could hardly wait to speak of him, for she knew instinctively that her mother would somehow understand the real man.

But even as she opened her mouth to begin, a little part of her held herself in check. What could she say to her mother? How much of her inner thoughts did she dare to reveal? Laramie was a wanted man. Yet Laramie was—a special man. Would she dare to confide in her mother that she thought—that she supposed she had fallen in love with her captor?

"Why did you bring this?" asked Ariana, her eyes wide with question.

"It's yours," answered her mother simply.

"But I don't need it—now," returned Ariana.

She heard her mother sigh. "Ariana," she said, "I'm not sure when I will be able to make this trip again. And when a girl reaches your age . . . then . . . one never knows just when—"

Ariana was not sure how she should respond. She was saved by the bedroom door opening. Aunt Molly stuck her head in.

"Tea's ready," she called merrily. Then she saw the gown in Ariana's hands. She pushed the door open and stepped in.

"What a beautiful dress!" she exclaimed. "Oh—my. Where'd you ever get it?"

Ariana let her hand slide over the material. It was beautiful. The most beautiful thing she had ever seen.

"It was my mama's wedding gown," Ariana answered simply.

Aunt Molly turned her eyes toward her sister-in-law.

"Oh, not mine," Laura Benson was quick to explain. "Ariana's birth mama. It was rescued from the wagon train after the raid. Ariana's second mama—Lucy Millard—saved it for her. It was one of the few things . . ." Her voice trailed off.

Aunt Molly stared at her with horror-filled eyes. Then she turned back to the gown. "Well, it sure is a beautiful thing. I've never seen such a pretty dress in all my days."

"Yes," said Ariana softly. "It is beautiful. When I was little I used to dream about the day—" She stopped. She wasn't sure now if she ever wanted to wear the gown.

"What is it made of?" asked Aunt Molly.

"It's satin—satin overlaid with lace—Spanish lace, Aunt Lucy told me," replied Ariana. "It was imported. Brought over special. Just for the gown."

"One sleeve—" began Aunt Molly, reaching her hand out to the gown.

"One cuff is missing," Laura Benson filled in. "See the

way it is made—this big puffed sleeve nipped into this slender cuff that reaches to the wrist. This cuff—on this side—buttons on with these tiny little buttons. That cuff must have been lost at the time. . . . It'll need to be repaired before Ariana—"

"I wonder if one can find matching lace," began Aunt Molly, who loved to sew.

"Oh, I don't think so," went on Laura Benson. "Lucy said she watched for material—and I've looked too. Mind you, I've not been to the bigger cities, but it was special material—ordered just for that gown. Imported, like Ariana said. No, I don't think one would ever match it."

"It's a shame," mused Aunt Molly, still studying the beautiful lace and the missing cuff.

"I've thought that one could just make two new cuffs—of satin. It wouldn't be quite as elegant, but it would do just fine. It's still the most beautiful wedding gown—"

"Well, there's plenty of time to be thinking on that," said Ariana suddenly. "I have no plans."

She began to fold up the gown with trembling hands.

"Is something wrong?"

Ariana stirred at the sound of her mother's voice. She did not know how long she had been sitting, gazing off into space, her thoughts far from the little log home that belonged to her aunt and uncle.

"What do you mean?" she managed to reply.

"I don't know. You just seemed . . . miles away. Rather . . . forlorn."

Ariana stirred listlessly again.

Her mother sat down beside her and placed a hand on her arm.

"I've noticed—something—ever since we arrived. What is it?"

"I'm . . . I'm not sure," Ariana began. "Perhaps I . . . just miss the school—the students. My friends from church. If I could have gone back home—"

"Maybe," replied her mother, not sounding too sure.

They continued to sit in silence, each occupied with her own thoughts.

"I thought you might be missing him," her mother finally commented.

Ariana swung around to face her, fully understanding her mother's remark. "He's an—"

But she couldn't say "outlaw."

"He's not . . . a believer," she said instead.

"I know. You told me," said her mother quietly. Her hand gently stroked the gingham sleeve. "That is what makes it difficult. You must dictate to your heart. You've made the right decision—but it isn't always easy to make the right decision—even when you know you must. Sometimes—sometimes—the heart needs some convincing, even though our faith says—"

"He was—"

"Your prison guard. I know. I've heard rather strange stories . . . about women and . . . and their captors. It really isn't at all unheard of for them to . . . to learn to love them."

Ariana brushed a hand nervously over her ginghamed lap. "Oh, Mother," she said quickly, "how could I? I mean, I was frightened of him—at first. I wanted the old man—Sam—to . . . to guard me. I certainly didn't—I mean, even after I . . . I thought of him as . . . safe . . . I still didn't—all the time at the camp—and even later on the trail I never—I mean, I never thought of him . . . in that way."

"And now?" prompted her mother. "Now that he is no longer your captor—but has become instead your liberator?"

Ariana shook her head and the tears began to fall, even though she fought against them.

"I don't know. I honestly don't know," she wept. "He was really . . . really a victim himself. He didn't choose that life. That way to live. His father . . . he was just raised to . . . and he had nothing to do with my . . . he didn't even know why I was there—at first. He really was . . . quite. . . . I . . . I know I shouldn't. I know he still isn't a believer, so I can't . . . but I . . . I'm afraid . . ."

She turned to her mother, the tears coming more quickly. "Well—it's a good thing he's gone," she blurted out and threw herself into her mother's arms.

The mother said nothing more, just held her daughter and patted her slender shoulder. It was as she thought. Ariana had indeed fallen in love with the young man. Her heart was still a prisoner—even though she had been set free.

Laramie managed to find work on a large ranch in the foothills. At first it seemed strange to have to report to the foreman, but he loved being out in the open. He even enjoyed working with the herd. And it was a new experience to line up once a month for his small stipend—earned wages—and know he had worked hard for what was rightfully his.

He didn't head for town and the saloon like the rest of the outfit. No one asked questions—though they must have wondered. Laramie didn't want to take any chances of being spotted by some lawman, though he was fairly sure he would not be known to anyone in the area as one of Will Russell's band.

Besides, he wished to save his money. Someday, he dared to dream, he'd have a little spread of his own.

"Preacher comin' to town," laughed one of the cowboys as he pulled off high-heeled boots and flopped down on his cot to sleep off the booze. "Can you imagine thet? A preacher. Here."

Hoots of laughter followed.

Soon snores replaced the coarse laughter. Except for

those who had duty riding herd, all would sleep for the rest of the day.

But Laramie was curious. Who was this preacher? When was he coming? And where?

He decided to saddle up and ride into town to see if he could find out.

The neighbors were thrilled to hear of the possibility of their children being taught.

"We need to build a school," one big man proposed.

"Maybe we could use it for the Bible lessons," offered a small woman timidly.

"Shore—a school an' a church—all in one," someone from the back of the room called out.

Laura Benson smiled at Ariana as she laid a hand on her arm.

"Perhaps God brought you to this community for a purpose," she whispered and Ariana smiled in return. She fervently hoped they would hurry with the building. She was anxious to get back in the classroom again. Perhaps it would give her something else to think about. Something other than Laramie.

Laramie looked up the preacher and was pleased to hear that the man was not just passing through the area. Laramie had lots of questions, and he was sure they couldn't be answered in a few short days. He began to attend the services whenever he was free. He even tucked his Bible in his saddlebag and took it with him as he rode the range. When he had a few moments as the herd contentedly grazed, he let his horse rest and feed while he sat in the shade and read the Bible, one eye on the lookout for trouble.

At last the pieces began to fall into place. He felt he was

beginning to understand what God had in mind for His creation—for him.

The sinner could be forgiven and the sin, not just forgiven, but forgotten, because of what Jesus Christ, the Redeemer, had done on the cross of Calvary. He had been the sacrifice—the atonement—for man's sin.

He, Laramie Russell, had to claim that gift of salvation—had to accept what had been done in his place. Had to vow to sin no more and make restitution—as far as possible—for sins of the past. Then he would be free to join one of the little groups that would be baptized at the small creek east of town.

It was not difficult for Laramie to acknowledge that he was a sinner. He had known that fact, deep down inside, for some time. Nor was it hard for him to ask for God's forgiveness. He had longed to be freed from his burden of guilt. It was going to be much more difficult to right past wrongs. He didn't quite know where and how to start.

Chapter Twenty

Truth

Ariana was thrilled when at long last the crude little schoolhouse was ready for use. Heart beating fast, she looked out over the small class of pioneer children. Their eyes shone with anticipation. Their faces looked to her with eagerness.

Perhaps Mama was right, she whispered to herself. *Maybe this whole chain of events was for this very purpose.*

It was nice to think that maybe there had been a reason—something good that could come out of the dreadful ordeal. *How wonderful to know that God never lost control*, she thought, *that He could be trusted even during the darkest times when there seemed to be no purpose to it at all.*

As Ariana looked into eleven pairs of eyes fixed on her face, she took a moment for a quick prayer. *Thank you, Father*, she whispered silently.

It was not much—but it came from an overflowing heart.

Laramie felt torn in three directions.

His first desire was to return to Ariana. He was anxious to tell her about his Bible reading, his talks with the pastor, and the fact that he now understood her faith. Yet he hesitated. He had no right to expect acceptance from her or her family. He had a past. A past that had not been put to right.

His second choice seemed to be to stay where he was and continue to grow in his understanding of the words in his mother's Bible. He had been welcomed into the small Christian fellowship group. The minister was most willing to lead him in his new faith. Other church members greeted him warmly and made him feel one with the little congregation. In fact, the eldest of the minister's daughters seemed more than willing to move the friendship beyond that. Laramie noticed that she often tried to catch his eye, flirting just a bit, and took advantage of every opportunity to speak with him. Had it not been for his feeling for Ariana, he may have felt flattered and perhaps even responded. Laramie simply did not give the extra attention much thought.

Yet, as much as he longed to return to Ariana, and as much as he enjoyed the fellowship of the little church, Laramie concluded that the only honest choice was for him to pursue restitution for the past. It was not an easy decision and one that troubled his soul as he battled it through.

"I've got to go back."

Laramie came to the conclusion after a long struggle. He had wrestled with the problem for many weeks, trying to find a good excuse for avoiding the return. After all, the trip could well cost him his life. He would not be welcomed back to his father's camp. Nor would he be welcomed in any of the towns where he had been part of the gang's activities.

But there was no way to escape the urgings of his conscience. He had done wrong. He had been forgiven—but he must—as far as possible, make right the wrongs of his past.

Laramie rapped loudly on the ranch house door and was admitted by the owner himself. The young man felt awkward and self-conscious as he stepped inside.

"Russell," the boss welcomed him and stepped aside for

him to enter. "Foreman says he's pleased with yer work. Know how to git the task done—without gripin' none. Been meanin' to have a chat."

Laramie removed his dust-covered hat.

"Jest came to thank ya for the opportunity of ridin' fer ya," he began. "I've appreciated it—but I have to be movin' on."

The older man looked puzzled.

"Somethin' happen?" he asked.

"Reckon it did," replied Laramie in his easy drawl. "Only—not here. Happened a long time ago."

The man waited.

"Ya see, sir," went on Laramie, fingering the hat in his hands, "I been ridin' under false colors. I . . . I'm wanted by the law."

The man shrugged careless shoulders. "So—" he said. "I don't ask no questions."

"No. No," agreed Laramie. "An' I appreciate it."

"Look," said the big man and took Laramie's arm to draw him farther into the room and toward a chair. "Likely ain't a cowpoke on the place thet ain't had a little run-in here or there. Thet doesn't mean the law's gonna catch up."

Laramie reluctantly took the seat, still twisting his Stetson in his hands.

"Ya heard somethin'? Somebody on yer tail?" the big man went on.

"No. Not thet I know of."

"There—ya see," said the rancher, looking relieved. "Likely no need to panic."

"Oh, I'm not panicky," said Laramie. "I jest want it cleared up. You see—I've been going to the little church—straightened out my life. Now—if I read my Bible right—I've got to do what I can to set the past straight. So—I've got to go back."

The big man looked shocked. "Ya mean yer walkin' right back into the hangman's noose?" he asked incredulously.

Laramie smiled and reached a hand up to the hat brim

that wasn't there. He scratched his head instead, feeling the scar that began on his forehead and stretched into the hairline.

"Well . . . now I don't know," he admitted. "I've no idea what my future holds. If I've got the hangman's noose to face . . . then I guess—"

"Don't do it, boy," the rancher said with great feeling. "It's a foolhardy thing. You'll never git a fair trial an' ya know it. It's good enough thet ya quit whatever it was ya was doin'. Thet's good enough." He put a hand up in some alarm. "Didn't kill a sheriff—or a marshal, did ya?"

"No," replied Laramie simply.

The rancher looked relieved. "There—ya see," he said, "likely nobody will even bother lookin' fer ya."

"You don't understand," said Laramie, and he stood to his feet. "The One who was looking fer me—the One thet really matters—He's already found me. An' He says yer sins will find ya out. He says, ya own up to 'em—make restitution, they call it—if it's possible. I plan to do that. An' I reckon what happens—well, thet's up to Him."

The rancher reached up to push back his thinning hair. He opened his mouth to speak and then closed it again, shaking his head.

He took a pace away from Laramie, then turned back to face him. "I think yer makin' a big mistake, boy," he said bluntly, then went on carefully. "But—iffen ya ever want to ride fer me agin—well you jest come on by."

"Thank you," said Laramie and he stretched out his hand.

"See the foreman. He'll settle yer wage." The two shook hands.

"I'll do thet, sir," replied Laramie. "I plan to leave before sunup."

All during the long ride back over the country that Laramie had covered with Ariana, he thought and rethought his situation. How could he get into camp without being seen by the sentry from the ledge? Would he be gunned down before he even made it through the chasm in the rock walls? How would his father respond when he came with his apology? If it was accepted, would he expect Laramie to become part of the gang again? No, he couldn't do that. Not even if it meant his death.

Should he go to the law first? No, he might spend the rest of his days in prison. First he had to talk with his father. Had to ask his forgiveness. Had to tell him about the truths he had learned from his mother's Bible—if indeed it had been his mother's. His father needed to hear.

In the end it was White Eagle whom Laramie first contacted. The young brave seemed excited to see him.

"Thought you die," he said, thrusting out his hand to shake Laramie's, white-man fashion.

Laramie smiled. "Thought you would have moved," he responded. "It's been a long time."

"Move village many times. Back again," said White Eagle.

"What happened after we left?" Laramie had to know.

White Eagle laughed. "Like ants," he said. "Then—long walk. Mad." He laughed again, remembering.

"Your father's black, good horse," he said seriously. "Carry squaw."

Laramie spun around. "Whose squaw? Yours?" he asked.

White Eagle beamed his pleasure. Laramie could tell that his friend was now a family man.

"Naw," he said, slapping the young Pawnee on the shoulder. "Ya don't say? Any papoose?"

"Soon," said White Eagle. His eyes shone.

Laramie nodded, acknowledging the man's good fortune.

"How's everything?" Laramie asked, changing the tone of the conversation.

"Bad year," said White Eagle seriously. "Much sick. Little food. Bad year."

"I'm sorry to hear that," replied Laramie. "Anything I can do to help?"

"Pawnee do not need help," he said simply.

Laramie nodded.

"Still the same chief?"

"Father, Half Moon, die. New chief. Brother, Broken Tooth. Maybe trouble," said White Eagle.

Laramie let his gaze drift out over the valley that lay beneath them. Miles of timbered hills stretched all the way to vast prairies. But the scene included small farmsteads—ranches—even a couple of tiny towns. Many more campfires than the Indians' lifted smoke to the sky. What would be happening in the years to come? Could the white settlers and the Indian tribes live in peace?

"Have ya heard anythin' about . . . my pa?" asked Laramie, shifting his attention back to the man beside him.

White Eagle's eyes darkened.

"Not good news," he said.

Laramie turned toward him. "What do you mean?"

"They raid. Bank. Not good."

"You mean . . . some of them . . . didn't make it?"

White Eagle nodded.

"My pa?"

"I not know. Only know not good. Only two horse come back. Funny little man."

"Sam?"

"Man makes much spit." White Eagle spit in the dust to demonstrate.

"Sam," said Laramie.

"One more. Hurt bad. Not new horse of father."

Laramie felt a lump come into his throat. He knew with a certainty that he had to get to his father's camp—quickly. He began to gather the reins of the buckskin.

"How long ago?" he asked as he mounted.

"Two—maybe three moons," said White Eagle.

Laramie reached down to clasp the hand of his old friend one last time. He might never see him again. They looked at each other steadily, then without exchanging words, they both turned to go.

❧ ❧ ❧

There was no man on the ledge that guarded the entrance to the camp. Laramie carefully studied the position before urging his mount forward.

As he rode into the little settlement he noticed how dilapidated the buildings all were. Bad before, they were even worse now. Everything seemed strangely deserted. Maybe there was no one around.

Then he noticed there were two horses in the corral. Someone must still live here.

He was dismounting when a shot rang out and splintered a pine bough just above his head. He dived for cover at the same moment that the buckskin reared and spun around, fear making the animal's nostrils flare.

Another shot. This one thumped into the tree behind which Laramie crouched. In the instant before Laramie ducked, he saw the shooter. It was Sam who leveled the rifle and was taking careful aim.

As soon as the echo stopped resounding off the rock walls of the valley, Laramie bellowed, "Sam. Sam, it's me. Laramie."

He waited.

"Show yerself," came a raspy voice.

Laramie wondered at the wisdom of obeying the command, but at last he eased out from behind the pine.

"Well, I'll be," said Sam, his rifle barrel gradually lowering. "It *is* Laramie."

Laramie looked around for his buckskin. The animal stood a few feet away, still appearing skitterish. The pack horse had run off several yards and was now feeding on the thick grass beneath a clump of birch.

Sam was walking toward him, his rifle lowered but still in his hand. His whiskered face was gaunt and his eyes dark and angry. "Ya got a nerve showin' up here," he growled.

It was not much different than Laramie had expected.

"I came back to see my pa," he said in explanation as he stooped to pick up his hat, which had landed in the dust.

"Yer pa," said Sam, and he spit in the dirt.

Laramie nodded and whipped the dust from his Stetson before putting it back on his head.

"Well—I'd say you were about three months too late," snapped Sam.

Laramie stared. "Ya mean—?"

"Dead! Like the rest of 'em. I'm the only one left." He spit again, his eyes glaring at Laramie.

The sudden pain in Laramie's heart was like a huge fist squeezing the life out of it. If only—

He turned away for a moment.

He turned back to Sam, swallowing hard. "Buried here?" he managed to ask.

Sam nodded. The gun had finally dropped down to his side. "Ya ain't brung a posse in here, have ya?" he asked gruffly.

Laramie's shock showed on his face. "Ya know better," he threw back at the old man.

Sam nodded his head toward one of the falling-down buildings. "Well—come in, then," he offered.

"I'll not be stoppin'," Laramie replied. "Just long enough to . . . pay my respects. . . ."

He gathered the reins of his mount and led him to a hitching post. The pack horse wouldn't wander far, he reasoned. Not with the other horses nearby.

"Now thet yer here, ya might as well come in," Sam said, spitting. Then he nodded toward the trees to their right. Laramie understood that his father had been buried there.

He found the grave. It was marked by a small homemade cross. On it had been written one word. "Boss." Laramie reached up and removed his hat. He felt choked. Saddened. He had wanted to talk to this man. To ask his forgiveness.

To tell of his newfound faith. And now he was gone. It was too late. Too late.

It was some time before Laramie felt ready to talk to Sam. He knew now that he would have to talk with him. He had so many questions. He needed some answers.

Sam had brewed an awful pot of weak coffee. They sat sipping it slowly, each deep in thought. Sam chewed on his dirty mustache and spit frequently into the corner, and Laramie toyed with his Stetson and rubbed unconsciously at the scar on his forehead.

At last Laramie spoke. "How'd it happen?"

Sam spit again. "Robbery went sour," he said simply.

"Where?"

"Over to Elk River. Bank there."

"What happened?"

"Yer pa figured Skidder sold us out."

"Skidder?"

There was silence for some time.

"Skidder—is he—?" Laramie began to ask.

"Yer pa shot 'im. He'd turned sides."

Silence again.

"Yer pa got shot. His horse was shot right out from under 'im. He had no place to go. Caught two bullets. I . . . I got him out but he was hit bad. We grabbed another horse an' lit out. We made it back. But he only lasted a few hours."

Sam clamped his mouth shut and chewed on his mustache. He had said his piece. There was nothing more to say.

Laramie sat silently, letting all of the pieces fit together. White Eagle had said that it wasn't his pa's horse. He'd been right.

Laramie could imagine the scene of the robbery. He'd been there himself on more than one occasion in the past. But he had never walked into an ambush. A double cross of one of their own men.

"Why didn't ya put his name on the cross?" he asked Sam softly.

Sam snorted. "His name? Which name? Which one of the five or six I knowed about was I gonna put on there?"

Laramie nodded. He had not realized his pa had changed his name so many times. Maybe he was one of the men listed in his mother's Bible. For some reason he could not bring himself to ask.

He stood and set aside his cup. "I'd better git," he said. "I've some ridin' to do."

"What ya gonna do?" asked Sam. "Thought ya might stay. This is still the safest place—"

"Not lookin' fer a safe place," Laramie responded. "I'm fixin' to turn myself in."

Sam jerked upright. "Did you come here to—?"

"I said, myself. Not you. Not anyone else. I came here to see my pa—thet's all." He looked evenly at the older man. "I'm not runnin' anymore, Sam," he said quietly.

"They'll lock ya away—iffen they don't hang ya," Sam said brusquely.

Laramie nodded. "They likely will," he agreed.

"Yer crazy, boy," spat Sam. "Plumb crazy."

"I was sorta hopin' thet you'd decide to join me, Sam. I hate leavin' ya here—all alone."

Sam shook his head. "Got a feelin' I'd rather finish my days here then at the end of a rope," he said firmly.

"Maybe there wouldn't be a rope. Maybe—"

"They'd be a rope," said Sam, and he spit to the side of the coveted chair with its many-patched wobbly legs.

"Sheriff wouldn't be in his right mind iffen he let me go," went on Sam simply.

Laramie nodded. Maybe it was so. He hated to think of it. He hated to leave the aging man all alone in the forsaken camp. It didn't seem right. But Sam had chosen his life. There was little that Laramie could do to right the wrongs. Still, he did at least owe him a glimpse at the truth he had found. The man would have to make up his own mind.

"Ya know, Sam," he said softly as he lifted his hat and fingered the hatband, "when ya found thet there trunk of my ma's . . . ya opened a whole new world fer me. A world of . . . good. Of law and order and . . . faith in God. I didn't know where it would lead at the time, but I've followed the trail . . . an' it led me to . . . forgiveness. It feels good, Sam. It feels mighty good."

Sam only stared.

"An' thet's what I came back to speak to my pa about," Laramie finished. "Now thet he ain't here—not much reason fer me to stay. But I want you to know about it, too, Sam. It really works. God can forgive. He can turn a man's life around. One has to ask fer the pardon He offers. It's as simple as thet."

Sam said nothing. He spit again, the brown liquid making one more stain on the already darkened wood of the floor.

"Think on it, Sam," Laramie prompted gently.

Sam didn't even acknowledge the words that were spoken. Laramie rose to his feet. Reluctantly he moved to go. He nodded toward the older man. "Thanks, Sam . . . fer the coffee an' fer . . . carin' fer me . . . as a boy. An' fer . . . lookin' out fer my pa." His voice threatened to break on the last words. He settled his Stetson back on his thick hair and turned to leave.

Just as he was stepping through the door, Sam called out after him.

"He wasn't really yer pa, ya know."

Chapter Twenty-one

Reunion

Heart thudding in his chest, Laramie swung around. "What are you sayin'?"

Sam eyed him coolly. He took another cut from his chewing tobacco. "He weren't yer real pa," he repeated.

Laramie stepped back into the room, moving slowly toward the little man. "You knowin' somethin' ya haven't come clean on—or are ya jest talkin'?" he asked tersely.

"Oh, I knowed all right," replied Sam. "I was there."

Laramie felt the strength draining from him. He fought for control, easing himself back to one of the log stools that had served the camp for many years. Sam now claimed the boss's chair.

Laramie swallowed, his eyes intense.

"Are ya sayin' thet wasn't my ma's trunk?" he asked Sam.

Sam fingered the tobacco before returning it to his pocket, spit in the corner, and tipped his head. "Oh, thet were her trunk, right enough," he said slowly. "Not much doubt 'bout thet."

"Then—" prompted Laramie.

"Thet scar ya got—" said Sam with a careless wave of his jackknife.

Laramie waited.

"Thet came in an Indian raid. Reason yer pa hated the redskins so."

Unconsciously Laramie's hand reached to the scar. One finger traced it back into the depth of his hair.

"We'd been out on a raid," Sam went on, finally seeming to warm to his subject. "Came upon this wagon train. Jest been ambushed. They'd done a good job of it too. Everybody dead—all over the place. Men—womenfolk—kids—all dead. Scalps gone—faces slashed. It was an awful sight. Near made a grown man sick to his stomach.

"They'd set the wagons afire—but the rain stopped some of 'em from burning outright. Well, we didn't much like what we saw. Some of the fellas was pokin' through stuff—seein' iffen there was anythin' worth takin', an' then I heard this—little mew sound. Thought it was a wounded animal of some kind. I looked in this here wagon—an' there ya was—yer head split open by a tomahawk—yer clothes soaked in blood—but still alive.

"Well, I didn't know what to do. I called to yer pa and he come an' took a look. Then he—"

Sam stopped and seemed to choke on the next words.

"Anyway, he picked ya outta there. I asked iffen he'd lost his senses, but he said we couldn't jest leave ya there to die. He told the fellas to see what they could find—fer yer care, an' Rowdy found thet trunk. It had some things fer a young'un an' we figured thet it'd help—so yer pa ordered it brought. Near killed the pack horse gettin' it back to camp. We shoulda jest took the things ya'd need, but we didn't have time to sort through it there on the spot.

"Well—he brought ya home and patched ya up the best he could—an' ya made it."

Laramie's head was spinning. He could not take in all that the man was saying.

"I told yer pa you'd never make an outlaw," Sam went on as though in argument. "Ya jest—never had the stomach fer it—ya could see thet from when ya was a kid. I mean—" Sam waved the jackknife in the air. "Ya was always patching up hurt things and cleanin' things an'—ya jest weren't made fer it. But he said he'd make ya what he wanted ya to be. Thet ya'd never survive elsewise. Someone would up and shoot ya in the back, or somethin'. He says—"

"How old was I?" cut in Laramie.

Sam looked startled, then annoyed. "How should I know? I don't know nothin' 'bout kids. Around two, I s'pose. What difference—?"

Then Sam stopped and stared at the young man before him. "Ya don't remember nothin'—?" he began, straightening up in his chair.

"Nothin'," replied Laramie, a frown creasing his brow.

"Well—I ain't surprised. Ya was hurt real bad. Ya didn't even start to talk fer a good piece after it. We wondered fer a time iffen ya'd ever git any sense. Shock—yer pa said. When ya came outta it—ya seemed bright enough."

"An' the trunk—?" insisted Laramie, leaning forward.

"Outta the same wagon."

Laramie managed to lift himself to his feet. "Is it still here?" he asked hoarsely.

"In thet cabin—where the girl was."

Laramie nodded and left the room in a daze. Inwardly he was being torn in two with separate identities. What could he believe? Was Sam right? Was he really not the son of an outlaw? Had his mother really been the sweet-looking woman in the picture? Was he the little boy?

He pushed his way into the cabin, memories of Ariana bending over her open Bible flooding through his mind. He made his way to the trunk and slowly lifted back the lid. The things were still all there. The garments that Ariana had worn, carefully folded on the top. He lifted the gown and stared long and hard. His mother's dress. She had been real. She had loved him.

Laramie buried his face in the soft garment, and for the first time since his babyhood he allowed himself the expression of tears.

❧ ❧ ❧

When his inner storm had passed, Laramie lifted himself from beside the trunk. It was over. He had emptied his soul of all bitterness, anxiety, and conflict. He was satisfied that he was who the book said he was. Burke Lawrence, son of Lavina and Turner Lawrence. He might never know more than that about his heritage—but at least he knew to whom he had belonged. It was something precious—a treasure to carry with him for the rest of his days.

He rose, folded the gown carefully, and placed it back in the trunk.

"Thank you, Mother," he whispered. "For yer . . . love. Yer prayers. I'm gonna be all right."

He closed the lid, gently, firmly, and left the room without looking back. He would call at his pa's—no—at his foster father's grave one more time. The man had saved him from certain death. He had raised him in the best way he knew how. He owed him respect—and one final goodbye.

❧ ❧ ❧

"Will Russell's gang, ya say?"

The crusty sheriff leaned back in his chair and lifted his feet up on the wooden desk.

Laramie nodded silently.

"Don't recall seeing ya when the bank got robbed," said the sheriff.

"I wasn't there," replied Laramie.

"Where was ya?"

"I had left—some time earlier."

The sheriff frowned. "Why?" he asked simply.

Laramie stirred. This was going to be harder than he had imagined. "There was a girl," he began. "She was kidnapped from Smithton. She was a prisoner in our camp. I took her—to her kin."

The sheriff's head lifted. He looked long and hard at Laramie, as though searching for his own answers, or looking for flaws. “What changed yer mind?”

Laramie frowned. “I never changed my mind—really,” he replied. “I hadn’t been in on the kidnapping.”

“Who was?”

“My—the boss. Will Russell.”

“What changed his mind?”

The man sure had a lot of questions. Laramie squirmed. Why didn’t he just get on with it? Get a confession, or whatever it took, and lock him up.

The sheriff was still waiting for his reply.

“Well . . . he didn’t change his mind . . . really. I . . . I took her without him knowin’,” Laramie confessed.

“This girl—?” The sheriff’s eyes narrowed and he lowered his feet. “Ya . . . harm her . . . in any way?”

“No, sir,” Laramie was quick to reply. “I jest took her to her uncle’s farm—in Montana.”

The sheriff seemed to relax. “Why?” he asked as he lifted his feet again.

Laramie could feel the anger flushing his cheeks. He was annoyed with all the senseless questioning. “Because, sir,” he said heatedly, “she didn’t belong in a camp with a bunch of outlaws. She had done nothin’ to deserve it. She was innocent and good and God-fearing. An’ there was trouble brewin’.”

He wondered if he had said too much. If he had become too vehement. He forced himself to cool down. He’d be getting the hangman’s noose for sure with such action.

The sheriff looked at him steadily, then nodded, lifted his feet from the desk, and opened a drawer stuffed with papers. “Don’t recall seein’ yer picture,” he mused.

“No, sir. Likely haven’t,” said Laramie in a softer tone.

“Why not?” asked the sheriff, putting his feet up again.

Laramie shuffled his feet uncomfortably. “Well . . . I reckon I haven’t earned a poster, sir,” he replied. “I was mostly left to hold the horses.” He flushed as he spoke the words.

"So," said the sheriff, not looking up. "You haven't killed a man—you don't have a bounty on yer head—ya don't even have yer face on a poster?"

Laramie nodded.

The sheriff's feet returned to the floor with a heavy thump.

"Don't look like I got any reason to hold ya, then," he said simply.

It took Laramie a while to grasp the words.

"I don't understand," he said when he could speak. "I was a member of the gang. I—"

"Now, how am I s'pose to prove thet?" demanded the sheriff. "Ain't nobody claimed to have seen ya—ain't no poster. Nothin'."

"But I have admitted . . . my guilt," declared Laramie.

The feet lifted again. The sheriff leaned back and looked at Laramie. He chewed on a straw that he picked from his pant cuff. "So ya did," he observed. "They say thet confession is good fer the soul."

He stared into Laramie's eyes as though his words carried some secret message.

"Son," he said at last, "ain't ever' day thet anyone comes to me tellin' me of past sins. Now I'm takin' from this here—confession—thet ya ain't plannin' on being a part of such—action—agin. Thet right?"

Laramie nodded dumbly.

"Thet ole gang—it's been—what shall we say—dismembered. An' from our little conversation—I don't think thet you'll be pickin' up with another one. Right?"

Laramie nodded again.

"Then—I suggest thet our conversation is closed."

At the stunned look on Laramie's face he went on, pointing one long finger at Laramie's chest. "But let me tell ya this, son. You mess with me—you're gonna swing. Ya got thet?"

Laramie stood to his feet nodding. He swallowed again.

"There's one more thing, Sheriff," he managed.

The sheriff nodded, but he looked impatient. "Make it fast," he said. "The coffee's gittin' cold over at Evita's."

Laramie lifted the little leather bag. "Money," he said simply. "This is stolen money."

"Stolen from where?" asked the sheriff.

"I don't rightly know. Here an' there. Most anywhere. I . . . have no idea. It was always divided up evenly. I don't know where this came from."

The sheriff swore. "Then how'm I to know where to give it back?" he said gruffly.

"Well . . . what am I to do—?"

"Look," said the sheriff testily. "Thet's yer problem. Not mine. Ya don't know where to take it back—then it's yer burden. You figure it out. I dunno."

He walked away muttering to himself. "Outlaws," fumed the sheriff. "Got no business gittin' religion. Makes more trouble then it's worth."

Laramie, holding his leather pouch of gold coins, watched him go and then stepped from the office. It took several minutes for him to realize that he was a free man.

Carefully Laramie counted out the money he had earned honestly as a ranch hand. He had already been giving his tithe to the little church where he had attended. Now the small pile of coins that were left did not look like much. Laramie sighed. They'd never put a down payment on his own spread, that was a sure thing.

He had seen a little church just down the street. He made his way to it now. A surprised minister answered his knock.

"Do you . . . do you help out poor people and the like?" asked Laramie.

"We help when we can, son, but our funds are limited," said the man. "Don't know that we can do much but—what can I do for you?"

Laramie lifted the leather bag and poured its contents

out on the wooden desk. "I'd like to make a donation," he said simply. The shining gold pieces glimmered in the afternoon sunlight streaming through the window. The man stood and stared.

"It was not honest money, but I've no way to git it back to those it was taken from," Laramie admitted. "Maybe you can undo a bit of that by puttin' it to good use."

The man still stared.

Laramie tipped his hat in respect and moved toward the door. "May the Lord bless you—an' yer church," he said with deep feeling, and he was gone.

Ariana moved about the schoolroom, cleaning the chalkboards, tidying the small desks, and putting the few books they possessed back on the one makeshift shelf.

She was finally able to hum again. It had taken many months for her to feel that the song was back in her heart. But the months had lessened her pain and disappointment—though she still prayed fervently for Laramie. God was in control. He had brought good from her ordeal. Never had she seen such eager students. And their enthusiasm for learning carried over into her Sunday school class, for most of them returned again on Sunday to have their Bible lessons in the same little building.

Ariana moved to put the last books on the shelf. It was a pleasant evening—with many promised hours of sunlight yet. She would have time to saddle the little roan and take a leisurely ride before Aunt Molly's supper was served.

A firm rap on the door brought Ariana to attention. She was not used to callers at the schoolhouse. Momentarily her heart began racing. She had not forgotten the men who had visited her over two years earlier and carried her captive. Ariana had a hard time finding her voice. She was not quite sure if she could bid the visitor enter.

The door opened—just a crack at first. Ariana watched

with her breath caught in her throat.

Then the door pushed open farther—and there stood Laramie.

He was clean-shaven with carefully trimmed hair. His clothes were not new but were clean and well kept. His eyes, which held a spark, seemed to look right into her soul.

She caught her breath again. One word escaped her lips. "Laramie."

He moved forward slowly, his black Stetson in his hands. "May I . . . come in?" he asked softly.

She nodded. She couldn't speak. He looked—the same—yet so different.

"You've come back," she managed to whisper.

He nodded. "You made me promise. Remember?"

"I . . . yes." Tears threatened to spill. He could see them coming.

He stopped a few feet in front of her. Just stopped and looked at her.

"You look . . . well," he observed.

She swallowed. "And you," she managed.

They stood in silence. Laramie struggled with words and then spoke softly. "You remember," he began, "that I was to . . . find some answers. Find myself."

She nodded.

"Well, I've done that," he said simply and then added, "an' in the process . . . I've found God, too."

She stood and looked at him and then the tears began to spill from her eyes. "Oh, Laramie . . . I've prayed and prayed. I was beginning to think—"

"I was . . . afraid thet . . . thet you'd have given up. Thet—"

She looked up into his face, her eyes shining in spite of the tears that still ran down her cheeks.

"Oh no," she said between tears and laughter. "I would have waited . . . forever . . . to hear those words, if need be. Nothing . . . could make me happier. We are . . . are . . . fellow believers now. Nothing . . . could bring me . . . more joy."

Laramie longed to reach for her. To brush the tears from her cheeks and bury his face in her hair. He did not dare. He knew he had no right to expect her to care for him in the way that he cared for her.

He swallowed hard and willed himself to remain at a distance.

Chapter Twenty-two

Adrift

Laramie found a job with a local rancher and settled into the community. He was welcomed into the small congregation that met at the schoolhouse, and Ariana saw to it that he was put to work. To his surprise, Ariana seemed to assume that the situation had now changed—that the past was forgiven and could also be forgotten. She even managed, in a subtle way, to convey the idea that she expected him to call.

Laramie was quick to oblige, and the young people were soon seen as a couple in the community. Even Uncle Jake and Aunt Molly expressed unspoken pleasure in the arrangement.

Laramie could not have expressed his deep joy. It seemed that his unthinkable dream might indeed come true. It was hard to keep his love for Ariana in check when she greeted him with sparkling eyes and welcomed, with open pleasure, his evening calls. They spent many pleasurable hours by the fireplace, sharing thoughts and dreams, talking about the events past and their dreams for the future.

Ariana would have been happy to marry quickly, and though Laramie was also anxious, he held himself back.

"But why wait?" argued Ariana. "We both know that in our hearts we plan to—someday—marry."

"Not until I have earned enough money to at least provide us with some of the things we'll be needin'," he countered.

Ariana smiled. "There's little I need to make me happy," she insisted.

"But you would like a roof over yer head," he teased.

Ariana tipped her head and grinned saucily. "It might be fun to sleep under the stars."

"Until the first snowstorm."

"Perhaps we could borrow a tent—from White Eagle."

"White Eagle needs his tent. By now his papoose will have joined him. He is a true family man now."

Ariana smiled. She had never been happier. She wished White Eagle even a portion of the joy that she herself felt.

"We do need to set a date," she said, and she was no longer teasing. "I want Papa and Mama to be here. Papa will marry us, of course. An' Mama and Aunt Molly will arrange the dinner for family and friends. They will need to know so they can make plans."

Laramie agreed.

The summer was moving into autumn.

"How about a Christmas wedding?" he asked Ariana.

Ariana thought about it. It seemed a long time to wait. At last she smiled. A Christmas wedding would be just fine.

"I'll let them know," said Ariana. "I do hope they will come early."

Laramie reached out to smooth back her windblown hair. They had ridden out to the ridge overlooking the small farm that belonged to her uncle. The day was just warm enough to be comfortable. The last of the summer crops bowed their heads to the passing breezes. The birds filled the afternoon with spirited chatter.

"It's so peaceful here—I love it," mused Laramie in contentment.

"Can we live here—always?" asked Ariana dreamily.

"Always," he answered.

Ariana moved in closer to him until her shoulder was touching his chest. "I never dreamed I could be so . . . happy," she sighed.

His hand dropped to her arm and pulled her closer against him. He lowered his head to place a kiss on the top of her tousled hair. "It is still like a . . . a dream," he said.

"When did you first know?" she quizzed him.

He smiled and gave her a little squeeze. "Is that important?"

"Sort of. I just wondered."

"I . . . it was after I'd shot the snake. I was afraid. I suddenly realized thet if somethin' happened to you . . . thet I would . . . suffer terribly. Thet you were much more than a . . . prisoner thet I was bound to free. I loved you. I realized thet then."

Ariana stirred dreamily.

"That's when I first knew, too," she told him.

She turned and reached up to run a finger gently along the scar. "And to think that I might have never met you. That you could have died . . . as a baby. You know, I owe Will Russell so much. For saving you, then for . . . for kidnapping me."

She giggled. "That sounds like a silly thing to say, doesn't it? But it . . . it turned out very well . . . don't you think?"

He nodded, his heart too full for an answer.

"You know," went on Ariana, "our backgrounds really aren't that different. Both orphans. Both lost our folks in an Indian raid. Rather ironic—or coincidental—don't you think?"

Laramie nodded, his head bent over Ariana's.

"Well, all that's behind us. Now . . . now we have the whole future ahead of us. We can . . . can make up for all the past . . . in the years ahead." She sighed deeply.

"God has been good," said Laramie.

"He has. Laramie—" Ariana caught herself and laughed softly. "You know," she hastened on, "it's hard for me to . . . to switch to Burke. I like that name. Burke. It's just that I've always thought of you as . . . Laramie. Will you mind if I slip now and then?"

Laramie smiled good-naturedly. "It's hard fer me, too," he admitted. "It takes some gettin' used to. I still have to stop and think when I go to sign my name or even when someone speaks to me. I guess we'll get used to it in time."

Ariana nodded. "It's hard to make a change—as an adult."

They stood in silence for a few minutes and then Laramie spoke. "What if we keep the Laramie? It seems thet . . . well thet I owe thet much to my . . . pa. He did do his best. He could have jest left me to die. It must have been an awful nuisance fer a man like him . . . to raise a child."

Ariana smiled. "Mrs. Laramie Burke Lawrence," she said softly. "It sounds just fine to me."

Laramie worked hard and saved his money for his upcoming marriage. They would not be wealthy—but neither was anyone else on the prairies. At least they would be together.

Ariana, too, was saving each penny she could from her small stipend as a schoolteacher. She was certain they would manage just fine. Her uncle Jake had given them a small parcel of land down by the creek and neighbors had promised a house raising just as soon as the crops were out of the fields. Ariana was fully confident they would have a snug little dwelling all their own by the time their important day in December arrived.

Her mother and father arrived two weeks before the wedding. Ariana was so excited when she met their stage that she thought she was acting like one of her first-graders.

"Oh, I'm so anxious for you to meet him," she bubbled. "I

know that you're going to love him just as much—well, almost as much as I do."

Her papa smiled and her mama held her close. "I knew it," she insisted. "I could sense you were in love with him when we were here before."

"Oh, Mama," laughed Ariana. "I scarcely admitted it myself then."

"Well, I knew it. You can't hide the look of a girl in love."

Ariana laughed joyfully. "We're going to need to fix that gown," she reminded her mother. "Did you bring the satin?"

"Oh yes. I didn't forget. Perhaps Molly will do the sewing. She is much better with a needle than I am."

Ariana fairly skipped her way back to the house. In only two short weeks she would finally be Mrs. Laramie Burke Lawrence. It still seemed like an impossible, beautiful dream.

"Ariana?"

It was Laramie who called.

"In here," she answered, her cheeks flushing with pleasure. She and her aunt Molly were busy at the kitchen table, studying the lace wedding gown, figuring just how to cut the satin for the new cuffs.

"I suppose we could undo this cuff and see just how it is put together. We would then have a pattern," Aunt Molly was saying.

Laramie stood in the doorway. Ariana looked up and smiled.

"It's okay," she assured him. "I'm not superstitious. You can see the gown before the wedding day."

He moved forward then. He knew nothing about gowns—but the gown that hung before him looked beautiful.

"You'll be . . . wearing that?" he questioned, his eyes traveling from the gown to Ariana and then back again.

She nodded, excitement flushing her cheeks and making her eyes shine.

He reached for her hand. "I had no idea—I mean, I've never seen a wedding gown before. I had no idea they were so . . . so . . ."

Ariana laughed joyfully. "They aren't—always," she admitted. "It just happens that you are seeing the . . . the most beautiful gown in all the Americas." She laughed again. "It's special—even for a wedding gown. Imported lace—right from Spain. Isn't it gorgeous?"

He nodded. "I can hardly wait to see you in it," he said quietly.

"Well, first, we have this little problem," stated Ariana.

"What is that?"

"This sleeve. See how that other cuff is? It buttons on. This one is missing."

"Can you make another?" Laramie inquired with a shrug of his shoulders.

"Not to match. We'd never match the lace. So we have to make two new ones—out of the satin. We're just trying to figure out if the cut is on the bias or—"

Laramie leaned closer and took another look. He frowned.

"Wait a minute," he said as he reached to finger the material. "I jest might have something to help you. I'm almost sure—"

Ariana looked at him in surprise.

"In my ma's little chest. I saw a scrap of material—almost like that. I don't think someone would notice any little bit of difference."

Ariana's eyes took on a shine.

"Could you get it?" she asked hurriedly. "It would be wonderful if we could keep the cuffs—"

"I'll go home and pick it up," he assured her. "I'll be back in an hour or so."

Laramie retrieved the small chest from its place of safety and flipped up the lid. He was anxious to get back to Ariana.

Hurriedly he put aside the small baby gown and fumbled through the hankies, searching for the bit of material he had seen in the box. He did hope that he hadn't inadvertently lost it.

He was almost at the bottom of the box before he found it. He smiled with relief and drew it forth.

Yes. He had been right. The lace looked very much like the lace of Ariana's gown. He smiled again. She would be so pleased.

Laramie was about to tuck the scrap of material in his shirt pocket when something caught his eye. A tiny button.

His eyes widened and he brought the material closer. Another button. And another.

He stared, not able to believe what his eyes were seeing. In his hand he held the missing cuff. It could only mean one thing.

His legs gave out on him and Laramie lowered himself to his bunk, his face in his hands. A wave of nausea passed through him, making him feel sick inside. Did he and Ariana share the same mother? It couldn't be. It just couldn't be. He loved Ariana. They were to be married. He felt inner pain as he had never felt before in his entire life.

His first temptation was to destroy the little cuff and say it had been lost.

But reason and honesty won the battle. That would not be fair. It would not be right. He could never live with the fact. Nor would Ariana ever forgive him if he tried.

One simply could not marry one's own sister. He lifted his head and stared—unseeing—before him. He would have to tell her. Would have to tell them all.

He hated the thought of the whole ordeal.

Why? Why? When everything seemed to have finally worked out for good?

Laramie dropped his head in his hands again and groaned. *Where are you, God? How could you let this happen? Why didn't you let us know we were brother and sister right from the start? Then our relationship could have been thet of family—good and proper.*

Laramie groaned again. He had never, in his lifetime, been struck such a cruel blow.

Ariana paced back and forth on the porch of her aunt's farm home. Laramie was taking longer than she had expected. Was he having trouble finding the material? It would be so nice to have the cuffs matching—or even nearly matching. It would be so nice to keep the dress as close as possible to the gown her mother had worn. She did hope that Laramie was right. That the cuff would not need to be changed to satin.

She hesitated and looked out over the country road in the gathering twilight. Laramie was still not in sight.

She sighed and paced some more.

She hoped nothing bad had happened. What if his horse had spooked? What if the law had suddenly appeared? No, that was silly. Laramie had said that he had confessed and been pardoned. Nothing like that would happen now.

Just as Ariana felt she could stand the uncertainty no longer, she saw Laramie's buckskin appear around the bend in the road. In her agitation she felt like running out to meet him. But that would be silly. She held herself in check. He would be with her soon enough.

She tapped one foot against the porch boards, impatience making it hard for her to wait. The warm evening breeze played with her hair, wisping it about her oval face.

At last Laramie pulled up and threw the reins over the

hitching rail. He came toward her. Ariana beamed and moved to meet him.

"Will it work? Is the lace pattern close enough?" she called as the distance between them closed.

In the semidarkness Ariana could barely see his face. When he drew near enough she saw he was pale and drawn. Something had happened. Ariana felt her heart beat faster. Was it just his disappointment that the lace wasn't right?

He said nothing—just reached out his hand to her. In his palm was the bit of lace. Ariana took it and turned it over in her fingers.

"It doesn't matter if it doesn't match," she began. "Don't feel badly if—"

Ariana looked more closely.

"It looks—very close," she said and looked up at Laramie.

He still was ashen—silent. She could not understand.

"Ariana . . . it doesn't just . . . match the cuff," he said softly in a choked, forced voice. "It *is* the cuff."

Her eyes widened. She looked into his face with disbelief.

"It *is* the cuff," he repeated. "Look. It has the tiny buttons."

Ariana's gaze went back to the bit of lace. She turned it over and over. First unbelief, then delight, filled her eyes.

"Why, that's wonderful!" she exclaimed. "Who would have ever believed it? Who would have ever imagined? The real missing cuff. Isn't it wonderful! Isn't God good!"

She threw her arms around Laramie's neck. Her warm tears of joy fell on his cheek.

Gently he pushed her from him. "Ariana . . . listen to me."

She looked at him, shock in her eyes. What had happened? What was wrong?

"I found the cuff . . . in my mother's box."

She nodded.

"My . . . *mother's*."

She looked puzzled.

"It matches your mother's dress. Exactly."

She took one tiny step backward, still staring at him.

"You don't mean—?" she began, but she did not finish.

He nodded.

"But it can't be," she almost screamed at him. "It—can't be."

"Ariana—"

She looked at him for one moment, her eyes wild and denying. His own tears were tracing the pattern on his cheek where Ariana's tears had been such a short while ago.

"It has to be," he said simply, looking away from the pain in her eyes.

"I don't want a brother," she cried. "I—want—" and then she turned from him and ran toward the house.

* * *

Dear Ariana,

I am leaving. I hope someday to return when I can think of you as a sister. I have decided that it is too hard for us to see each other now. I will pray for you. I will love you always, but that love must change now. Perhaps someday we will be able to say that God has worked it for good.

Love, Laramie

Ariana held the letter in a trembling hand, tears flowing freely down her cheeks. Across the room she could see the lovely gown of Spanish lace—its second cuff now securely in its place.

"I will never wear it," she whispered to herself. "Never! I loved him so."

She stirred and looked at the gown again, brushing at the tears on her cheek with the back of her hand.

"If only I had *known* he was my brother. We could have . . . have shared so many things. Learned to love each other . . . in a different way. But this? This is so . . . cruel. I will never be able to . . . to accept him as a brother. Never. I love him far too deeply."

Ariana began to weep again.

Her eyes fell back to the final words of Laramie's note. "Perhaps someday we will be able to say that God has worked it for good." That seemed impossible. Impossible. God seemed . . . seemed so far away. So . . . beyond her reach.

Trust, came the quiet message to Ariana's heart—but at the moment she found it beyond her capability.

Chapter Twenty-three

The Diary

For the first week Laramie just drifted in a daze, except for the pain deep inside that constantly reminded him he was still alive. Even when he would rather not be.

It had all been so unexpected. Though looking back, Laramie wondered why he hadn't begun to put some of the pieces together much earlier.

The wagon train. The massacre and burning. The fact that both of them were without their real parents. Yes—it should have made him wonder. Yet who would have thought?

Laramie looked at the small chest with a mixture of love and hate. It had held one too many secrets. One that had torn his world apart.

"It was best that we know," he told himself over and over. "It would have been a dreadful thing if . . ." But secretly, Laramie wondered.

He found it hard to pray—so he read. At least he could still manage to concentrate when reading his mother's Bible. *Our mother's Bible,* he corrected himself. Perhaps someday—with a lot of help from the Lord—he and Ariana would be able to read it together.

No. No, he concluded. I just can't—can't think of her as a sister. I just can't.

After a week had passed, Laramie mentally took stock.

"I've got to get out of these doldrums," he told himself. "I've got to go on with my life."

At first he had a hard time deciding what he would do, and then he remembered the rancher. The man had said if he ever wanted a job—well, he needed a job now. Laramie saddled up his mount, tied the bundles to the pack saddle, and headed off.

When he rapped on the ranch house door, Laramie was welcomed.

"Hopin' ya'd come on back," said the big man. "'Bout given up on ya. But it couldn't have been at a better time. Foreman jest quit. Fixin' to have his own spread. None of those yahoos I got out there is worth their salt. I was afraid I'd have to be my own foreman. Hate the thought of all thet ridin'."

He stopped for breath and looked at Laramie. "Ya want the job, it's yers."

Laramie nodded. It was the only contract needed.

"The foreman has his own bunk," the man went on. "Thet little shack down the lane. Throw yer bedroll in there."

Laramie was thankful to be on his own. He much preferred it to bunking in with a bunch of card-playing, snuff-chewing, booze-drinking cowhands.

"Maybe I'm jest a coward," he chided himself, "but I sure don't feel ready to socialize yet."

He tossed his bedroll on the bunk, unpacked his few belongings, turned his horses into the corral, and went to look for some kind of a broom. The small shack was a mess. He planned to clean it thoroughly before claiming it as his own.

Ariana stumbled through one long day after another. She previously had quit her position in the little school, so there wasn't even that to think about. Besides—it was the Christmas break. She wouldn't have been teaching anyway. She would have been getting married.

Now there was no wedding to think about. She didn't even want to think about Christmas. It was going to be very empty—meaningless.

Ariana shook her head. No, she mustn't think like that. She mustn't. Christmas would still have the same meaning as always. It was Christ's birth they celebrated. Nothing in her circumstances had changed that.

But as Ariana looked at the pocket watch she had purchased for Laramie, she found it hard to feel in the Christmas spirit.

She had to do something. Something to take control of her life again. She couldn't just stay in her room and weep and mope. That was not honoring to her Lord.

Two days before Christmas, she donned her nicest gown, bathed the puffiness from her eyes, and joined the family at the breakfast table.

Everyone seemed to hold a collective breath. Dared they speak? What topics were safe to address? What meaningless comment might start the tears flowing again?

Ariana managed a wobbly smile. She reached over and took her mother's hand.

"I've made a decision," she said simply. "I'm coming home with you."

Everyone at the table looked surprised. Four pairs of eyes turned toward her to see if she was in her right mind.

"It only makes sense," she went on calmly. "With the gang gone, there is no reason for me to hide myself away here. I've resigned from the school. They already have a new teacher engaged. I . . . I'll just go on home with you."

Gradually those at the table began to see that she was thinking quite clearly. Quite capable of making a decision. Her mother squeezed her hand. Her father beamed his pleasure. Her aunt Molly looked about to weep, while her uncle Jake just cleared his throat noisily.

"We'll miss you, dear," said Aunt Molly.

"It will be so good to have you home again. I've been so lonely," her mother admitted.

"You leave on the third," Ariana went on. "I will have no problem being ready." Her eyes clouded.

"There is only one thing I haven't figured out," she went on.

Her mother's hand tightened on hers. She was afraid there might be tears again.

"The little roan," went on Ariana, and though her voice cracked slightly, she did not begin to cry.

Her uncle Jake was quick to speak. Perhaps he feared a fresh outburst of tears as well. "Happy to keep him here—until such time as you can get him," he said, and then cleared his throat again.

Ariana smiled softly in appreciation. "Thank you, Uncle Jake," she said evenly.

The matter seemed to be closed.

Laramie settled into his new responsibilities. For the first months, through the last of winter and into spring, he spent his days in the saddle from sunup to sundown. He wanted to discover the lay of the land—to survey the entire ranch and know thoroughly each draw, each hill, each valley. He checked the water supply, the grass supply, each head that grazed, each new calf that arrived. He could not manage well what he did not know well, he reasoned, and his boss took great pleasure in watching him take the job so seriously.

"Make a good rancher," he informed his elderly wife. "Too bad he don't have a spread of his own."

"He's young," his wife reminded him. "He has lots of time fer thet."

As the days lengthened, Laramie felt well enough in control to assign the range riders the tasks that needed to be done.

That gave him more free time—something he did not welcome.

He resumed his worship in the small church, and the

preacher's daughter took up her role of flirting again. Laramie tried to avoid direct contact with her. He was sure she was a fine young woman, but he just wasn't interested.

He began to look for things to do. They were not always easy to find. He spent more time reading his mother's Bible. The lessons he learned helped him get hold of his life again—but he still could not forget Ariana. He still was not able to think of her as his sister. He began to wonder just how long it was going to take.

One day, in his loneliness, he drew out his mother's little chest. Would he find healing there? Would he find the link that would finally enable him to think of Ariana as a part of his family?

Listlessly he turned over each hankie, each button, each little memento. There was nothing. Nothing that changed the feelings in his heart.

He had emptied the little chest and was about to put all of the contents back in place when he noticed that a bit of the lining was coming loose.

He wasn't skilled in mending and fixing, but he wondered if there was some way he could repair it so the little chest wouldn't continue to come apart.

He ran one finger along the spot and felt something he had not noticed before. He lifted the box for a closer look. To his amazement there was a little clasp hidden from casual view. He pushed on it. Wiggled it gently and pushed again. Then he lifted it—up and in. To his surprise the bottom of the chest flipped upward on a small spring. There was a false bottom to the small chest.

Laramie could not believe what greeted his eyes. The whole bottom of the small box was covered with bills. Money. Stacked thick—though crisp with age. Strange money. He was not familiar with it. But it was money, of that he was sure.

"I don't believe this," he said to himself. "Mama had a whole stash here."

He looked over his shoulder. He did not wish to be observed. The door was closed. He moved to pull the curtain over the one window. Then he sat back down at the table and began to lift out the crinkled bills.

At the bottom of the pile he discovered a small book. Was this her record of account? Laramie lifted the book and flipped the pages. No. There were no numbers. Simply writing. Some sort of—record. Or journal. He laid the book aside and began to count the money.

There were thousands of dollars. Enough for a ranch of his own. Enough to give Ariana—

His thoughts stopped there. When would he ever stop thinking of Ariana?

He stirred from the table and paced about the small cabin. The money had lost all its appeal. What good was it?

Yet it was there. He should do something with it. He placed it, all but a single bill, rather roughly back in the secret compartment and carefully fastened the false bottom into place. He did not return the little book. He laid it in with the hankies and buttons and brooches. He should send the things to Ariana. They were more suitable for a lady than for a man.

Laramie put the chest back in its hiding place, opened the covering on the window, and checked his hair in the cracked mirror on the wall. He would just ride on into town and visit the banker. Perhaps the man could shed some light on the strange currency.

"Where'd you get this?" asked the cigar-chewing man behind the desk.

"My mama left me a box," replied Laramie. "I didn't realize it had a false bottom in it—until today."

"This was in it?"

Laramie nodded. There was no need to tell the man that the bill was only one of many.

"Haven't seen these for some while," said the banker as

he turned the bill over and over in his hand.

"Real money?" asked Laramie.

The man twirled his cigar with his tongue. He looked up and smiled in an amused fashion.

"Real money, all right," he said, and Laramie was about to let his breath out with relief when he continued. "Ain't worth a lick, though. Confederate. Union decided it's not legal tender. Might as well use it to start yer fire in the morning."

So Mama's box held no treasure after all, Laramie thought to himself as he rode home. It had been a disappointment—but after what he had already been through, it didn't matter all that much.

He let his mount pick his own gait. He was not in a hurry to get anywhere. What was there to do when he did get home? Nothing? Perhaps he'd ride on out and check the west spring. Or maybe he'd see how that new colt in the east pasture was doing. Or maybe he'd just loaf. He didn't know—he didn't really care.

And then he remembered the little book. *Maybe I should take a look at it,* he concluded. *Looked like a woman's writing. Maybe it's Mama's. If it was her diary—it might hold some information. Maybe even some answers.*

Laramie urged the buckskin forward at a faster pace. He was rather in a hurry after all.

Chapter Twenty-four

The Answers

By the time Laramie reached the ranch he was anxious to get his saddle horse put up for the night so he could get to the small journal. His inner tension had been mounting with each mile he traveled.

He could hardly wait to discover just what the little book was. What secrets of his past—Ariana's past—it might hold.

He entered his small abode and shut the door against the noise and dust of the day. It was rather dark after he had pulled his curtain firmly across the little window, so he lit his lamp before lifting the small chest from its hiding place, withdrawing the small book, and settling himself at the wooden table.

He flipped open the first page.

"To my dear daughter Lavina Ann Bradley on the occasion of her fourteenth birthday. July 10, 1836," it read in a crisp script. Beneath the penned inscription were the words, "Always be the godly woman admonished by Scripture in 1 Peter 3:4. Your loving father, Winston P. Bradley."

Laramie turned to the next page. The writing had changed. He could almost envision a young girl sitting at a polished writing desk, her smooth brow puckered in concentration.

"July 10, 1836. Today is my fourteenth birthday. I cannot

believe it. Mama gave me the most beautiful blue gown. It is my first real grown-up dress with charming puffed sleeves and a full skirt with lots of petticoats, and blue ruffles upon beautiful blue ruffles. She also said that when I wear it I will be able to pin up my hair. Imagine. Me—grown-up. Papa gave me that horse I have been teasing for and a sidesaddle so that I might ride her in ladylike fashion. He also gave me this book. To keep a diary, he said. I think that he feels I am terribly impulsive and he hopes that it will teach me a bit of discipline. (He wishes me to write an account in it daily, but that seems like a very big chore. Almost like a school assignment. I think that I shall write in it only when something very important happens.) Like today. Today has been so exciting. Even Ethan shared in my joy. And brothers do not do that very often."

Laramie turned the page.

"July 11, 1836. I wasn't going to write in my diary today, but Papa asked me at the breakfast table if I had. Since I had not, I assured him quickly that I would. He seemed satisfied. But I really have nothing important to write about. It looks to be an ordinary day, and after having such an exciting day yesterday, it is difficult to endure. And it is so miserably hot and stuffy. I think that I shall die of the heat. I have asked Papa if we might go to our house in Charleston, where the ocean breezes help to make things a bit more bearable. He wouldn't give his answer.

"July 12, 1836. It is still hot and miserable. Even Mama is annoyed with the heat. I hope that she joins me in persuading Papa. Perhaps then he will take us to Charleston.

"July 13, 1836. We are going to Charleston. Oh, joy! I can hardly wait. Mama said that she simply could not endure the swampy heat of the plantation. I will take along my new blue gown and pray for a party so I may wear it. Ethan is fussing because Papa said that he cannot go. He has to stay home and help with the plantation. Papa says that is a man's duty. I don't think Ethan enjoys being a man—at sixteen."

The next date was not until September 29, 1836.

"It has been wonderful in Charleston. Every day there are new people to meet. I have never been to so many parties—but Mama is well-known here. Papa went directly back to the plantation. Mama has added more gowns to my wardrobe. She says that a young lady must be properly attired. I cannot believe how grown-up I now look, in just one short summer. I feel grown-up too, and I have had many nice compliments from the young gentlemen. Mama still will not allow me to have callers. She says I must wait until next year. That seems a long time to wait. We must leave for home tomorrow. It will seem very quiet and boring after life in the city.

"February 15, 1838. A most wonderful thing happened to me today. I had always thought that the most exciting thing that could ever happen to a young lady would be a proposal of marriage. Well, I was wrong. I discovered another love. All of my life my parents have been very diligent in making me attend services in our local church, in reading portions of the Scripture before our breakfast, in insisting that I read sections on my own and memorize the same. I had always accepted their faith as a matter of course. But today, today I understood the truth of God's Word for the first time. I really understood—with my heart as well as my head. I prayed the prayer of repentance, and such peace and joy flooded my heart. I will never be the same again—nor do I wish to be.

"March 2, 1838. My faith has continued to grow. It fills me with overwhelming joy—at the same time that it breaks my heart. I can't help but grieve for all of those who have not yet heard and believed. I have Papa's permission to start a little class of Bible lessons for the children of the slaves. They are so sweet and so quick to pick up the truths that I was so slow in learning.

"March 22, 1838. My first little 'black sheep' accepted the teaching of Scripture. What a joy it was to lead this little one in a prayer of repentance. I think that her mammy had already prepared her heart.

"September 12, 1838. I have just met the most wonderful

young man. Maybe I should have noticed him long ago. His father owns the plantation across the river from us. We have known the family for years and I do recall him faintly—but I had never really noticed him before—in this way. He's tall and very nice looking, with the most gentlemanly manner. I am quite taken with him. I am not sure how he feels about me. I have added him to my lengthy prayers. God knows what is right for me. I must learn to trust Him in this matter as well.

"April 4, 1839. Turner Lawrence III asked my papa for permission to call—and was wholeheartedly accepted. I am so thankful. I can scarcely believe my good fortune. (Papa says I am not to use that term. It is not good fortune for one of God's children—it is the grace of God.)

"July 19, 1839. We are leaving for Charleston as we do each summer, but this year I hate to go. I have enjoyed getting to know Turner. Our conversations have shown me that we are of one heart and mind. He, too, deplores the ownership of slaves. He says if he had any say in the matter, he would free his. His father still runs the plantation, though. Turner lost his mother to the swamp fever when he was only eight. How sad for a child to be raised without a mother. He does love his nurse. She is a big woman, with love for all God's children. I can understand why Turner feels the way he does about her.

"December 8, 1839. Papa has agreed to a spring wedding. I am so happy. I never knew that one's heart could be so full.

"May 10, 1840. Today is my wedding day. Papa sent to Spain for the lace for my gown, and Mama had it sewn in Charleston. It is the most elegant thing I have ever seen. It is ivory satin, overlaid with this gorgeous lace. The sleeves are full and puffed, nipped in with soft satin bows, with slender long cuffs buttoned underneath and reaching to each wrist. The skirts are full at the back with yards of bustle. The bodice is fitted with the lace gently sculpturing the natural lines. The neckline is high and simple and will show off the new sapphire and diamond pendant that Papa has given me.

Someday I will pass this beautiful dress on to my daughter to wear at her own wedding. I can almost see her walking down the aisle."

Laramie stirred restlessly in his chair. In his mind he was seeing Ariana in that same lovely gown, walking the aisle of the little church to join him at the altar. It was all he could do to continue reading.

"Mama is sure that all of Charleston will rave about the gown and the wedding, and I have a secret feeling that is important to Mama. I certainly would be ungrateful if I did not appreciate all that Papa and Mama are doing for us—but I would have been quite happy to just marry my Turner. He is so wonderful. This promises to be the beginning of a wonderful life. We have prayed together, many times, asking God to bless our union—to make us truly one in Him.

"Papa's gift to me was a new family Bible. He was so sweet as he gave it to me. 'Every home must have a Bible,' he said. 'A home cannot be safely built on any other foundation—no matter how much love is shared by the homeowners.' He also flipped to the pages for records and advised me to be diligent in keeping my posting up to date. I promised him that I would.

"August 15, 1840. I am a wife. I still find it hard to believe. After a wonderful trip abroad we settled into life at Roseberne plantation. Turner's father has informed me that I am the full mistress of the manor now. I am thankful that Mama took her teaching duties seriously and I know how to go about the task. Nevertheless, I am still a bit nervous. Turner is wonderfully reassuring.

"December 2, 1853. Today was a very difficult and sad day. Father Lawrence passed away suddenly last evening. The doctor said it was his heart. Turner feels it deeply. Though he has not always agreed with his father, he loved him dearly. I'm not sure what the future holds for us now.

"September 5, 1854. It has been decided. Turner is selling Roseberne. He cannot bear the thought of owning slaves—yet the plantation could never be run without them. It is an untenable situation. However, he refused to sell the slaves along with the property but granted them full freedom and gave them each an amount of cash to get established elsewhere. It was a sad time. We all cried together. I struggled with the decision. I do not like slavery either, but I could not but fear for our future. Turner is confident. We are to move. He has picked St. Louis. He does not like the unrest that is sweeping the South. He is afraid there will be war. He tried to talk to Papa and Ethan about it, but they both are adamant in their resolve to stay as they are. I feel so mixed up and confused—but Turner constantly reminds me that God will lead us.

"June 6, 1855. We are well settled in St. Louis. It is a fine little city, though it cannot compare in any way to Charleston. I miss the plantation life and I dearly miss my family. Sometimes I wonder if we have done the right thing. But rumors keep circulating. Turner is sure it will end in war. I pray that he is wrong.

"I had hoped to be a mother long before now, but that has not been. Turner keeps reminding me that God can still answer our prayers. It seems that each year that passes just breaks my heart a little bit more. It is hard to be patient.

"February 3, 1860. I cannot believe it. I am to be a mother. I had almost given up. At age thirty-seven it seemed that motherhood had passed me by. (I will be thirty-eight by the time our little one joins us.) I can only bow my head and my heart and thank God.

"August 10, 1860. The miracle has actually happened. I am a mother. What joy I feel! Our son arrived at ten o'clock this morning. I cried as I held him. He is beautiful. I think he will be a big man, like his father. But Turner insists he will have my eyes. He has only just arrived—and yet I would gladly give my life for him. God has been so good.

"January 2, 1861. Christmas was so special this year. Little Burke has given us the true meaning for all of life, but the thought filling my heart was that of the great love of God the Father. How could He love me enough to give His Son?

It is a love I cannot comprehend as I look at my own precious baby boy. To love enough to die for him—yes—a thousand times, yes. But to love enough to send him to die—I never could love that purely—that strongly. What a magnificent love is the Love of God! I pray that God will keep my boy safe—protected and in His care—always."

Laramie felt his eyes dampening. His mother was speaking of him. How he wished he could have known her. How he longed to feel the beat of her mother-heart.

The next page was not dated. The usual even script looked hurried, agitated.

"It is as we feared. Our beloved country is at war. North against South. Brother against brother. Ethan has gone. Mama says it was his duty. I don't understand about duty that would lead a man to fight his own countrymen. My heart is grieved. I am glad I didn't have a son earlier. He, too, might need to fight. Little Burke is still safe in his cradle. I pray that the day may never come when he has to use a gun to save his own life.

"October 14, 1861. Turner has decided we will move farther west. He is afraid that the effects of the war will even touch St. Louis. I pray that he is wrong but I have not argued. I am willing to go wherever he sees as best. Little Burke is my only thought. My only joy. He is growing so quickly. Turner was right. He does have my eyes.

"November 18, 1861. Turner has located a group of people who are planning to move west. He is making arrangements for us to join the train. I went with him to one of the meetings. He insisted. He did not want me to feel pressured into going farther west if I was against it. I was favorably impressed. They seem to be a kind, God-fearing group of people. The wagon master and his trail riders seem to be competent. I will feel quite safe in their company.

"November 26, 1861. We had another meeting of the people from the train. I met the sweetest young woman. Her name is Morgan Oliver. She and the man she plans to marry will be joining the train next spring as well. She is so anxious to marry her Preston that she reminds me of myself several years ago when I was all starry-eyed about my Turner. But she does not have a mother to help her with her wedding plans as I did. She would like to be married on Christmas Eve. I have told her that I would help in any way I can.

"December 25, 1861. What a lovely wedding we attended last evening. There was only a small gathering in the local church. The guests were mostly the people of the wagon train who are busy preparing for the spring trip to the West. Morgan married her Preston Whitehall. She was a radiant bride. I was glad that I had thought to offer her the use of my gown. I am sure my future daughter will not mind that we shared the dress with another. Morgan is such a sweet little thing. I am looking forward to having her on the train for those long, tiring days of travel.

"March 4, 1862. The war still rages. News is not good. Mama tries to keep us posted—but each letter that makes it through breaks our hearts a little more. I fear for the safety of my family. Turner was right. I am so thankful we have left so that Burke might be kept safe. Each time I look at him my heart swells with love.

"March 6, 1862. Morgan came by today with some delightful news. She is expecting a baby. We are both praying that our trip might go well and that we will have arrived and become settled before the little one is born. What a delight it would be if it is a boy. It would be wonderful to have a playmate for Burke. True—Burke would be two years older, but two years will not seem like much in years to come. I am praying daily for Morgan. I feel I am uniquely sharing her joy.

"June 4, 1862. Next week we begin our long trek west. Our days will be filled with all of the last-minute purchases, sales, packing, and planning. Turner has secured two sturdy wagons and an additional driver so that I can take some of my treasured possessions with me. He says that there is no need for me to feel I have forsaken civilization. He wants his son to grow up to have the social graces of a southern gentleman even though we have been forced to leave the South.

"I suffered a deep disappointment yesterday. The doctor has confirmed that I will not be able to have another child. I wept well into the evening, even though Turner tried to sweetly comfort me. Then I looked at Burke. I chastised myself. God has already blessed me much beyond what I have deserved."

I don't understand, mused Laramie. *How could that be? What about Ariana?* Laramie turned his eyes back to the book in his hands and read on. The doctor must have been proven wrong.

"August 16, 1862. We have been on the trail for what seems forever. Sometimes I wonder how much more I will be able to stand. I was not prepared for this. It has been much more difficult than I would have guessed. Bad weather has kept us from making the progress we had hoped. I worry for Morgan. She is due in September, but the trip has been hard for her. I fear that the rumbling wagons might bring the baby earlier than it is supposed to come. Each day I include her in my petitions. It seems that we keep God so busy with our many prayers. I am glad He is able.

"August 29, 1862. Morgan's baby arrived last night. She is a good two weeks early, and though she is small she is wiry and seems strong. Thanks to God. Morgan is so excited. I know the feeling. I felt the same way when Burke arrived.

"September 17, 1862. We had hoped to have reached our 'Promised Land' by now, but more bad weather has delayed us. However, Turner assures me we are getting close. I am concerned about Morgan. She does not seem to be getting back her strength as quickly as she should. A dear woman who lost her husband in a horrid drowning at a river crossing, Mrs. Millard, is helping her. We are constantly reminded that we are in Indian country, but our wagon master assures us we have little cause to worry. I keep reminding myself of the verse that I have carried with me, 'Trust in the Lord with all thine heart.' Sometimes that is all I have to cling to. I am not afraid for myself. I just pray that Burke will be kept from the evil of the world. He is all that matters. I pray each day that God will protect him.

"September 26, 1862. Morgan was up today but she is still weak. I pray that God will give her strength. We have decided to meet each day, in the time that we have left together, to pray for our babies. Their safety. Their futures. But most of all, that God will keep their hearts open to His voice and protect them from the sinful ways of the world. The West seems so frighteningly crude to me that I sometimes fear for my son. But God kept the young Moses. Surely I can trust Him with my precious Burke.

"We are soon to come to the parting of our ways. The Whitehalls plan to head south, while Turner has decided that we will travel north. I was so disappointed I wept for most of the day. I tried not to let Turner know—but I fear he guessed. I have made a decision. I will give Morgan the wedding dress."

Laramie's heart quickened and he hurried on.

"September 27, 1862. I bundled up my beautiful gown and took it to Morgan today. This is the last night that we are to be together. Tomorrow we are to go our separate ways. She was so touched when I made my little presentation that she wept and I wept right along with her. I had already shed tears alone. It seemed that I was giving away not just a dress, but my memories and my future hopes and dreams. However, I am not sorry. I will never have a daughter to wear it, and little Ariana seems almost like a daughter to me. I know that someday she will make a beautiful bride."

Laramie, breathing heavily, read the passage again. Ariana. Ariana was Morgan's baby. Morgan's daughter. She was not his sister. Could it be? Was the book telling the truth? He turned back anxiously to the little diary.

"I was disappointed to discover that one of the cuffs was missing. At first I was mystified and then I remembered that I had noticed one of the tiny buttons was loose. I laid the cuff aside until I could fix it. I can't recall where I put it unless it is in my little chest in my trunk.

"Later. I found the cuff. It was in the small chest that holds my 'treasures'—including this diary—between my recording days. (I haven't been as faithful as Papa would have liked, but I do see this little book as something very precious—even though I don't fully understand what gives it such value.) I fixed the button, so I'll be able to deliver the cuff to Morgan in the morning before she leaves."

There were only empty pages following the notation. He looked back at the last date entered.

Morning had never come for his mother. At sunrise the Indians had attacked.

Laramie felt physically sick. His mother—his dear mother—she who had loved him and wrapped him securely in her daily prayers—had not lived to see another day. He could not even think of it. And Ariana—she had lost her mother, too. Morgan. Morgan Whitehall. They both had been left orphans—Ariana hidden by the widowed lady whom she lovingly called her second mama.

Laramie stirred from his reverie.

Ariana. *Ariana needs to know.*

His thoughts moved from the horror of the wagon massacre to the fact that Ariana was not his sister. They had two different mothers—women joined only by friendship and the sharing of a beautiful wedding gown. It was a miracle. A little miracle. No, a great big, wondrous miracle. The secret compartment of the little chest had held a treasure far more precious than confederate money. It held the key to the secret of his past. Of Ariana's past.

He shoved the book into his pocket and began to pack a saddlebag. He could not wait to get to Ariana. Could not wait to share the knowledge the little book held. They were free. They were not bound by kinship. They were not brother and sister. They were free to join in marriage. They were free to love each other as husband and wife.

Ariana stood with one hand on the window ledge and looked out at the young squirrels frisking about on the grass in the backyard. They looked so playful, so filled with energy. In spite of her still-heavy heart, she could not hide a smile.

"Ariana," her mother called from the front of the house. "You have a caller." Her voice sounded excited. Ariana wondered about it as she turned from the window and let the curtain fall back into place.

She walked down the hall to the parlor expecting to see one of her Sunday school class members or perhaps, she thought, with a quickening of her pulse, the school board chairman. Maybe they had found they could use her in the local school after all. She did hope that it wasn't Bernard Dikerson. He had been making a nuisance of himself ever since her return.

But it was a tall young man who stood there, hat in hand. Ariana could not have mistaken his identity, even though his face was shadowed.

"Laramie!" she gasped.

Her head began to spin. He had said he would be back when they could accept the brother-sister relationship. If he had worked it through, he was much ahead of her, she decided. She still was not ready to see him as the brother she had never known.

He stepped forward and reached for her hand, but Ariana drew it back. She wasn't prepared for this. She wasn't. She cast a look over her shoulder, willing her mother to interfere, to support her in some way. Her mother was nowhere to be seen. Ariana felt a moment of panic.

He did not try to reach for her again, though his eyes showed—what?

"I found something," he said, pulling the small book from his pocket. "I thought I would explode before reaching you. I traveled first to your uncle's. I—"

Ariana let her gaze look out the window. His buckskin and a pack animal stood tethered to the hitching rail, and by their side stood the little roan pony. Yes, he had been up to her uncle's. Tears began to form in her eyes. She turned back to him. But she still couldn't comprehend what he was saying.

"It's all in here," he began, his voice full of excitement as he tapped the small book he still held in his hand. "It's—"

He stopped and looked at her longingly.

Ariana slowly shook her head. "You said you wouldn't come until—" She stopped and licked her lips. "I'm sorry," she continued in a shaky voice. "I . . . I'm not ready . . ."

He moved forward then and placed his hands on her arms. "You don't need to be," he hurried to say. "This book. It gives the whole story. We are *not* brother and sister. Our parents—two totally different families."

Ariana drew back and looked at him with wide, startled eyes. She could not speak.

"Honest!" he continued. "Our mothers—our families—were not the same. It's all in here."

She was in a total daze.

"You're sure?" she managed to whisper.

"I'm sure. Honest."

And then she was in his arms, weeping against the pocket that had held the small diary with its precious secret.

"I can't believe—" she began, but her tears stopped the words.

"It's true—it's true. Our mothers' prayers have—kept us—fer . . . fer some special reason. I . . . I feel thet. I'm not sure jest what—yet. But we'll find it. We are free to serve Him—together—now. Honest."

His arms tightened around her and he lowered his face to bury it in her hair.

"Mama's book said it, too," he whispered. "Thet special verse of yers—'Trust in the Lord with all thine heart.' She said it, too."

Ariana lifted a smiling but still tear-stained face to Laramie, and he drew her closer and bent his head to kiss her moistened cheek.

Two hearts lifted in deep thankfulness to God. They were not brother and sister. They would soon be husband and wife.